HALF COCKED

SYBIL KNIGHT

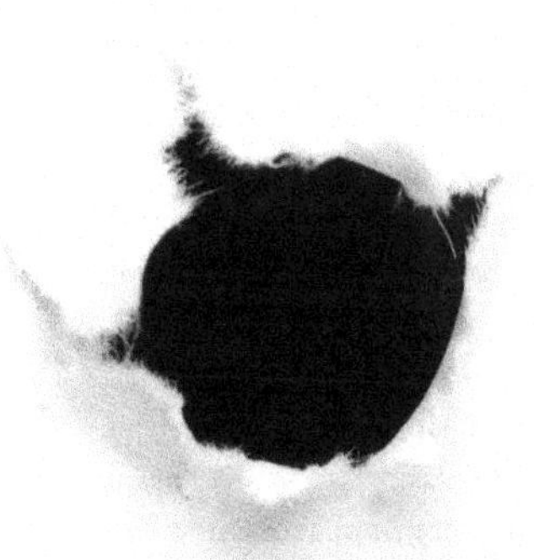

COVER CREATOR: 3CROWS AUTHOR SERVICES LLC
EDITING: KAT PAGAN, PAGAN PROOFREADING
FORMATTING: DAHLIA REIGN LLC

SOCIALS:

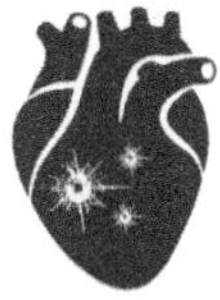

EMAIL: AUTHORSYBILKNIGHT@GMAIL.COM

NEWSLETTER: WWW.SENDFOX.COM/DAHLIAANDSYBIL

FACEBOOK GROUP:
WWW.FACEBOOK.COM/GROUPS/DAHLIAANDSYBILSLITTEDEVILS

INSTAGRAM: WWW.INSTRAGRAM.COM/AUTHOR.SYBIL.KNIGHT

FACEBOOK PAGE: WWW.FACEBOOK.COM/AUTHORSYBILKNIGHT

TIKTOK: WWW.TIKTOK.COM/@QUEENSOFCHAOSBOOKS

AMAZON: HTTPS://WWW.AMAZON.COM/STORES/SYBIL-KNIGHT/AUTHOR/B09QW5R3MB

Stop!

Unless you're willing to trade in all that pearl clutching for a pearl necklace.

Then, by all means, welcome to the shitshow. Where the pies are cream-filled and so are you.

Or at least you will be… by the time we're done with ya.

TRIGGER WARNING:

A SHIT-TON OF SEX AND TWICE AS MUCH VIOLENCE.
IF NEITHER IS YOUR THING, JUST DON'T.

BLURB:

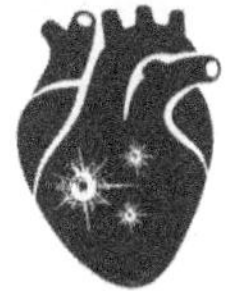

If there was one thing I knew for sure, it was that good guys finished last. But smart women? We finished on top.

It made for a quick climax and an even quicker escape. Especially when you left 'em zip tied to the headboard with a wink and a wave of the middle finger.

Mine wasn't a love story. It was a cautionary tale. A field guide for exactly what not to do if you ever found yourself in my size six riding shoes. A reminder in case you needed another reason you sure as fuck shouldn't fall for the bad boy who promised you the world and left you with a bullet in your skull instead. Or the glorified bodyguard who thought catching a knife to a gut meant he deserved a ring. And how to not use sex and adrenaline to cope with either. *Both?*

Yup, my life wasn't just complicated. It was fucked. And so was the pretty boy with the green eyes and the greener

COMPLEXION. THE SAME ONE WITH A LIMP IN HIS STEP AND A SLIGHTLY TENDER SET OF BALLS BECAUSE HE WAS DUMB ENOUGH TO STAND BETWEEN ME AND MY NEXT PAYCHECK. WHICH LEFT ME TO WONDER HOW THE DUMB FUCK STILL THOUGHT I WAS GIRLFRIEND MATERIAL.

SOMEONE WAS ABOUT TO LEARN A HARD LESSON. I COULD ONLY HOPE THAT SOMEONE WASN'T ME...

PROLOGUE

T he dark, tacky substance stuck to my skin like honey, my eyes fixated on the way the translucent film popped when I pinched my fingers together before prying my thumb from my middle digit.

Blood.

At this point, I didn't know if it was mine or not. If I'd killed someone or met the jagged edge of a beer bottle after one too many bar fights. If I was in the middle of a job or working on the cleanup. Not that it mattered. Now or ever really. I lived and breathed this shit. Embodied the sort of lifestyle that was less than... *aboveboard.* Thrived on the corruption that was pumping through my veins like second fucking nature.

Couldn't tell you how old I was the first time I felt the rhythmic bolt action of a 357 Magnum beneath my grip, or inhaled that biting sulfuric smell of a crisp copper jacket whirling through a freshly primed barrel, or even watched some fucker's brain splatter red against the gray of a concrete wall. Shit was ingrained. Like a core memory that had always been there. What I *could* tell ya is I was born for it. For the violence my last name brought to the dinner table with a side of depravity.

So, no, none of the gory details bothered me. Going for the jugular was just another ugly part of what made mankind tick. Let ya survive in this dog-eat-dog world, where the only thing that mattered was how sharp your teeth were. Sure was funny how easy your morals could twist, bend, come undone with just the right amount of coaxing... when you suddenly realized it was you or the other guy. Yeah, I had no doubt humanity was nothing more than one fuck-up away from total anarchy—you were lying if ya told yourself otherwise.

However, the not remembering, the not knowing what I was doing right now? That shit was a real kick to the lady balls.

"Bitch, you shot me!"

Well, that answered that. Not my blood.

"Please, it barely grazed you." Because if I actually shot the fucker, he'd be dead.

Shoot to kill, Dani. Always shoot to kill. There was a lot less chatter that way.

"Hey! Headcase!" The man-child with barely enough stubble to deem it a five o'clock shadow was squawking in my ear again. "Are you going to untie me or what?"

My glare dropped to the fresh red streak pooling on the fucker's cheekbone before skimming along the blood that was already beginning to coagulate. I cocked my head to the side, noting how his hands and feet were hogtied using my preferred brand of flex cuffs, and then glanced out the window that told me we were closed inside one of my many storage units, each registered under an alias. And couldn't help but wonder how much time had passed.

My best guess was two to eight minutes. Two to eight

minutes of lost time. The blackouts were getting more frequent. Not that it really had much effect on my operation. My body would switch to autopilot, muscle movement, and instinct. It was my brain that always seemed to remain a little foggy.

Wish it had the same effect on my hearing. Because he was spitting mad now.

"Hey! Bitch!"

Good looks, if you could even call 'em that, sure as hell didn't make up for bad manners. Someone should have taught the fucker as much.

The sound of his nasal cavity caving in beneath the force of my ruptured knuckles was worth the throb now radiating up my arm.

Guess I was that someone.

1

I peered up at the neon green sign flashing over the door of Mollies, a club I had no business standing outside right now. Or ever really. Not in this area of the city with a name like mine. Which I had to admit was also a big part of the appeal. I especially enjoyed the things in life that weren't good for me. And quickly tugged my ID from my pocket and passed it over to the bouncer.

"Sorry, no dice, dollface. Better luck next time." The boy too pretty to be called a man smiled and winked while shooting out one of his overly inflated arms to nudge me back a step. Farther away from the fucker I'm sure was hiding out somewhere just beyond the tacky velvet rope that separated me and my next paycheck.

"I don't need luck, *dickwad*. My name's on that list of yours. So, go on. Tuck your cock between your legs and let a lady through."

"Lady?" He quirked a brow, and I didn't appreciate the way the word came out of his mouth more as a question.

I could be a lady if I wanted to be. I glanced down at my leather riding pants and matching vest. The black ankle-high boots that had seen better days and over to my broken nail beds that still had dirt and blood staining the cuticles.

All right, not a lady. But that was beside the point.

"Yeah, lady." I crossed my arms, knowing that the stance would pop up my tits in that way that was irresistible to the male brain and the hormones that were sure to flood it as soon as pretty boy got an eyeful.

"Okay, then, *ma'am,*" the fucker mocked. "This name most certainly is on the list." He paused to tap my ID card against his clipboard. "But it ain't yours." My posture sank and he raised a brow. "Should probably invest in a better fake. I know a guy... if you're lookin'..."

"Really?" I shouldn't have sounded so eager. I knew it even as I said it. But a good counterfeiter was hard to find.

"Fuck no!" He laughed. A real, genuine laughter that accentuated the creases around his too-fucking-pouty lips. "But you dropped that scowl for a second, didn't ya, baby girl?"

Son of a...

I stared up at his strong jawline through a fan of black lashes while allowing the strain to prick my eyes. It didn't take more than a few seconds for the bullshit tears to fall without thought. "You don't understand... he's in there... and if I don't bring him home... I need him home. He's... my brother is the only one who can talk Papa down when he's been drinking..."

I watched as pretty boy's features softened, as his posture seemed to relax. "I... are you being serious?"

"Fuck no!" was my response as my already damaged fist made contact with his glass jaw.

It was cliché but the big ones always did fall the hardest —the force of gravity and all that.

Onlookers gasped and cooed but not one of 'em

stepped forward to intervene when the glorified door guard toppled to the ground. I smiled. It was always the same. That was the one constant you could count on. People and their cowardice.

The combination of strobing lights and overused bass along with the noxious odor of perspiration that made up the VIP room at Mollies was the thing of my nightmares. And far worse than any bogeyman I could conjure up.

At most, I had a few minutes to lock eyes on my mark before: one, the bouncer came to or two, the son of a bitch manning the security cameras called out "man down" and recognized some asshat had let a Rossi into a Mulligan club. Either option was an inconvenience I just didn't have the patience for tonight.

My head was still pounding from the altercation this morning—I really should have passed off this case. But my work was like a drug and I needed a fix. A distraction. Liquor and faceless sex just weren't doing it for me anymore.

Shocking, I know.

I glanced down at my watch and let out an exasperated huff. I had to make this shit quick. In and out like a short dick on prom night. And recited the profile for one John Porter.

Thirty-four-year-old male: shaved head, generic tribal tattoos (bilateral arms) and an eyebrow piercing (left).

Call sign: Douche with a side of mommy issues.

Okay, I might have made up that last part but it was fitting nonetheless.

Ticktock, Dani Girl, you ain't getting any younger.

"Here, kitty, kitty," I purred among the waves of body odor and pheromones as my eyes scanned the room before honing in on their target.

Two minutes in, and it was almost as if the mugshot had jumped off the folded piece of paper and materialized in front of me, an arm slung along the bar top and six empty beer bottles acting as witness to the fucker's misplaced masculinity.

"Long time no see, lover boy," I hummed, dropping the instinctual edge that tended to pleat my voice.

"Aren't you a sweet little thing?" His grin curled like something out of a horror flick, his eyebrows so narrow they looked drawn on. Like he woke up that morning and decided that today was the day he was gonna take on the world with his sister's leftover lip liner.

"Oh, Johnny, Johnny, Johnny." I cocked my head as I sidled up next to Mr. Mommy Issues on the empty barstool and skimmed my mouth along the arch of his ear, trying not to choke on the punch of stale cigarettes and cheap liquor that assaulted my nostrils with each forced inhale. "Five minutes. Meet me out back." It wasn't a request and the sick bastard liked it. The male species really had no chance of survival if the sons of bitches didn't start thinking with the larger of their two heads.

I didn't hesitate before beelining it for the neon EXIT sign. My steps fast. But not so fast they'd raise suspicions. *Do not look back. Do not stand out.* I needed to remain just another silhouette in the swarm of buzzing partygoers.

I pushed out the door, my cheeks immediately slapped by the crisp night air at the same time I glanced down to see the pointer finger and thumb clasp around my wrist and drag me to the side of the building.

Well, ain't that a bitch? Looks like someone's mama blessed him with chiseled features and *a quick recovery time.* A double threat if I ever saw one.

"Miss me so soon?" I grinned. Because fuck if I didn't like pushing buttons just because I could.

"Not so fast, dollface..." This time pretty boy's endearment was a little less, well, *endearing* as he yanked me backwards and against the bite of the cold brick wall that lined the alleyway.

"When you say doll, what are we talking about here? ʼCause you know there's a difference between Precious Moments and the Bride of Chucky." I tapped my chin with my free hand while puckering my lips and biting the inside of my cheek.

"More like fucking Annabelle." It was clear his tone was meant to straighten my spine, but the fucker's play at having brass balls only had me raising an eyebrow instead.

"The cinematic version or the good old-fashioned Raggedy Anne doll?"

"Enough with the games."

"Games? Yeah, you're not exactly my type when it comes to playing." I smirked. "I'm just trying to determine exactly how condescending you're lookin' to be right now. But it seems your ego is just as fragile as your jaw."

"Awfully proud of that cheap shot, aren't ya, baby girl?"

"Nothing about me's cheap." I winked, mimicking his patronizing gesture from the door and wasting more time than I had to spare.

Something about this fucker left me sidetracked,

veering off a course that should have been locked on cruise control. While the slew of expletives flung in our direction were exactly the slap to the face I needed to jerk the steering wheel back on the road.

"What the fuck!" Johnny Boy hissed under his breath, his jacket flung over one shoulder and his jeans already unbuttoned as he made his way towards what he was assuming was a sure thing.

The only thing *sure* about tonight was supposed to be the easy cash in my pocket.

I used the momentary distraction to impart a good old-fashioned knee between the legs and quickly dislodged my wrist from pretty boy's collapsing frame, before returning my attention to my target. But the dilation of Johnny's eyes and the set of his jaw told me it was too late. My cover had been blown.

"Oh, fuck no." Mommy Issues threw his hand up in a dismissive wave before pivoting towards the asylum of the open club door. "Not sure what the fuck you are into, but that ain't my thing," he grunted with a shuffle in his step that told me he was clamping his thighs together. Attempting to safeguard his family jewels even from afar.

"Fuck! Do you even know how much money you've just cost me?" I crossed my arms and glared at the figure currently hunched over a trash can, his hand in the air wordlessly suggesting that I "hold that thought." Or so I could only assume with the way speaking wasn't much of an option for 'em at the moment.

Pretty boy slammed his palm down on the metal lid, brandishing a slew of vocabulary colorful enough to make a sailor blush before sucking in a steadying breath.

"What are you? Some kind of hooker or something?" He choked out the insult as tears burned his lash line.

"Do I look like some kind of hooker?" The cocky bastard's hesitancy as his eyes raked along my silhouette led me to add, "It's like you want another kick to the balls... Is that *your* thing?"

It didn't take long for the rest of the club's security detail to surround me following the little incident in the back alley. I allowed the fuckers to do it, of course. That messed-up part of me wanted to see what the boys had been up to over the years. If the Mulligans were still as slimy as I remember 'em being. I also may have needed the distraction—the entertainment—to compensate for the wasted time.

I watched my bald, burley, self-imposed warden (who wasn't nearly as pretty as his counterpart) dial out to the local precinct. And my smile grew as his diminished. I didn't have to hear the other end of the conversation to know what words were spoken once I'd name-dropped and urged the fucker to: *go on ahead and call the fucking cops if his dick was so hard for bacon.*

They might as well have told the desk clerk I said hi while they were at it. Officer Gallagher had a list of my favorite aliases memorized by this point. And she hated these Irish fucks almost as much as I did.

Better than their inability to detain my ass was the picture of a younger version of me taped up by the bastard's head next to the other sons of bitches banned from entering any Mulligan establishment. The one none of the guys on staff seemed to recognize as the chick sitting cross-legged in one of their cushy office chairs.

The big guy slammed the receiver down and grunted through the door. "Mac, get your ass in here!" Suddenly eye contact was off limits as the Vin Diesel wannabe dished out orders to the bouncer still bearing the gait of a man with too much to prove and the sore testicles to match. "Drop her ass out on the sidewalk. And no one would blame ya if ya wanted to look away when she happens to trip during the stroll to her cab."

"Mac?" I laughed, my eyes reflecting back in the green of his irises. "Way to stick to a stereotype. That's commitment, I'll give ya that. Let me guess..." I paused, pointing at each of the other two men glaring at me like I kicked their puppies. "Tank and... Axel. Am I right?"

Vin Diesel sneered while Mr. T (obviously the most cordial of the group) stifled a laugh before correcting, "Rocco." He pointed first to baldy, then gestured to himself. "And Zeke."

I snapped my fingers while half a smirk played on my lips. "So close!"

Yanking me up by my forearm, *Mac* lifted me to my feet in a gesture that was ninety percent bravado and ten percent irritation. He wanted to show his buddies that he took my little show at the door real serious but I had my suspicions that he actually liked being bossed around. Probably enjoyed that shit in the bedroom too.

"So what? A honey trap? Is that what this is about?" he urged when the cold night air assaulted my nostrils for the second time in less than twenty minutes.

"That would suggest I'm sweet. Do I seem sweet to you, *Mac*?" I rolled his name along my tongue before discharging it with a click of the C.

"Connor."

"Pardon?"

"Connor *Mac*Cullagh," he clarified.

"So, Connor *Mac*Cullagh," I echoed. "Do you always share your personal information with complete strangers?"

"Pretty sure everyone's a stranger until you do, dollface."

"Touché." Had me there but that was as close to a win as the bastard was gonna get.

"And you are?"

"Busy... very, very busy," was all I offered in return as I spun on my heel and disappeared into the comfort of the thick Chicagoan fog well after I should have been kicking it down the street. Couldn't tell you why I kept the banter going for as long as I did, other than the fucker made it easy. And like I said, shit 'round here had gotten boring.

2

I remembered the soft glow of the red block numbers on my analog clock.

Five AM. It was when I'd usually wake up, throw on some workout gear, and gun it to the gym. Where I'd stretch, hit the bag until it swung so hard it might hit back, then ease my muscles into a hot shower.

By seven, I'd choke down a quick breakfast somewhere local, order my coffee (black, always black), then scan my files. Looking for a case that piqued my interest. A challenge.

It was seven thirty. And I remembered doing jack shit after staring at the red dashes of the number five as it blinked back at me. Two and a half hours of nothingness— the longest period of time yet.

I didn't dream. I never dreamed. It was more like whispers of the past would bide their time until I finally lost consciousness. Then they'd worm their way into the dark, unoccupied crevices of my fucked-up brain, the instances where my neurological system would misfire and forget to maintain its usual shield.

By the time the glow of that clock bore into the gray of my irises, those voices had slithered away. Retreated to whatever bullshit rock they crawled out from under just long enough to torment me for a few hours.

The coffee tasted stale and my neck was stiff. I must have gone too hard on the bag in my haze. My bandaged knuckle bolstered that sentiment. This ringing in my ears was new, but it subsided as the buzz of the city streets took over.

I didn't have my files with me and I could only hope that I hadn't dropped them on the ride over. Maybe I'd reviewed them and found zip? Fuck if I knew. The pickings had been slim. Too fuckin' slim for my own good.

I thirsted for the chase, especially after Johnny Boy got away. If I didn't have something to occupy my time, I went stir crazy. I could already feel my knee bouncing under the table, the pent-up energy clawing at my insides and begging me to let it the fuck out.

Fucking and fighting. They were the only two outlets that fed this innate hunger that festered beneath my surface. And last night I'd left with neither. Something that wasn't boding well for the growing tension in my muscles. Hitting the bag was about as satisfying as my vibrator. Nothing compared to the real thing. The feel of skin on skin, the release of bodily fluids, the push and pull.

I had to get out of this café, find a target, and spill some blood or cum. *Which* it would be was entirely dependent on whoever the fuck I ran into along the way.

There were three things a girl needed to remember in order to give the most unforgettable blow job.

First, you had to grab the base. Think of it like a joystick. *Control the cock, control the man.*

Second, always choose the corner of the room with the best vantage point to keep one eye on the door. *To avoid unexpected surprises, of course.*

Third, and probably most importantly, never—and I mean never—use your teeth... *Until the last possible moment.*

Then bite down like your life depends on it. 'Cause sometimes it would. And I promise you, when he's flopping around like a gutted bluegill, your name will be the only one to part his lips. That and perhaps a few other choice words...

But you catch my drift. *Un-fucking-forgettable.*

And that was how I ended up where I was presently, with that familiar copper taste in my mouth and red coating my teeth.

Sucks for him that tonight the answer was blood. It was dirty work but someone had to do it. Besides, the screaming really did it for me when the cock couldn't.

Whatever remnants of the man remained in my mouth were easily killed off with a quick swish and spit of 151. While I wasn't one to waste alcohol, there was a caveat to even my most steadfast rules.

Did I have to go down on the fucker?

Probably not, however, it was a tried-and-true method that had yet to fail me in a crowded room when other options for seclusion weren't available. And, when done properly, it was a good way to distract your target while giving him a thorough pat-down. Though I could see how the method could be problematic for law enforcement. Good thing I had no interest in wearing a badge. Too many rules and regulations. And, to put it mildly, *fuck that.*

I'd feel bad for the son of a bitch if it didn't take more than a quick contacts change and a blonde wig to make myself unrecognizable. I didn't pity stupid. Envied it sometimes, but you got what was coming to you when you thought with the shit between your legs instead of the shit between your ears. Believe me, I was case and point. But at least I learned.

My target was doubled over, clutching what was left of his cock in one hand while trying to staunch the bleeding with the other. He was screaming but no one could hear his cries over the beat of the music. This was one of those few instances where a crowd was to my advantage.

I flipped Johnny onto his stomach and drew out the pair of zip ties from my pocket, forcing the bastard's arms behind his back with one knee securing him in place. Then dragged him through the closest exit, towards the paneled van I left parked in the alley. I made it three steps out the door, Johnny whimpering in front of me, before a familiar voice had me stopping in my tracks.

I knew it was a risk to come back here so soon. But when I saw a new bouncer at the door and realized the asshats were too dumb to remove my fake name from their list, the thrill of the hunt had me tempting fate.

My boy here had a 10K bounty on his head. Chump change in the grand scheme of things. But it was one of those few instances where the client didn't care if the fucker was brought in dead or alive. I didn't know what Mr. John Porter had done to piss off the Russian mob. But between the FBI and the Volkovs, every bail enforcement agent and hitman in the city was looking for this one target

—some dumb fuck who was apparently either too stupid or too horny to stay in hiding.

Me? I walked that fine line that separated the good guys from the *not-so-good* guys. I was neither hitman nor bounty hunter. If anything, I'd call myself a hired hand. A recovery specialist? Fuck if I knew. I didn't exactly have an office or a business card. What I did have was no interest in making a name for myself. I liked keeping to the shadows, spilling a little blood, making a little more cash, and calling it a day.

Sometimes I would take down a target. My hands sure as fuck weren't clean. But I didn't like to stick to one thing. I enjoyed the change of pace, never knowing what I was walking into. And what I loved were the words *dead or alive*. It meant anything could happen and there was no way to predict what the day would bring me.

I didn't have a boss exactly. Well, I did. My boss was me. But outside of myself, I reported to no one. I'd drop my target or what was left of 'em off to a third party that would pay me cash. Up front of course. Double the listed bounty. And then make a deal with whatever side submitted a better offer. Sometimes that meant handing the mark over to the coppers. Other times, well, you could see where this was going...

Which was exactly how I fell between the two sides of the law. Not really bad, but not so much good either.

Oh, right, but I was in the middle of something, wasn't I?

I looked down at the floor of the panel van. I hadn't even remembered knocking the fucker out and shoving him inside. But here he was. Though I wasn't sure if that was another blackout or if I had been so lost in thought I went into autopilot again.

What I did remember was someone calling out to me. A voice I recognized.

I slammed the back doors in place and secured the outside lock before glancing over my shoulder at the darkened alleyway behind Mollies. There was no one in sight. Had I imagined it? Wouldn't be the first time I heard voices, though usually they were made up by my subconscious. A way to self-regulate and kick my ass into gear.

I cracked my neck from side to side and popped a piece of chewing gum into my mouth. Needed to get the taste of cheap soap and ball sweat off my tongue. Apparently there were some things even alcohol couldn't kill. Then I jumped into the driver's seat and shifted the van into reverse.

"So, where we going, B?"

The question had me choking on my Spearmint and aiming a fist at whoever the fuck thought it was a good idea to stowaway in my truck and then get close enough to whisper in my ear.

3

My ma always told me I was thick-headed. Some kids only had to get burned once and quickly learned not to touch the stove. Not me though. Third time was the charm. Usually. I liked odd numbers. Call me curious, experimental, a *dumb fuck*. Didn't matter. I needed to make sure the result was always the same before I cemented it in stone. Before I accepted something as fact rather than chalked it up to being the luck of a 50/50 coin flip.

So when I saw a certain she-devil in a cheap blonde wig dragging a fucker twice her size out the back door and into the alleyway, I did what any wayward son of a strict Irish Catholic mother would do. I followed them. And watched the slight thing that she was heft the guy onto her shoulder and shove him into the back of one of them pedophile vans —the kind with blackout windows that might as well say *free candy* across the sides.

Of course, my ma also raised me to be a gentleman. So I called out and asked blondie if she needed a hand. She looked in my direction before continuing on with her evening plans like all six-foot-four of me wasn't there.

My metaphorical flame was so lost in her head she didn't even notice when I opened the passenger door, climbed inside the van, and waited for her behind the driver's seat.

Why? Because I was a dumb fuck and she was a pretty girl, remember?

"So, where we going, B?" I caught an elbow in one hand and then a fist in the other before she could land either.

Some things I picked up after the first try—one was an odd number too. And I wasn't about to let her knock me on my ass twice in less than twenty-four hours. Nope, learned my lesson quick when she got the drop on me at the door last night.

Before I realized what she was doing, blondie released the parking brake and was speeding out of the alleyway, which had me clutching the headrests to stay upright.

Yeah, couldn't say I thought this through very well. I must have missed my ma's lecture on getting into creepy-ass vans with strangers. Because here I was, holding on for dear life with a chick who appeared hell-bent on ending it.

"B?" she questioned over her shoulder while her eyes remained fixed on back roads that appeared too tight to fit the likes of us in this big-ass van. Especially as her speedometer teetered dangerously close to eighty.

I smirked. "Yeah, short for *busy, very busy.*"

"Cute..." she replied in a tone that told me she didn't

think it was cute in the least. Which honestly just made it cuter.

"I thought so."

"I don't do cute."

"Got it, lovebug," I hummed by blondie's ear before nipping at her lobe. She smelled like vanilla and… gunpowder?

She reached a hand behind her head and swatted me aside.

"I wouldn't need to come up with my own if you'd given me your name when I asked for it."

"Not gonna happen," she said, without bothering to spare a glance in my direction.

"Guess I'm gonna have to keep playing around until one of 'em sticks." I shrugged.

"Or you could get the fuck outta my car."

"Van."

"What?"

"It's a van, not a car, dollface."

"Do you get off on correcting everything I say, asshat?"

"*Connor*. And, nope, I get off on watching that thing your lip does whenever you're trying not to smile."

"Pretty sure you mean snarl."

"Tomato, tomahto. Fact is it's fucking adorable."

That one had the tires screeching to a halt and Little Miss NASCAR turning around to land me with a glare. Followed by the cold steel of a barrel pressed to my forehead.

"How fucking adorable is it now?" she hissed between two of the plumpest lips I'd ever seen.

I paused for a moment, envisioning all the dirty things that mouth of hers could do to me. All the dirty things I wanted to do to her. Before returning my focus to the very real threat of the gun in her hand. "In all honesty? I don't think I've ever been more turned on, baby girl."

"You're a sick fuck, you know that?"

"Yup. And a good one too, if ya give me the chance to prove it."

Her eyes seemed to flick down my body, taking in everything I had to offer before slowly raking back up again. "Maybe, but you talk too much for it to be *that* good."

I had a clever retort teasing the tip of my tongue, my jaw dropped and my lips with the makings of a panty-melting smirk. At least I was pretty certain I did. Until I felt a prick on the side of my neck, my limbs went numb, and that sensation of falling took over as my world turned upside down and I found myself staring up at the ceiling instead. My eyes shifted from side to side, my brain attempting to gain its bearings while a warm haze traveled up and down my spine.

"You smell nice," I whispered to the angel standing over me. Her dark hair glowed like a halo beneath the van's overhead lighting before everything went black, as the last thought on my mind was...

What the fuck happened to blondie?

4

You know those real vivid dreams you have after you've drowned your sorrows in a cheap bottle of whiskey and more pussy than you could count? The type of dreams that were so fucking realistic you'd swear you could feel your balls tighten on the verge of a mind-blowing orgasm. Almost like you were a prepubescent boy again and you fell asleep with one of your old man's nudey magazines clutched to your chest?

No? Just me?

Doesn't matter. Let's just say that I felt pretty fucking primed and ready, my brain trying to catch up with my body, which was well enough awake to be throbbing in the best way possible. I couldn't quite remember what kinda shit I'd gotten myself into last night. But the hangover was a son of a bitch and my head was pounding.

I knew I needed to get on with my day, open my eyes, and force my ass to take a cold shower before my rock-hard cock found its release between the wrong pair of thighs. There was nothing worse than when the fucker had a mind of its own, leaving the rest of me to deal with the consequences of his good time.

Who needed kids when the asshole between your legs found enough trouble on his own? Swear to Christ I would have gotten snipped if it wouldn't have broken my poor ma's heart.

I had every intention of rolling over and dragging myself out of bed when a couple of warm palms landed on my chest and I felt the instinctual grind of female hips against my bare pelvis.

My first thought was: *Mm, fuck yeah, baby. Just like that.*

My second thought was: *Why the fuck are my wrists zip-tied to the bed?*

Followed by: *Kinky?*

Every muscle in my body screamed at me to grab her waist and sink that tight cunt down where I needed her. When I was confident that wasn't possible, I finally forced my eyes open and stared up into the face of blondie. Who wasn't blonde at all, mind you. I just didn't know what else to call the chick with so much pent-up aggression I bet she'd fuck like a champ. Though something told me I was about to find out...

If this was a dream, goddamn it, I didn't want to wake up. Not before I got a taste.

"Never considered myself much of a bottom, but fuck it. I'll try anything once. You gonna fuck me good, dollface?" I grinned up at her. Despite my thrumming temples, I never felt fucking better. So fucking good, in fact, I didn't bother to question the hotel room or how the fuck I got here.

She rolled her eyes as she leaned forward to rest her hands on the headboard so that her lips were just a breath away from mine. "I liked it better when you didn't talk."

Then she shoved two fingers into my mouth, only to

huff when I met her challenge with a few careful flicks of my tongue around the tips. Blondie's eyes widened before she quickly schooled her features again and returned the palms of her hands to my chest.

It was almost as if she were waiting for me to ask her what I was doing here. I didn't care. I liked where this was going and I wasn't about to look a gift horse in the mouth. Nope, I knew a good thing when I saw it. *Felt* it. And this was fucking magnificent.

She ground her hips against me a second time, and I groaned at the sensation. If she kept that up, I was gonna come before she did and that would be a real fucking shame —as well as a blow to my pride.

When it was clear I wasn't taking the bait, and that my consent flag was waving like it was the final lap at the Grand Prix and I was fucking Andretti rounding the bend, blondie grabbed my chin between her thumb and pointer finger. "I brought you here to see if that giant ego is well-deserved or not. So keep that mouth of yours shut or I'll shut it for you..."

"Don't threaten me with a good time, baby girl..." My smart-ass remark trailed off as she ripped her black tank over her head and tossed it across the room.

I had seen a lot of tits in my day. Some up close and personal, others from the sanctity of my computer screen. But these ones? Fuck, were they works of goddamn art. Award-winning. Nobel Prize worthy. Too damn perfect to be real and I couldn't even touch 'em.

Now I got the full picture. Blondie was looking to torture me. And it was working.

5

After escorting my mark to the drop site, I had a few hours to kill and a lot of steam to blow off. You'd think lugging two hundred plus pounds of muscle from the back of the van and up to the twenty-ninth floor of the Fairmont would be enough to do me in for the night. But a trusty luggage cart and access to the freight elevator did most of the grunt work. Which left me with an itch the evening's takedown didn't quite scratch.

At first, I was gonna leave my stowaway tied to the bed, sans his wallet and keys—and a lot less clothing. A little lesson when it came to sticking your nose where it didn't belong. But after I stripped him bare and saw what he was working with, temptation got the better of me. I mean, the fucker had been talking a big game all night... and the game was *big*. I'd give him that much.

He was knocked out cold. The quick-acting sedative had a half-life of four to six hours, give or take, depending on the individual's body weight and metabolism. But the rest of him seemed to work just fine, respond to my touch as readily as someone with their wits about them. So I threw a thigh over his waist and climbed onto his lap while staring down at the finely sculpted planes of his abs, which led up to his prominent pectoral muscles and over to a pair of broad shoulders that could likely throw me around like a goddamn rag doll... if I let 'em.

Like I said, the fucker was pretty. A little too pretty if you asked me. And he knew it too. His arrogance was visible even in his sleep. He had this stupid half smirk on his face that told me he was more than aware of his good looks. I fought the urge to slap that smirk off his lips and not because I didn't want to hurt him. But because it would ruin the mood if the fucker woke up and started talking again.

I'd already showered—needing to get the stench of Johnny off my skin—and changed into a black tank top and a pair of lace underwear. So there was nothing more than a thin layer of fabric separating me from the pretty boy beneath me, and I found myself grinding my hips against his pelvic bone before I could stop myself.

It wasn't smart. I didn't have a file on this guy. Didn't know where he'd been or who he'd been with. But that was the problem with us thrill-seekers. We knew the risks and we thrived on taking them. I mean, the fucker looked pretty clean, smelled it too, and most of the other stuff could be killed with a heavy dose of antibiotics. That's what I told myself anyway as I considered sinking down on the fine specimen of man meat in front of me.

And by consider, I meant my hands were grabbing for the joystick when the son of a bitch woke up and looked me dead in the eye. Instead of the terror I was hoping for, I saw surprise followed by a hefty serving of lust. I should have put the brakes on my libido right then and there. Climbed off the bed and offered Connor MacCullagh the one-finger salute as I slipped the *do not disturb* sign on the door and slammed it behind me. Leave the fucker with blue balls and the bag of coke I tossed in the bathroom for housekeeping and the authorities to find at checkout.

But I didn't do any of that. Because before I could think on it, I was tugging my shirt over my head and dropping it onto the floor. It would be a shame to waste a good cock. They were hard to come by these days—pun intended—and God knew I needed a decent fucking.

I was already worked up, so it didn't take more than shoving the lace aside and sliding down onto nine inches of smooth dick to have me halfway to the point of coming. A handful of back-and-forth motions to have me swallowing my moans. And a few rotations of my pelvic muscles to bring me to the brink of bliss.

The sound of Connor's voice grated on my nerves, but the little grunts he made as I used him like a fuck doll were more of a turn-on than I'd ever admit. I could almost imagine his large palms resting on my hips, guiding my movements, slamming me down faster, harder, as I edged us closer and closer to that orgasmic cliff. Though if the fucker came before I did, he'd better be prepared to lick me clean because I would ride his face until I got mine or he suffocated. I didn't care which.

I needed this. Fuck, I needed this. I needed the stretch, the burn, the pain mixed with pleasure. I needed the darkness in my head to recede and just to feel nothing for a little bit. I needed more than nothing. I needed something. And I needed this fucker to give it to me.

It wasn't until I leaned forward again, shifting his cock into that perfect angle, that he met me halfway, sucking my nipple between his teeth and biting down. That delicious sting traveled from the nerves in my tit straight to my core and sent me flying. I was near giddy as I rode out wave after wave of pleasure until sweat drenched my forehead and chest, and my neck tweaked with the sudden chill running up my spine.

He was on the verge of coming too. I could feel it in the way his thigh muscles clenched where my knees had them pinned against the mattress. See it in the way his jaw tensed and his teeth ground together. Hear it with each quickened breath that parted his pussy-sucking lips. But his pleasure had never been my prerogative... or my problem. Which had me hopping off the bed, throwing on my clothes, and exiting the hotel room while his pent-up, drawn-out "fuck" followed me down the hallway.

"Maybe next time you'll think twice before jumping into cars with strangers." I grinned to myself.

6

"Pretty sure I'm in love, man." I slammed my beer onto the bar top, using my free arm to slap a palm against Zeke's shoulder.

I recognized the incredulous look he gave me. The one that said "what the actual fuck" before he ever had to utter a word when it came to what he was thinking. I could read my childhood friend quicker than the latest article in Maxim magazine—*hint: we never read the fucking articles.* Any fucker who told you otherwise was lying through his teeth.

"So, I just wanna make sure I got this straight..." Zeke gestured a hand in my direction, a single brow cocked in that condescending way he did while one side of his mouth lifted into something that resembled a snarl. But not quite. Almost like he smelled something rank and was trying to figure out where it was coming from. "This chick drugged you, tied you to a bed in some random hotel room, fucked you almost good, then left your ass with the worst case of blue balls and a bathroom filled with enough coke to land yourself some distribution charges. And the immediate response in that fucked-up brain of yours is to call it love?"

"Yup." I popped the P, shrugging through my grin while Zeke eyed me like I had two cocks sticking out of my forehead. "The heart wants what it wants."

"Right... and I'm sure this has nothing to do with the fact that you're bored and get your rocks off on taming yourself a brat."

"Man, there ain't nothing bratty about this one. Baby girl could bring me to my knees and have me lickin' her boots like it was just another Sunday afternoon for her." I rubbed a hand against the back of my neck, picturing all the things I never got to do to her in that hotel room.

Lucky for my squeaky clean record, the nice housekeeper lady took pity on my predicament and cut me free before turning on her heel and walking back out the door. My guess was that it had something to do with the apologetic dimples I flashed her while trying not to *flash* her the rest of me. I did always have a way with the cougars—something about my boyish charms called to their primal side or so I'd been told.

"Need I remind you, you don't even know this chick's name?"

"What's in a name? That which we call a rose by any other name would smell just as sweet?"

"Yeah, how about you don't use that Romeo shit on me? Save it for the college girls who like all the corny-ass lines you feed 'em."

"Actually, it's Juliet's shit, not Romeo's."

"Okay, and now I understand why she drugged your ass. That's annoying as fuck, you know that, right?"

"And yet, here you are, stuck to that ass like fucking glue through the years. So who's the real masochist?"

This had 'em chuckling around the rim of his beer as he knocked back what was left of it. Zeke liked to give me shit, but at the end of the day, the fucker had my six better than any blood brother ever could. He just didn't want me doing anything stupid. Kid always had a level head on his shoulders while I enjoyed the chaos. Likely had to do with the different ways we were raised.

I was an only child while Zeke was the eldest of six. Which meant he was the mother hen of our group of misfits at the club. Always pecking at our feet when we strayed from the straight path. We appreciated his efforts—really we did—but it also made 'em a bit of a Debbie Downer whenever one of us was looking to be a little reckless.

Still, Zeke was the one bastard you could rely on to pick up the phone if you needed bailing out. Also the first guy to grab a shovel if someone were looking to hurt you. The only time I ever saw the fucker truly unhinged was when some drunk fuck threatened Zeke's sister. My friend went full-on apeshit and nearly landed himself in the clink. Took a lot of persuading to get the dumb fuck to drop the charges and for the nightclub owner to make the whole thing disappear. We might have kept our noses clean but we weren't naïve to what went down behind closed doors in our place of employment.

The streets were mob territory and anyone who grew up in these parts also knew better than to get between the Irish and the Italians and whatever turf wars had them feuding this time around. You turned your head and pretended you didn't see shit. Because seeing shit dragged you into deeper shit. And deeper shit landed you in the kind of shit you couldn't dig yourself out of. It sounded way more complicated than it was.

But you could catch my drift. *Shit was bad. Avoid shit.*

Which was exactly what Zeke, Rocco, and I did to the best of our abilities. Until women were involved. And then we lost whatever brain cells we had in these skulls of ours. Hence my present predicament.

It had been two days since blondie left me tied up in that hotel room, and I hadn't been able to stop thinking about her or the way she moved those hips... The feel of her tight-as-fuck pussy gripping my cock like it was meant to be there... How sweet her nipple was when I was finally able to get a taste... How perfect her heart-shaped ass looked in lace while I was forced to watch her walk away...

If she had waited long enough for me to finish, I would have called it the best sex of my life. Even so, it was high up there on the list. I was hard just thinking about it. Imagining a take two that ended with my cum coating her ass cheeks when I bent her over the bed... or the counter... or whatever piece of furniture was within arm's reach the next time I saw her.

Because there would be a next time. Baby girl just didn't know it yet.

7

The jobs had been nonexistent, the tension in my head growing louder with each day that passed without some form of outlet. I'd be lying if I said I hadn't thought about the pretty boy with the piercing green eyes.

Okay, I'd more than thought about him. I'd woken up in a cold sweat, in desperate need of a colder shower in the morning, my body plagued by the phantom touch of his cock between my legs. I'd found myself seeking him out in the crowd, even knowing I shouldn't, that he wouldn't be there.

I knew better. Attachments were a weakness in my line of work. Left you vulnerable and stupid. Something I knew firsthand. And couldn't forget thanks to the little souvenir I still carried with me after my last relationship.

Funny enough, I didn't think about Leo often. Whenever I did, it was as if the bullet still lodged in my brain would punish me. My temples would throb, my jaw ache down to the base of my neck, and I could feel the tension building in my shoulders. All of which reminded me of a time in my life when I threw common sense out the window and trusted the dick between some fucker's legs more than the gut feeling in the pit of my stomach.

I didn't miss the bastard. Far from it. I was angry. And pent-up rage had a way of fucking with your nervous system, increasing the stress hormones coursing through your body while causing the veins to restrict and the pressure to build. In a way, our bodies were our own worst enemies. Because we did that shit to ourselves. And there wasn't a goddamn thing we could do to fix it.

My nails were tapping on the kitchen table when I finally decided to say "fuck it" and give good ol' Officer Gallagher a ring. I didn't like reaching out to Laney's side of the law, unless I absolutely had to. And right now, it felt like a necessity more than anything else.

I didn't wait for her to speak before I was breathing into the receiver. "Please tell me you have something off the books..."

"Either we're doing an impeccable job at keeping the streets clean or being dirty ain't paying like it used to. You could always come over to my neck of the woods. Wouldn't mind having another female in the ranks."

I could hear her grin through the phone. The woman loved to bust my balls but she was a decent egg as far as cops went. Even if bacon was my least favorite flavor. She also understood that the world wasn't black and white and the rules needed to be bent every once in a while to benefit the greater good. It just so happened that my version of *good* revolved around keeping a roof over my head and my liquor cabinet filled.

I mean, we all couldn't be superheroes. What use were they without a few villains in the mix?

"Thanks but no fucking thanks. I wouldn't last two days

in the bullpen without putting one of those bastards on their asses—IA would have me outta there quicker than a greased pig at a southern barbecue."

"Your loss." She sighed before adding, "Let me see what I can do... I'll give one of my contacts a call and get back to you."

"Thanks, Lane." It was better than nothing. Though not by much.

"Stay outta trouble, Dani. And away from that club. Those guys have your face plastered across every back room and you don't want that kinda attention in your line of work."

"Yeah, I saw that. Speaking of..." I knew I shouldn't. But the words were tumbling out of my mouth before I could stop them. "Can you look someone up for me? Wanna see if the fucker is worth the effort it'll take to bring him in?"

"Sure... Got a name?" I could hear her rummaging through her desk, likely looking for a pen and a pad of paper.

"Yeah, MacCullagh. First name Connor."

She hummed to herself and I wasn't sure if it was a sound of familiarity or a lack of. "Never heard of 'em. Part of Mulligan's crew?"

"Possibly. But I wanna know what I'm getting into before pissing off the Irish." I was lying. And something told me she could sense it too. It wasn't like me to give a fuck about the repercussions, not when there was a paycheck waving at me from the other side of the same line I was more than willing to cross for the right price.

She didn't call me out on it though. Which meant one of two things. She was being polite; the Gallaghers were known for it. Tried to fuck her brother once and the bastard turned me down. Offered to take me on a proper date first or some shit—lost my lady boner real quick with that one. Or Little Miss Detective was playing hardball and wanted to figure out my angle before presenting her case.

At the moment, I didn't care what her reasoning was as long as it got me results.

Who the fuck are you, Connor MacCullagh? And why the fuck do I even want to know?

8

"Who the fuck let Danica Rossi into my goddamn club?"

You could practically see the steam coming out of bossman's ears as he tapped on the CCTV footage from a few nights back, his fingertip aimed at my mystery woman while his nostrils flared in a way that told me my ass was about to get chewed out. I couldn't be bothered to care at the moment. Because I finally had a name.

Danica. I liked the way it tasted on my tongue. It suited her somehow. Pretty but not delicate. And an ironic testament to her driving skills when she was weaving in and out of those back alleys in that van of hers.

Benny rewound the film a few hours before turning his glare back on Zeke and me, seeing as we were the ones in charge of checking IDs on the nights in question. "Not once. But fucking twice!" he hissed.

My mouth always got me in trouble and right now was no different. I didn't understand what the point was of getting so worked up over something you couldn't change.

Judging from the vein pulsing in his forehead, I could only assume this guy's blood pressure was through the roof.

"She someone important?" I could feel Zeke's eyes boring a hole through the side of my face. But it wasn't like that was ever enough to stop me. " 'Cause I ain't ever heard of her, Benny." I shrugged.

"What that girl is, is fucking trouble. The Rossi family is blacklisted—something you two fuckwits should know by now."

"Right, 'cept baby girl used a fake ID, then landed a cheap shot when I called her out on it." The grumpy fucker in a suit two sizes too small raised a single eyebrow at my use of a pet name. I ignored him and shoved my foot farther into my mouth. "Not much we coulda done about that. Once we caught on to her game, we followed protocol to the letter. The cops told us to drop it before we could get anything outta those tight lips of hers."

"Fuck the cops. Why didn't anyone call me?" There was that vein again. Fucker was on the verge of an aneurism at this rate.

"And say what?" Rocco chimed in. He was standing by the door, watching while doing fuck all to help us. "The chick never mentioned she was a Rossi, and my guys know better than to bother you with low-level bullshit like fake IDs."

"Who was the cop?" Benny asked, his eyes narrowed in on me. God only knew why.

But at least the heat was off Zeke. He was the one who let my girl through in that cheap wig—even a blind man coulda seen through that disguise. Fucker probably got distracted by a nice set of tits. And, honestly, I couldn't blame 'em. The memory was enough to have me swipe my tongue across my lips and check for drool.

"Gallagher," Rocco answered for me.

"Fucking hell. Her uncle was on the books, but Delaney's been a tougher one to break." Benny was rambling now, saying more than he should in front of Zeke and me. Which meant my girl must really have him on edge. "Bet that bitch pig knew exactly what she was doing when she told you to let Danica go. I'm gonna..." His eyes flicked in our direction, almost as if he forgot we were in the room, before the rest of his words died on his tongue. "Get the fuck out of here. I'll call in my nephew to clean up your mess."

Great. Baby Mulligan was the opposite of what we needed right now. The kid was a halfwit with tiny prick syndrome—I'd never seen it myself but that shit was obvious the moment he opened his mouth and tried to throw his toddler-size balls around. His last name was his only saving grace. People feared it, not *him*.

I pushed to my feet, tempted to ask a little more history on the Rossis—or at least one in particular—when Zeke tugged me through the door, down the hall, and out the back entrance.

"What the fuck is wrong with you?" he grunted the moment the fresh air smacked us across the face.

"A lot." I shrugged. I wasn't sure why he was acting like this was news to him.

"Fucking right there is." He was pacing up and down, raking a hand across his recently shaved head like he'd forgotten there wasn't any hair left to tug. "I mean, you've always been a dumb fuck. But now all of a sudden you have a death wish too?" His eyes were wild. I hadn't seen him this worked up since that incident with his sister.

"What the fuck is your problem, Z? Benny's always been an ass. This ain't nothing new and it's not like he said he was gonna fire us or anything. It was a fake ID for fuck's sake. What's the big fucking deal?"

This was apparently the wrong thing to say. Though it did stop his pacing. It also had him pivoting on his heel and pinning me against the brick wall. "The big fucking deal, dipshit, is your dumb ass dragging us into the middle of this mafia bullshit because you wanted to get your dick wet."

"Me?" I shoved at his chest, just enough to send his ass back a few steps. I wouldn't hit 'em. But sometimes he needed to remember that I could. I just chose not to. "Pretty sure I followed your ass here and not the other way around, *brother*."

At the same time, it didn't hurt to remind the fucker that he was like family to me. It helped get him out of his head when he was overthinking. It came from a good place. I knew as much, but it didn't make his *mother hen* act any less annoying.

"I never asked you to do that." He sighed and cast his eyes to the ground.

I draped an arm over his shoulder and led him over to the door. "Didn't have to. Where you go, I go." I grinned in that stupid way that forced him to do the same, tugging Zeke inside and getting our asses back to work before our necks really were on the chopping block.

9

DG:
Your guy's clean.

> **ME:**
> What do you mean clean?

DG:
I mean exactly what I said. He doesn't have
a record. Sealed or otherwise.

> **ME:**
> That doesn't make sense. An Irish fucker
> working for the Mulligans who doesn't
> have a record?

I hit send before I realized what I'd done, cursing under my breath when my phone immediately started ringing in my hand. I could ignore it, but she'd just keep calling. Or worse, she'd dig into what my interests were in some nobody without a record.

My thumb swiped up on the call and Laney didn't wait for me to greet her. "I told you to stay the fuck away from that club, Rossi."

"Yeah, not sure I'm too keen on being told what to do. Thought you'd know that by now."

"It's not funny, Dani. Those fuckers already want your blood. Stop giving them a reason to take it."

"If MacCullagh isn't on their actual payroll, then they have no reason to fuss, am I right? You said it yourself. The guy doesn't have a record."

"Then why's he got a price on his head?"

"Never said he did."

"No, but you sure as fuck implied it. If this isn't about money, then what's it about, Dani?" She had her detective hat on now. I could hear it in her tone, almost picture the way her eyes would narrow in whenever she was thinking too hard.

"I told you it was a job. Doesn't mean he's the target."

"Right... well, if you have a DOB..." she started, and I stopped her before she could finish her train of thought.

"Yeah, haven't gotten that close yet."

"It's not in your file?"

Fuck, she had me there. But I couldn't let her know she'd backed me into a corner. That's exactly what she was hoping to do.

"Already said he wasn't the target, just a weak link," I was quick to remind her. "Anyway, thanks. Hit me up when you got something interesting to say," I added before disconnecting the call.

Shit wasn't making sense. Pretty boy was way too dumb to stay clean. Lacking street smarts and not so much a dull crayon fresh outta the box. Which meant it was unlikely he could avoid trouble for long. If he didn't find it, it sure as fuck would find him.

He'd climbed into my van for fuck's sake. I could only

imagine the sort of shit he'd stumbled upon hanging out with Mulligan's crew. The fact the guy was still breathing was a wonder—might even call it the luck of the Irish if I weren't so sure that shit was an old wives' tale.

If the Irish did have luck, Mulligan's ran out a while ago... around the same time his nephew put a bullet in my head. Maybe it was just karma finally catching up with the slimy son of a bitch and what was left of his fucked-up gene pool. Or maybe this was God's way of tellin' me I should speed things up a bit.

My head was pounding, the fluorescent overhead lighting flickering as my vision came into focus. My eyes instinctively dropped to the time on my watch. It was 10 PM. I'd lost another two hours and I didn't even know where the fuck I was.

This wasn't good. Sure, losing time was nothing new. But part of my subconscious usually took over and I followed a routine, never ended up somewhere I didn't recognize, doing God only knows what.

I choked down a deep breath and forced myself to take in my surroundings. I was in a... supply closet?

There was a row of industrial-style brown paper towels lined up on a shelf behind me, a mop bucket in the corner while the monogrammed cocktail napkins gave me the first real hint to my location. I was back at Mollies. With no clue as to how the fuck I got here.

The last thing I remembered was Laney's call. A

thought that had me patting down my leather jacket in search of my burner. It was nowhere to be found, the jacket or the phone, which meant I'd either left 'em behind or someone had taken 'em from me. Though the latter wasn't likely, seeing as I didn't spot any blood on my knuckles. I wouldn't have given 'em up without a fight and my body didn't feel any worse for the wear.

My hand was reaching for the knob, looking to make a quick escape from whatever bullshit I'd gotten myself into tonight, when the door flung open from the other side. Large hands pressed on my shoulders and forced me back a step as a figure crossed the threshold and closed us inside. It took me a second to recognize him, the throbbing behind my eyes making it difficult to focus.

"What the fuck are you doing here?" It was not the brightest thing to say but it was the only question that came to mind as I tried to regain my bearings.

"Here, as in inside this closet? Or here, as in at the club? 'Cause the answer to both is I work *here*, Danica."

I didn't remember ever telling the fucker my name while the smirk he was presently wearing confirmed I hadn't. Bastard looked way too proud of himself.

So I decided to change tack. "What do you want, Connor?"

He shrugged before taking two more steps forward, caging me against the back shelf. His breath mingling with mine so that I could almost taste him. "I could ask you the same thing, dollface, seeing as you're the one who came here insisting on seeing me."

"I did not." The words sounded childish even to my own ears. But I couldn't stop myself. I didn't come here for him. I wouldn't have, would I?

No, there had to be another explanation. A case, a file, money on the line. I just needed to try harder to remember.

Conner reached out, lifting my chin with his thumb while running his forefinger along my bottom lip. The tension in the air had my eyes drifting closed as he lowered his mouth to mine and whispered, "Oh, but you did, baby girl. Heard you were beggin' for it too."

10

TWENTY MINUTES PRIOR

"Yo, Mac." O'Brien's voice crackled through my earpiece.

"What's up?" I called back.

It was a full moon, which meant it could be anything from a fight breaking out at the door to a bunch of dudes ODing in the bathroom. I wasn't superstitious or into any of that tarot card and crystal crap Zeke's baby sister was always goin' on about, but shit was too constant to be unrelated. The crazies always came out when Mercury was in retrograde or whatever it was Annie called it.

"Some chick is asking—more like demanding to see you out front. She ain't half-bad looking either."

"What's she look like?" I couldn't help the smirk already tipping up the sides of my lips. Only two women would have balls enough to come to my job looking for me—the girl whose name I couldn't get outta my head or my sister. And I didn't have a sister.

"Small thing with a big attitude. A brunette."

Looked like this particular crazy was mine.

"Keep an eye on her. I'll be right there," I responded through the light static.

"I'll do ya one better and keep two on that ass."

I could hear the fucker's grin, and ground my teeth to stop myself from saying something I might regret on an open comm line.

I wasn't sure what baby girl was doing here. Especially with everyone and their uncle warned about allowing a Rossi into the club for a third time. It was now deemed a fircable offense but still totally worth the risk—if you asked me. Zeke might argue otherwise.

We were lucky enough that O'Brien was a dumb fuck, easily distracted by anything in a miniskirt or, in this case, a pair of skintight riding leathers.

I took a moment to appreciate the view from where I was standing by the side door. I had no doubt she expected me to come through the front, which allowed me a few minutes to take in the little hellcat with naturally chocolate-brown hair that begged to be wrapped around a fist and tugged, a tiny waist my palms were just itching to grip until each of my fingers left an indent, and curves that rivaled Marilyn's on a good day. And were even fuckin' better on a bad one.

Danica Rossi was like every man's wet dream. At the very least she was mine. Cliché as fuck to say aloud but no one was stopping me from thinking it. I could see the goose bumps forming across her arms, her top half bare except for a tiny leather vest that was no more than a bathing suit top in size. Baby girl looked like she was freezing her tits off, despite the matching leather pants and black ankle boots.

Something told me she wasn't planning on going out tonight...

Her dark gray eyes flicked in my direction almost as if she could feel me watching her from afar. But it was like the lights were on and no one was home—she was doing that thing where she sort of stared through me again.

It wasn't safe for her to be hanging 'round outside the club; it was less safe to drag her inside along with me. But apparently neither one of us cared about our well-being at the moment.

It took two steps for me to close the distance and zero fucks to ignore O'Brien's raised brow as I threw my jacket over Danica's shoulders and guided her through the employee entrance. She didn't say a word, or really even acknowledge my presence as I led her down the dark hallway before pulling her inside the first door I found. All while hoping the guys in the back room weren't paying too much attention to the security feed. Thank fuck most of them were on Mulligan's payroll and didn't give two shits about their "day" jobs. The club wasn't anything more to them than a front, a place to fuck around and clean their dirty money. Whereas it was my and Zeke's goddamn livelihood.

I glanced behind me before shoving the supply closet door shut and pivoting to face Danica, my back pressing against her only escape and my hands free to do as they pleased this time around.

But first thing was first. I needed someone to cover me, and there was only one someone I trusted enough to ask almost as much as I dreaded asking 'em.

I raked a hand through my hair, far more stressed about approaching Zeke than I was about someone finding me and my little stalker tucked away in this closet. The same girl who had yet to acknowledge my presence, mind you.

I reached out a hand, tipping her chin up and forcing

her to look at me with that dead expression on her face. "Stay right here. Do not leave this room, got me?" When she didn't immediately respond, I added, "Blink if ya understand me, dollface."

Something about the words I said or the tone I used had her lashes fluttering in my direction. Which I took as the closest thing I was gonna get to a *yes* at the moment.

There was more to Danica's sudden appearance tonight, almost as if she wasn't just looking for me but some part of her was asking for help. Because whatever was going on in that head of hers, it wasn't normal.

Lucky for us, neither was I.

I pressed a kiss to her forehead, the only thing that felt right when baby girl was nearly catatonic, turned around, grabbed the knob, and slowly clicked the door closed behind me.

This wasn't a conversation I wanted to have, but lying to my best friend wasn't an option either. Unfortunately another one of my quirks was that I was honest to a fault— at least that was what everyone liked to tell me. Though I always thought it had more to do with the realization that I was a shit liar, so why bother tryin' in the first place?

Zeke gave me shit for a good five minutes before the fucker waved me off and told me to hurry the fuck up or he'd *hand my ass over on a silver platter*. It was bullshit and we both knew it, but I had the decency to at least pretend like I believed him.

I didn't have much of a plan in mind when it came to

what I was doing here, how I'd get her out without being seen, or what I'd say if someone spotted us. But honestly that was pretty par for the course with me. Planning just meant you expected things to go wrong, and my last name gave me the benefit of having pure dumb luck on my side.

11

PRESENT

"Oh, but you did, baby girl. Heard you were beggin' for it too." My words seemed to echo around us as I edged my little troublemaker closer to the back shelving.

Danica appeared much more herself now—what parts of her I'd gotten to know anyway—as she jutted her chin defiantly, her glare searing like she was hoping she could burn a hole in the center of my forehead.

"How do you know my name?" It sounded more like an accusation than a question. Which was funny when you thought about it, seeing as baby girl was the one stalking me and not the other way around. Not saying I had any qualms about hunting her down. It just seemed near impossible when this woman disappeared like Cinderella at midnight.

"Apparently, you're a legend around here, dollface. Something about you having a beef with the Mulligans?" I quirked a curious brow, even knowing damn well she wasn't about to clue me in to the history there. One thing I knew for sure was that Danica Rossi liked her secrets.

"More like they have a beef with me," she grumbled, her top lip curling into a snarl. Her eyes flicked to the door and I could almost see the wheels turning in her head. My girl was looking to bolt, and I didn't even know why she sought me out in the first place. "And if you know what's good for you, you'll stay away from both of us."

"There's something you need to understand, dollface. I don't know what's good for me. Never said I did. Or gave you any inclination that I cared. If I want an extra piece of cake before dinner, I'm gonna fucking eat it. Because it tastes goddamn good. Same goes for you. If I wanna fuck your ass six ways to Sunday while playing a game of Russian roulette, I'm gonna do that too. I don't give a fuck if it's good for me or not. Not when we both know it feels fucking fantastic." I leaned forward, pressing my body closer to hers. "And no one, not even you, can do a damn thing to stop me."

Distraction was the only tool I had at my immediate disposal. So I pried her legs apart with my knee, feeling the warmth of her cunt even through two layers of clothing, and propped my right arm on the shelf above her head. I knew she could fight me off if she was really looking to get away but my gut told me her feigned reluctance was a front. A fight-or-flight response because I made her feel uncomfortable in all the right ways. It was hard for someone who was used to relying on themself to admit they wanted something from someone else. Almost like they thought it made them weak.

I had no problem admitting it, though. I wanted this woman more than I needed my next breath. Enough to risk my life and my livelihood just to steal a few minutes alone with her in this closet.

Her head tipped up almost subconsciously. Like she didn't even realize she was leaning into me, her hands no longer pushing on my chest to shove me away but clutching my shirt to tug me forward as her hips started to grind against my thigh. She would never say it aloud; she didn't have to. Her body language spoke volumes.

She wanted me.

My free hand crept up and around her throat before gently drawing Danica's head forward to close the millimeters of space between us. I could have just lowered my lips to hers, but something deep in my psyche needed her to come to me. To submit in some fashion when the woman hungered for control.

The moment her mouth met mine, though, all bets were off. I slammed my body against hers, not even bothering to look when I heard the distant sound of glass shattering as various items rolled off the shelving unit and hit the floor. Danica wrapped her legs around my waist in a frenzy of thrashing limbs and gnashing teeth. I yanked her head back to give me a better angle, and she moaned against my lips. The sound like music to my goddamn ears.

Obviously we'd fucked already—or rather she fucked me—but this was different. So much better. Especially as my hands pulled and tugged at her too-tight pants as I propped her ass on the ledge and struggled to shove the material down her thighs. But fuck if it wasn't worth the effort. Like finding the prize at the bottom of the box after weeks of eating the same bland cereal. I fumbled around between her legs before yanking her underwear to one side and dipping a finger into her wet cunt.

I groaned as Danica threw her head back, seemingly

unfazed when she cracked it against a metal bracket. She continued to twist her hips and ride my hand until I pulled it free and reached for my belt buckle. One snap of a button and a quick release of a zipper later, and I was pulling my cock free and driving forward.

The first thrust was nothing short of nirvana—especially after how she left me the other night—while the next three had me counting dead kittens in my head to keep from coming. "Fuck, baby girl, you feel so fucking good," I grunted between thrusts.

"Dani," she hissed in reply. Though I could tell she was struggling to get the words out.

"What was that?" I pulled back to look her in the eye, hoping it wasn't the wrong move, seeing as I was pretty sure my balls would shrivel up and die if I didn't get to come this go-around.

"My name. It's Dani. Not baby girl or Danica. Or whatever the fuck else you like to call me. It's just Dani. Four letters. Simple enough for your Neanderthal brain to remember."

"The thing is, Dani." I grinned, slamming forward again before she changed her mind and left me hanging. "I plan to fuck you until neither one of us remembers our own names."

Her hands found purchase in my hair as she twisted her hips to the rhythm of my strokes, likely looking to bring herself to that edge with or without me. "Big talk for a man who was on the verge of coming the moment he walked in here."

I captured her lip between my teeth, biting down just enough to sting, before releasing her on a grin. "What can I say, dollface? Guess I get off on being chased down."

12

This was the last thing I should be doing. More like *he* was the last thing I should be doing. Again. But the fucker was right. It felt way too fucking good to stop now and I was a hedonist at my core. Over-indulgence way more gratifying than doing what was expected of me. It was how I got here.

And I didn't mean this storage closet. I meant my position in life. Doing what I wanted when I wanted was what had the eldest heir to the Rossi bloodline leaving it all behind to fuck around with some Irish prick who put a bullet in her head less than six months later, because his family didn't like his choice in women. Or the lineage that came with her last name.

Apparently I had a preferred flavor though. Seeing as I now found myself in an Irish club getting my brains fucked out by a certified leprechaun. But something about Connor was different, endearing almost, in the way he pursued me. Despite his claim that it was the other way around.

I might not have remembered riding over here, but the fact that he knew who I was and wasn't hand-delivering me to a Mulligan meant the guy was a little more than infatuated. My head was worth a pretty penny, probably why I found so much enjoyment in slipping in and out unnoticed whenever given the chance.

He was risking his own neck just to get his dick wet. Which meant that he was either brave or really fucking stupid. Okay, maybe *endearing* wasn't the right word. But for some reason, this felt like more than that. Like more than just a quick nut...

Shut the fuck up, Dani.

I couldn't help but scream at myself. Thoughts like those, emotions—yeah, they had no fucking place in my fucked-up world. And pretty boy was better off staying well the fuck away from my orbit and the shitstorm that came with it.

Connor's mouth slammed down on mine again, his tongue darting inside and tasting me, as he groaned with each forward drive of his hips. It was that sound he made that geared me closer to the edge of climaxing, that had my thighs trembling and a moan escaping my lips before I could stop myself. The man had more stamina than I would have given him credit for.

Guess that time in the hotel wasn't a once off.

He grabbed my ass, angling himself so that he was somehow thrusting deeper, as he pulled almost all the way out before diving back in again. His strokes alternated between slow and languid to fast and punishing. Which left me teetering on the ledge. I could feel it. I was almost there. But not quite. And that seemed to be his intention as a slow grin spread across his face.

I used one hand to brace myself on the shelf while I reached out with the other, gripping his back through his shirt and embedding my nails through the thin material. He hissed with the initial contact but apparently it wasn't enough to get my point across, as the fucker decelerated to a goddamn snail's pace.

I wanted to be fucked, not edged all goddamn night. The bastard was turning this quickie into a tantric sex session.

"Patience, baby girl," Connor whispered into my ear, his minty breath sending a chill down my spine. "Remember, you're the one who gave me something to prove." He punctuated his words with more slow thrusts of his hips, this time hitting that deep spot that meant I could feel him in my lower abdomen. It was uncomfortable and so good at the same time, especially as his pubic bone brushed against my clit in a circular motion.

He had me there. Right fucking there. But I wasn't about to let him know that and have the fucker stop, thinking I deserved it and trying to get back at me after the little incident in the hotel.

I could feel my toes curling, my muscles tightening in a way that told me my legs would feel weak later, followed by the delicious pressure in the pit of my stomach.

Fuck, yeah, I was com—

13

A sudden pounding on the door had me pulling back from Dani and shoving her behind me as a voice hissed out from the other side. I ignored her grumblings, and the aching of my pussy-drenched cock, as I listened for the fucker to speak first.

"Hurry the fuck up and nut already. Junior is on a warpath." I could hear the panic in Zeke's voice and my throbbing dick cursed him for it.

It was my own damn fault. I was trying to make a point with my girl and ended up giving myself an even worse case of blue balls instead.

"Would be a lot easier to do if I didn't have your voice in my ear," I yelled back, tugging my pants into place before dropping to my knees in front of Dani. I should leave her hanging. Would serve baby girl right after what she did to me at the Fairmont. But I wasn't about to gain the reputation of being the kind of guy who didn't know how to please his woman.

I needed to give her a reason to come back after all. And a soul-shattering orgasm would be just one of many.

I could see the frustration on Dani's face as I peered up at her from between her slick thighs. My cock was begging me for a few more strokes—the woman fit me like a goddamn glove—but I didn't have time and she didn't have the patience at the moment. I needed her to come quickly so I could get her the fuck out of here before Mulligan's nephew got his sights on her. I didn't know what the fuck was going on between the two families and honestly I didn't want to know. I was sure I wouldn't like it. And I didn't need more of a reason to hate the fuckers I worked for. Not when their money kept the lights on.

"Look, this has been fun and all but—"

A quick flick of my tongue cut off whatever bullshit Dani was gonna try to feed me as she threw her head back on a moan, her hands reaching out to shove my face closer to her cunt. Her deliciously bare, perfectly pink cunt.

I dove in, licking, sucking, and biting in all the right places. While the taste of my precum was a stark reminder that I'd forgotten the little matter of protection. Which wasn't like me. But fuck if this woman didn't know how to get in my head and have me losing all reason; contraception was one thing I wasn't so reckless about. The last thing the world needed was a bunch of toddler-sized MEs running around.

Fuck that.

I needed to remember to keep a few extra condoms in my wallet, for whenever my girl deserved a good fucking in a nearby closet. A thought that had my mind returning to the mouthwatering task at hand.

I took a deep breath, her scent filling my nostrils and her arousal dripping from the tip of my nose. So much so I had to fight my urge to reach a hand up, swipe it off, and lick my fingers clean. Because, once again, time wouldn't allow for that little indulgence. Dani's thighs were cinching around my head, holding me in place, like I had any intention of going anywhere before I had her soaking my face while crying out my name.

I'd love to say my girl tasted sweet, but that would be a fucking lie. She tasted like pussy, which just so happened to be my favorite flavor. I could drown in her pussy juice with my nose pressed against her lips and my tongue deep in her cunt, and it still wouldn't be enough. I had to will my hands to not deter from their path, one ensuring her thighs stayed spread wide for me while the other circled around her clit, to keep from reaching down and finishing myself off. My cock was begging for a few more seconds of bliss but I had a job to do... before I had to do my job.

One, two, three more carefully drawn-out figure eights and Dani was sucking the air out of my lungs as her thighs clamped closed and she convulsed against my mouth. There was no better feeling, no more intoxicating a sound than hearing my girl come undone by my doing. Except maybe if I had been coating those perky tits with my cum. But there would be time for that later. I'd make damn sure of it.

She'd barely come back down from that climactic high before I was tugging her pants up her thighs, pulling her onto her feet, and patting her ass towards the door.

"As much as I'd love to enjoy that post-orgasm afterglow I see on your face right now, it's time for us to go, baby girl." Then I scooped a hand under her thighs and picked her up bridal-style, refusing to give her a moment to protest.

Zeke looked none too happy to see me on the other side of the door, my grin wide while Dani appeared dazed—in a good way this time. But the motherfucker would have to get over it. It wasn't like I asked for favors often. And I'd done more than my fair share for him.

"If anyone asks, we had a fainter," I grunted in Zeke's direction, not waiting for a reply as I made a beeline for the door.

"What the fuck are you doing?" Dani hissed, her fists beating against my chest as she tried to wiggle free.

"Gettin' us the fuck outta here before Junior uses your ass to try to get in good with his uncle. Something tells me you know exactly what I mean by that, don't you, Dani?"

Her silence gave me the inclination that I was right; but it was the moment she stopped fighting me that really confirmed it. I could tell it wasn't out of fear—nah, nothing scared my girl. Except maybe commitment. But that was an issue for another day. It was her stubbornness and inability to allow the Mulligans a leg up that had Dani giving in to me right now.

"When'd he get here?" she asked instead of arguing.

A fact that had my eyebrow lifting in question as I carried her back through the side door and out into the alleyway. It was the only spot without live CCTV, seeing as Benny was too fucking cheap to get the feed out here fixed so the stupid fuck used a dummy camera instead.

"This afternoon, why? You two have history?" I countered, setting Dani on her feet before backing her against the building's weather-worn exterior.

I should have had my fill of her by now, but my rock-hard cock had other plans while the devil on my shoulder urged me to say screw it and just fuck my girl against the brick wall. If it weren't for the chill in the air, I just might. But my jacket slung over that tiny vest did little to protect her from the elements. And something about the idea of her being cold didn't sit right.

I took care of the people who meant something to me. A lesson Danica Rossi would learn soon enough.

"You could say that. I'd call it current events though. History suggests it's in the past and I'm not ready to leave it there quite yet." She pivoted on her boot, likely looking to make another quick getaway.

Not gonna happen.

I reached out and tugged her back to me. "Should I be jealous, dollface?"

I didn't like how needy the question sounded but the way she called Junior her current anything left a strange weight on my chest. I'd knock the fucker out myself—paycheck be damned—if it meant keeping him well enough away from the girl I was seeing more and more as mine.

"Jealous of the man I plan to kill? That depends on if you have a death wish, MacCullagh. Do you?"

I brushed a loose curl from her face and tucked it behind her ear. "Something tells me when it comes to you, I just might."

14

"You gotta death wish or something, Rossi?"

Leo's deep timbre put a smile on my face despite my best efforts to press my lips into a tight line.

"Or something, Mulligan." I shrugged, trying to appear nonchalant as Leo crept up behind me and tugged my back to his chest. The recognizable scent of his woodsy cologne had my chin tipping up, my bare neck his for the taking.

Lust definitely had something to do with it. I wasn't so naïve to think it hadn't been a factor that drove me into enemy territory. The lure of the forbidden was definitely a part of it too. I'd always been drawn to the sort of things I shouldn't have. Like my father's favorite whiskey and my mother's secret stash of Virginia Slims—smoking wasn't ladylike. And a mobster's wife had an image to maintain. But that was her problem, not mine. My brother was the heir and I was the wild child. So breaking rules was kinda my thing. A calling of sorts.

Though this wasn't just a rule. It was mafia law, and I was crossing the metaphorical picket line. Fucking around with an Irish boy. And not just any Irish boy. Their golden child, the next in line to take over the Mulligan Gang. It was as Romeo and Juliet as you could get, right down to the rival families both out for blood.

At the start, it was an infatuation. A curiosity. Plus, the Irish-Chicagoan accent did wonders to my panties. I was soaked before Leo could even pry 'em off me that first night. But over the last six months, it had grown to be more. Which made things... complicated. A fling could be had and forgotten. But a full-blown relationship was becoming a tad bit of a challenge. We each had our responsibilities, different sets of eyes on us, opposing playgrounds, and lines drawn in the sand at all times. Me, on the Italian side of town. And Leo, with his merry band of leprechauns—my father's words, not mine.

Yeah, the animosity was long-standing and deep-rooted. But it had little to do with us. We were just two horny-as-fuck teenagers with too much time and money at our disposal.

"You're gonna get caught one of these days, Dani..." Leo grunted as I shoved him backward onto the mattress and threw a leg over each of his hips.

"Doubt it. Your pops may want to train your security team better." I grinned as my hands reached for his buckle, unfastening the clasp before tugging the belt free. It landed on the area rug with a muffled thud. Before I set my sights on his buttons next, and then unwrapped my favorite present.

Those myths about the Irish sure as fuck weren't true, at least when it came to this particular boy wonder. Leo's cock was like something out of my favorite lady porn, too perfect to be real honestly. And fuck if it didn't stretch me in all the right ways.

A couple quick strokes of my palm earned me my pot of gold—the head of Leo's cock throbbing and just begging me to ride his rainbow. I tugged off my leggings and underwear in one go before reclaiming my position on his lap. He grunted deep in his chest as I lowered myself down inch by fucking inch. I might not have been a virgin but it sure as fuck felt like my first fuck every time.

"Fuck me..." he groaned. His head thrown back on his pillow, and one arm clutching his bedsheets while the other rested on my waist.

"Pretty sure that's exactly what I'm doing," I hissed between clenched teeth as I ground my clit against his pelvic bone. I liked the penetration but I needed the double stimulation.

With each bounce of my cunt on his cock, Leo thrusted upwards, punching against my guts so deeply I could have sworn I felt the man in my throat. Or maybe that was just because his size left me gasping for air.

I bit my bottom lip to keep from crying out and causing an army of gangsters to come running into Leo's bedroom. It wasn't the first time I'd sneaked past the Mulligan's less-than-tight security details and climbed into my boyfriend's window. And something told me it wouldn't be the last either.

Wonder if that made me Romeo in this scenario?

Leo tapped my thigh, forcing me back into the moment. The silent gesture was his way of telling me he was close and we'd forgotten protection. Something that was both the most and least dangerous thing we were doing right now. I reached out a hand and wrapped it around his throat.

"Don't you dare come before I do." My words died on a moan, as his cock swelled in that way it did just before he finished. "Ladies first," I was quick to remind him as I lowered my free hand to my clit, circling a finger across my favorite barbell at just the right rhythm. Three more rotations and I was soaring over that ledge and bouncing off Leo's cock before he could infect me with his bastard offspring. My luck, we'd both be super fertile and the Irish were known for reproducing like fucking rabbits.

I waited a beat for my breathing to even out before rolling onto my side and collecting my leggings—I would leave my underwear as a parting gift, since my boy had behaved. I could feel Leo's eyes on my back as he watched my every move. He was oddly quiet tonight, though I assumed that had more to do with me fucking loose what was left of his brain cells.

I had one leg thrown over his windowsill, ready to jump down and make a mad dash across the front lawn, when Leo's words had me pausing on the spot.

"Hey, Dani..." He waited for me to peer up at him, at the barrel he now aimed in my direction, then added, "I just need you to know that I love you..."

The sound of Leo's voice was the last thing to ring through my head before the sharp sting of a bullet followed its path.

15

PRESENT

My head was throbbing. I could practically feel my brain pulsing inside my skull, and it took everything in my power to stop myself from clawing at my scalp and peeling the layers of skin back. Anything to relieve some of the pressure building up in my temples.

I'd been cleared by all the quacks years ago. They told me removing the bullet would do more damage than good and that it wasn't interfering with my cognitive abilities. Somehow the dumb Irish fuck had missed my brain and now I was stuck with a metal cylinder rolling around inside my head. Though there were nights when I'd swear I could hear it clanking around in there. But the docs told me it was impossible, insisting it was encased by fluid or some shit.

About as impossible as all the blackouts, right?

I could hear the distant shouting but my eyes refused to focus on anything, forming blobs and colors instead of actual images.

By the time I got my bearings, I realized I was in a car with a blown-out windshield, the distinct scent of gunpowder wafting over the interior. I didn't see blood. Which was a good sign. But I also wasn't driving...

"Dani! You with me?"

I glanced to my left, my nails sinking into the faux leather seat as Connor weaved in and out of back streets and alleyways. Guy was trying but it was obvious he didn't know shit when it came to evading a tail.

"Dani!" he repeated, his eyes flicking in my direction before returning to the road.

I needed to think, not talk. But I could tell that was a luxury I didn't have at the moment. We were running from something... more likely someone... and I had no doubt it had to do with me.

"Pull over," I grunted as I tried to blink the spots away from my vision.

"Like fuck am I pulling over. Are you insane?"

"Actually, I just might be. But that has nothing to do with what I'm telling you. Pull the fuck over and let me drive before you get us both killed."

"Baby girl, you ain't in any position to drive—something we need to discuss later. In the meantime, keep your pretty little ass in that seat, that smart mouth closed and fucked-up head down."

Yeah, like any of that was gonna happen.

I glanced over my shoulder and spotted a pair of headlights tailing us in the not-so-distant distance. I couldn't determine the make and model with all the fog. But that was to our advantage. It was hard to shoot what you couldn't see.

"Who'd I piss off this time?"

"Don't you remember?" Connor muttered under his

breath, his knuckles turning white as he clung to the steering wheel like it was a lifeline.

"Not exactly..." I shrugged. Though it was more like not at all. I remembered the storage room, my pussy sure as fuck remembered the sex—I could still feel my thighs quivering—and I remembered popping out into the back alley.

After that, I materialized in this car. Speaking of...

"Where's my bike?"

"Yeah, didn't exactly have time to ask you all the specifics."

"I loved that bike, you know. And some asshole is probably gonna scrap it for parts."

Conner pinned me with a glare that told me that was exactly the wrong thing to say. "Sorry. Next time we're getting shot at, I'll make sure to grab your shit first."

"That's all I ask." I grinned, because why the fuck not? Being miserable wasn't gonna get us out of this situation any quicker. I had to admit it was nice seeing pretty boy so rattled. That cool as a cucumber facade was getting old.

A sharp left turn had me slamming against the passenger door before wiping the smirk right off my face. Guess I touched a nerve. Either that or my new favorite sex toy really was terrified.

"Look, Connor, just pull over and let me out. We both know they're after me, not you. I'll lose 'em on foot and you can go on pretending like this didn't happen."

"What the fuck is wrong with you? Dani, they shot up my fucking car! You really think I can just pretend that didn't happen?"

Fuck, I hated feeling guilty. I usually didn't feel anything at all. So it was like a weight sitting on my chest.

"I'll get your car fixed up—I know a guy. I know several guys and they all owe me favors. Give me a few weeks..." I patted the seat for emphasis. "And your baby will be like brand-fucking-new."

A second sharp left had us nearly teetering on two wheels before Connor slammed on the brakes, backed into a garage, and jumped out the driver's side door. He stalked towards the far entrance, peering through the glass before sending a shitty glare in my direction.

"You really think I give a damn about the fucking car?" he hissed as I slammed the passenger door shut louder than I should.

"You said—"

"I know what the fuck I said. I don't need instant replay."

I held up my palms in mock surrender. I must have really pissed him off. I honestly didn't think it was possible. "My bad…"

Connor took a few deep breaths, a hand raking through his disheveled hair as he pivoted back towards me. I could only assume we lost whoever the fuck was following us. Either that, or lover boy had decided it would be easier to use me as a bargaining chip. Wouldn't blame him for it. It was actually the smartest thing he could do right now.

He didn't speak again until we were nearly toe-to-toe, and I could see the stress lines wrinkling his forehead. Fucker wasn't just scared. He was terrified. I'd forgotten not everyone was as used to being shot at as I was. I actually couldn't remember a time when there wasn't a target on my back.

"Hey, I'm sorry for yellin'. My ma would be the first to tell you I wasn't raised like that." He reached out and cupped my jaw in his palms. Which were slick with sweat but I decided to keep that observation to myself. Connor lowered his mouth to mine and kissed me in a way that felt different from the few times before. I couldn't put my finger on it. But somehow this was both sweeter and more possessive. Chaste with an undertone of something carnal. "I didn't care about the fucking car, Dani. I don't care about the fucking car."

Now I was really fucking confused. "If it wasn't because of the car, then why were you so upset?"

"I wasn't upset. I was pissed the fuck off. I saw it in your eyes. You honestly expected me to pull over and leave your ass to the wolves. They were trying to kill you, Dani."

I shrugged. "Yeah, it kinda comes with the territory, Connor. All part of the game."

"For fuck's sake, this stopped being a fucking game the moment those fuckers started shooting to kill. Why the fuck would you show up tonight knowing they were after you like that?"

Good question. I'd love to know the answer to that one too...

16

A FEW MINUTES PRIOR

I'd just pressed Dani up against the wall outside Mollies when Zeke came running up behind us. I could see the panic on his face and immediately knew I'd fucked up. It wasn't just my own neck on the chopping block; it was his as well. And I knew more than I wanted to admit that I was being a selfish bastard.

I would love to say Dani brought that side out of me, that it wasn't a bad habit of mine, but that would be a lie. My penchant for going with my gut meant I often ignored my brain. Which made it far easier for me to forget about how my actions affected others.

Not being able to control your impulses was a son of a bitch.

Zeke doubled over, trying to catch his breath as he gestured a hand towards the alleyway. "You need to get gone, and quick. They know she's here, Mac. Pretty sure I heard Junior say something about strapping up."

We both knew the kind of men we worked for. But knowing it and seeing it were two different things. The realization that we were part of a full-on mob war felt like a punch to the dick. Zeke and I were no strangers to the occasional bar fight—it came with the territory. And neither one of us got squeamish at the sight of blood. I mean, we'd spilled plenty of our own over the years. But as a rule, we didn't fuck with guns. We couldn't afford the high-price lawyers like the rest of ʼem and my ass didn't look good in orange.

It looked worse dropping the soap...

I glanced back to Dani, who of course appeared unfazed. Nope, not the right word... because, fuck, she was doing that staring into nothing thing again. I needed to get her the fuck out of here before Baby Mulligan took advantage of her in this state. That thought alone had my teeth grinding in my jaw, and my shoulders tense with pent-up energy.

But I'd have to run inside and grab my keys from my locker first. I eyed Dani's riding gear. Something told me baby girl didn't own a car. As if reading my mind, Zeke tossed a set of keys in the air and gestured for me to get going. I owed this guy more than my life. I owed him hers too.

I took two steps forward, my hand wrapped around Dani's wrist, before pivoting back towards the club. "They're gonna know you had something to do with this..."

Zeke shrugged, his way of saying: *I know.*

"Come with us," I urged him, because something in the pit of my stomach told me this wouldn't end well for either of us. He didn't bother responding as he turned back around and disappeared through the side door. I knew it was pointless. They had his sister by the cunt and Zeke wasn't about to leave her there to flounder, as much as I reminded him that it was her choice.

But you can lead a horse to water and all that. The stupid son of a bitch needed to figure it out on his own. Much like I did when it came to a certain chick with very similar problems.

We didn't make it to the back lot before bullets were flying in our direction. No warning, no goddamn option to surrender—not that I would have but it would have been nice for the fucker to at least offer.

When a stray round ricocheted off a streetlamp, shattering the bulb and shadowing us in darkness as we navigated around the fresh scattering of broken glass, I had to wonder if they really had that bad of an aim or if these were meant to be warning shots.

It was hard to tell.

Dani still hadn't spoken a word but her reflexes seemed to be working overtime while the rest of her remained stunted.

By the time my car was in view, I could make out the distinct sound of several pairs of boots crunching behind us.

"Rossi, ain't it about time you stopped running? Why don't you turn around, get that tight little ass of yours back here, so we can discuss things like civilized adults?" Junior's voice was grating on my nerves more than usual.

You'd assume it would have had something to do with the fact the fucker was trying to kill us, but if I were being completely honest, I was pretty certain it was the "ass" comment that had me wanting to grab the bastard by the balls and twist.

"Yeah, that ain't happening," I called over my shoulder before shoving Dani into the passenger seat and climbing behind the wheel. Then I rolled down my window just enough so that I was sure the slimy fuck could hear me.

"Talk to her like that again and you'll be drinking out of a straw for the rest of your life." I threw the car into reverse, barely missing mowing down the little shit with my Buick, before taking off as quickly as the '86 engine would let me.

It was an idle threat. He and I both knew it. And not because I wouldn't try but because the son of a bitch would never face me like a man. He always had his goons hanging around. Worse than Benny ever did. But it still felt good to say.

Though it felt a little less good when those same goons lit up my back windshield. I didn't have much to my name. My old man's car was about it, and now she was taking on more lead than I could count. Lucky for us, this girl was built like a tank.

The sound of metal on metal, followed by more shattering glass, made it hard to focus on anything besides not getting dead. There were a couple of shards embedded in the back of my right arm, but other than some dampness, the adrenaline pumping through my veins kept me from feeling much else.

Something told me it would hurt like a son of a bitch in the morning though.

I had no clue as to where we were headed, just that I had to put Mollies as far back in my rearview as was humanly possible. I knew what my split-second decision meant. What the consequences would be.

I didn't have a job to go back to, a place to live, or much left of a car. Zeke and I shared a little spot down the street from the club—returning meant putting him in more danger than I already had. Plus, Junior would be waiting for me before I made it through the front door.

The fucked-up thing about it was how much I didn't care right now. My life was turned inside out and pissed on, and that was fucking rainbows and butterflies. Because my girl was safe.

My eyes alternated between watching the road and peeking in her direction. Besides a few scrapes, and that dazed look in her eyes, Dani appeared no worse for the wear.

Now I just had to figure out what the fuck was going on in that head of hers...

17

PRESENT

"Where are we by the way?" My eyes flicked around the room, bouncing over the various tools and car parts piled up on every available surface, before landing on Connor again.

It was great that he'd lost our tail and all but staying holed up in a tiny garage wasn't much better. We were sitting ducks without a breadcrumb in sight.

Connor scratched the back of his neck, a nervous tick that told me I wasn't gonna like whatever it was he had to say. He closed both eyes, popping one open to peek at me when he replied, "My uncle's garage."

I barked out a laugh. Because, honestly, it was such a dumb move it was comical. "Your idea of hiding out is driving directly to your family's place?"

"Look, it ain't like I do this shit every day, dollface." He shrugged.

"Clearly." I pivoted on my boot heel and took a better look around, my fingertips grazing over several torque wrenches, a few ratchet extenders, and a worn sledgey before landing on a nice heavy-duty ball-peen. I twirled the weight in my hand a few times before settling on my weapon of choice. "I don't suppose your uncle has any guns stashed 'round here, does he?"

When Connor's only response was to lift a brow, I cocked an arm back and sent the hammer flying. It completed a few rotations in the air before embedding itself in a piece of drywall with a thud.

"It'll have to do, I guess."

Not that a ball-peen would do much against a barrage of bullets, but shit worked for close-quarters combat when a knife wasn't at your immediate disposal. I'd bashed a skull in once with nothing but a beat-up hammer. The six-foot-five, three-hundred pound biker fell like a sack of cocaine-laced potatoes. He'd complained about a headache before going dead quiet—though I was honestly surprised he'd felt anything with the amount of blow they'd found in his system.

It wasn't like me to leave the house without at least a blade or several tucked into my boot and secured to my thighs, which told me this whole blackout thing was worse than I cared to admit. I was reserved to the idea that I was doing things on autopilot and just not remembering them, but now I was leaving myself vulnerable too. And that just wasn't okay.

It was fucked.

Connor didn't say much, but I could feel him watching me as I strapped myself up like I was looking to go to war with the villain from that kiddie movie with the talking cars —or was it a toaster?

I honestly couldn't remember. Disney's obsession with bringing inanimate objects to life freaked me the fuck out as a kid. Never could look at the refrigerator the same again.

"So what's the plan, Rambo?" Connor's question broke me from my thoughts about murderous kitchen appliances and returned my focus to the potential casualty in front of me.

"The plan is I go out there, and you stay in here."

He folded his arms over his broad chest, and I wasn't too proud to admit I liked the way his shirt pulled tight across his sculpted pecs. There was a reason I called him pretty boy. There was no denying that the cocky son of a bitch was easy on the eyes.

"Yeah, and exactly how long do you expect me to sit around with my thumb up my ass?"

"I mean, if that's what you're into, have at it." I grinned.

"That's not what I meant, Dani. And you know it," he grunted, and I could tell his patience was waning again—*guess I was only cute until I became irritating?* "How long?"

"A few hours, maybe days, might wanna stock up the canned goods for a couple of weeks while you're at it? Why?"

Instead of answering, Connor stalked forward, grabbing each of my makeshift weapons from my person and dropping them to the floor with an audible clank. I couldn't tell you why I didn't stop him. But it likely had something to do with how his sheer audacity had my jaw dropping and my feet frozen to the cement floor.

"What. The. Actual. Fuck," I hissed when I was finally able to form words.

"Whatever you're thinking, it's not happening, Dani. You're not running out in the middle of the night looking like you rolled around in a junkyard a few too many times. Because unless you're the Bionic Man, ain't none of that gonna keep them from putting a bullet straight through your head."

"Poor choice of words," I grunted.

"What?"

"Nothing." I shoved at his chest and forced a couple of steps between us. "If you had an issue with my plan, why'd you watch me strap up?"

"Was tryin' to determine the level of crazy I'm working with. Which is on the high end by the way." He shook his head, and I quirked a brow.

"Like you're surprised?"

"Not in the slightest."

I should take offense, but what was the point? He wasn't lying. "Okay, Captain Kirk, if you don't want me to go outside and you don't want to stay put, what *do* you have in mind?"

"Never said I didn't like the part about staying put, just the part about you going out there."

"Right, well, I'm gonna go out on a limb here and assume Junior and his merry band of misfits are on my trail." I still didn't have any recollection as to whether that was true or not. But pretty boy didn't need to know that. "And the fuckers also caught me runnin' off with one of their employees, who, going by his lack of a record, has his real emergency contacts and home address listed in his HR file. I'm no Sherlock Holmes, but I'm guessing we have less than twenty-four hours before someone comes knocking on that door." I flung an arm out in front of me for emphasis, as Connor's lips curled into a slow grin.

"How'd you know I don't have a record?"

18

I watched Dani scramble to answer what I thought was a very simple question.

"Hm?" she hummed, likely attempting to buy herself some time while hoping I would get the hint and stop pressing her.

Too bad I was about as dense as a preacher in a whorehouse on Sunday morning—don't bother asking me what that meant. It was just something my ma used to say to me whenever she felt like I was being stubborn just for the sake of it.

"I said... how do you know I don't have a record?" I tipped up Dani's chin, forcing her eyes on mine when she was trying to look at anything else.

"I notice things. I could just tell."

"*Ernt,* try again. How do you know I don't have a record, Dani?" I repeated for the third time in a row.

"I already told you I didn't know for sure. I assumed. You just don't have those bad boy vibes."

"Liar." I grinned, before dropping my hand and allowing her to put distance between us again. "A pretty liar but a liar all the same. You looked me up, didn't you, baby girl?"

The slight twitch in her lower lip told me I was right, while the way her nostrils flared and her jaw clicked as she ground her molars in the back of her mouth suggested she was more than a little annoyed about it.

Guess Danica Rossi wasn't the only one who noticed things.

"I didn't look you up. It's my job to collect information, put files together on... people," she muttered under her breath.

"On *people* without records?" I fired back. "And what is it that you do again, Dani?" When it was clear she wasn't gonna answer that one either, I added, "Yeah, that's what I thought."

"Okay, smart-ass, pretty sure we've wasted enough time playing Twenty Questions. Where do you suggest we go from here?"

"So now there's a *we*? I think I like the sound of that, dollface." I clapped my hands together to cut off whatever snarky comment was forming on her lips and quickly steered her thoughts in another direction. "Whelp, seeing as we can't very well drive around in something that resembles a block of Swiss cheese, our best bet is to lie low, get a few hours of sleep, and regroup in the morning. I mean, you said it yourself. We have what? A good twenty-four hours or so before Benny lights a fire under Junior's ass and they both come looking for us again?"

I glanced back at Dani, who responded with a noncommittal shrug, and something told me I had better sleep with one eye open and my wrists tucked under my head. Not that I didn't appreciate a little kink. I just had a feeling it would have more to do with baby girl trying to sneak out in the middle of the night than her wanting to take full advantage of riding my cock.

"Right, well, guess we can flip for it," she said while one of her hands dug into the pocket of her too-tight riding pants. "There's a buncha glass in the back. So, heads for the trunk and tails for the front?" Her lips curled into a near sinister smirk as she flipped the coin into the air and expected me to call it.

Not only was I certain that the game was rigged. But she'd surpassed crazy at this point if she thought I would trust her enough to climb my ass into that trunk and expect her not to lock me inside. Besides, I had no intention of sleeping in my beat-up Buick tonight.

I needed a cold shower, a warm meal, and someone to pluck the glass from my arm because right now it stung like a son of a bitch.

The coin bounced off the concrete floor with a clink before rolling under a large red tool box. Dani followed its path, then eyed me like I'd just popped the last balloon at her birthday party.

"Yeah, I have a better idea. How about we just go inside and sleep in a bed? Unless you'd prefer to freeze your ass off out here, then by all means, the trunk is yours." My grin widened while hers dropped.

"Inside? There's an inside?" she grunted.

"More specifically, an *upstairs*. But, yeah, you catch my drift." I didn't wait for her to argue as I strolled up to the far door, ran a hand through the dust collected along the top of the frame, and grabbed the key that was waiting there.

I'd never been more thankful for my uncle's forgetfulness. The man had been prone to locking himself out of his apartment more times than he could count and resorted to keeping a spare down here to avoid the locksmith costs he was constantly racking up. Uncle Mickey was retired now, his tools rusting away and the space sitting vacant. But the old man just didn't seem to be able to let the place go.

Dani huffed and puffed the entire way up the back staircase, and not because she was out of shape. Nope, the little sounds she was making were completely intentional, her way of expressing her displeasure without having to verbalize 'em to me. Or so I could only assume.

The woman was no better than that kid throwing a tantrum in the middle of the toy aisle at the department store. All because she was stuck inside when she was itching to get out and spill some Irish blood.

Then again, mine was still up for the taking. I was more than aware that my sex kitten had claws. And that she liked to use 'em too.

Dani hit the landing with a childish boot stomp. I shook my head, brushing past her before sliding the key in the lock, jiggling the knob around a few times, and shoving the door open.

It took a couple swipes of my hand for me to break up the dust particles floating in front of my eyes and get a good look at the place. My uncle's loft was nothing short of a grease monkey's paradise, with a beer fridge in one corner, a pair of oil-stained overalls balled up in the other, and air so thick and stale with a hint of cigarette smoke that it clung to the back of your throat until you were forced to swallow it. I flicked on the nearest lamp, tugging Dani in front of me and securing the door before turning around again.

I scratched the back of my head while shrugging my apologies.

"I mean, it's no Four Seasons but guess it beats sleeping in an icebox." Dani plopped down on the 70s style plaid sofa, a cloud of dust popping into the air as she crossed her boots at the ankle and rested them on the coffee table.

These mood shifts were like something out of a made-for-tv movie, but I had to admit some sick part of me enjoyed not knowing which version of Danica Rossi I'd be seeing next.

19

I wanted to be annoyed—no, that was a lie. What I wanted was a taste of blood. Instead, we were shacking up in a little one-bedroom apartment, sharing space with dust mites and more than likely a horde of rats and cockroaches. Not that I was all that picky.

I might have grown up with a silver spoon in my mouth and more cash than I could spend in a lifetime, but I also knew what it was like to sleep on the streets and fight for my next meal. A reverse rags-to-riches story if you ever saw one...

Some people called what happened to my family karma, while I considered it a life lesson about getting too comfortable. Luxuries made you soft and soft made you dead. It wasn't some cosmic power enacting its revenge; it was simply survival of the fittest.

And my parents and brother didn't make the cut.

My eyes flicked around the room as Connor disappeared behind a door to scope out the sleeping arrangements. My guess, it was a one-bed situation. But I was too aggravated to point out the obvious to a man with a skull thicker than clam chowder. Pretty sure the only reason the fucker was alive was because he was too stubborn to die.

That made two of us.

When Connor didn't pop back out after a few minutes, I assumed he'd fallen asleep or fallen in, and pushed to my feet to check out the rest of the apartment. The beer fridge was painfully empty, so were the cabinets minus the occasional mouse dropping, as was the small pantry. It was clear his uncle hadn't been here in years.

Maybe the old guy was dead? A fact that could play out in our favor when the Mulligans came looking for us. Not that I had any intention of staying put. Three hours of sleep and I'd be golden. Though the dried sweat sticking to my skin told me a shower wouldn't hurt either.

I took two steps towards what I assumed was the bathroom and collided into Connor's shirtless chest. He winced as his right arm shot up to steady me. And my eyes dropped to the ace bandage wrapped around his bicep. It wasn't there before. I would have felt it when I was clawing at his chest like a cat in heat back in that storage closet.

"Glass." He shrugged, as if he could see the wheels turning in my head.

"You get it all out?" I asked, though I still wasn't sure why I cared. But I did.

"Fuck if I know. Stopped fishing around when it looked like I was doing more damage than good." Connor forced out a laugh, but it was clear the dumbass was hurting more than he was letting on while earning himself a one-way ticket to infection.

I shook my head and spun him back towards the bedroom. "I'm assuming your uncle has a first aid kit?"

"Nah, I keep gauze and tweezers in my pocket for whenever my girlfriend decides to piss off a bunch of mobsters." He offered me a stupid grin, quickly dropping it when I shoved a finger into his open wound.

"First of all, not your girlfriend. We fucked—twice-*ish*. Second, keep being a smart-ass and I'll just let that arm of yours rot and fall off."

"Who said I was talking about you, baby girl? Unless you *want* to be my girlfriend. That's it, isn't it?" The smirk was back as I shoved him down on the toilet seat a little too roughly.

"Not happening," I hissed before swinging open the medicine cabinet and pulling down a half-empty bottle of rubbing alcohol and a pair of rusty tweezers.

"Okay, what about fuck buddy? Fugitive with benefits?"

I refused to take the bait, but that didn't seem to stop his rambling.

"Or how about I get myself a bike and you can be my ol' lady?"

Instead of answering him, I unraveled the bandages around his arm, poured a heavy dose of alcohol onto the gashes running up and down his right bicep, and watched his eyes widen as he cursed under his breath and squirmed on the creaky toilet lid.

"You gonna behave or should I flush it out one more time?" I asked, and Connor grunted in reply. "That's what I thought. Now, let me see if I can get some of this glass out so you stop whining like a little bitch."

By the time I'd finished extracting the tiny pieces of windshield with the precision of a skilled surgeon, watered down blood was running down Connor's arm and he looked like he was on the verge of passing out. To his credit, he didn't moan and groan all that much—though, judging by how tight his jaw was set, it was evident he wanted to.

"Now, just alternate between leaving it covered and letting it breathe. Doesn't look like you'll need stitches, but keep an eye out for any redness or pus. The first sign of infection, and we'll have to shoot your ass full of antibiotics."

He flexed his upper arm before eyeing me from across the small bathroom. "It actually feels surprisingly better," he said, and I shook my head.

"Yeah, I mean, who woulda thought that removing the jagged pieces of glass before covering the wounds would actually help?" I replied, my voice thick with sarcasm.

"Right, well, the shower's yours if you want it. Though I'm not sure if they'll be any hot water. And I changed the sheets on the bed." Connor stood to his full height, towering over me, as he reached out his good arm to push the bathroom door open. He brushed past me before pausing at the threshold. "I'd offer to take the couch. But I'm not a gentleman and we've already established you're sure as fuck not a lady. So I expect to see your ass in that bed, Dani." He grinned, and I watched the muscles in his back ripple with each step he took as he walked away.

20

Since I was old enough to listen, my da stressed the importance of finding myself a good woman and settling down. I was the only son, the heir to nothing but the family name and a fondness for the black stuff.

Common sense should have told the old cunt that the last thing we needed was more mouths to feed. But my da was traditional, straight off the boat Irish, and the fact he and my ma only had one kid might as well have been a curse on his bloodline. Ironic, considering the man loved fuckin' and fightin' and not so much the family life. But his name—that was a thing of pride—and I was expected to breed like the rest of 'em.

"Connor," he'd say in that thick brogue of his, which got thicker with the more whiskey there was under his belt. "First, ya need to taste 'er ale pie."

Get your mind outta the gutter. He didn't mean that kinda pie.

"Second, ya need to see how she keeps 'er house. Never marry a lass whose floors you can't lick."

Yeah, not the best choice of words there either, Da.

"Third, ya watch how she is with the babes. Marry the lass ya want rearin' yer wean."

Okay, I was startin' to see a theme here. But us Irish were a different lot—everything we said sounded dirtier than it actually was. We liked it that way.

The point was Daire MacCullagh painted a very specific picture of the type of woman he wanted brought home to Sunday dinner with a horde of yougins in tow. And Danica Rossi was not it.

Didn't know if she could cook, but something told me I was more likely to get a pot of boiling water tossed on my lap than a hot meal served at my table.

As far as licking her floors? Pretty sure the only way that would happen was if her boot heel was digging into the back of my skull. Though, add a little bondage, and I wasn't totally against the idea.

And when it came to children, my girl seemed like the type who'd throw the babe out with the bath water. And listen for the *splat.*

All of which, my old man could have looked past... if only she were Irish. That part went without saying.

"Find yerself a nice Irish girl, son."

If my da were here right now, I'd tell 'em nice was boring. I didn't want nice. I wanted the girl presently stalking towards me with fire in her eyes. The girl who hurled insults at my face while using a gentle hand to tend to my wounds. The girl who couldn't decide between hating my presence and loving my cock.

Because that girl was *it* for me. I just needed to hang around long enough for her to realize I was *it* for her too.

"Why are you looking at me like that?" Dani grunted as

she approached the bed in a towel so small she was better off wearing nothin'.

"Like what?" I grinned, my arms resting against the wall with my hands clasped behind my head, as I sprawled my legs out over the tiny mattress.

"Like the cat who ate the canary," she said, and I laughed.

"I mean, I'm more than willing to eat something, doll-face, but it ain't no canary." I shrugged, watching as her gaze honed in on my mouth before traveling lower. There was no hiding the way my cock was currently tenting the near translucent bedsheet I'd thrown across my lap. Though, after she dropped the sliver of fabric from her body, my dick might as well have been a flagpole waving her forward.

Fuck, just one look and I was so hard my toes were going numb. Or maybe I'd just lost a little too much blood. Either way, I was certain a good fucking would fix me right up.

"Just so you know, this..." Dani waved a hand up and down her body. "...isn't for your benefit. Have you ever tried sleeping in leather pants?" she asked as I quirked a brow. "Trust me, it ain't fun."

"I'll have to take your word for it, baby girl," I said while gesturing her forward. It was clear she was fighting herself, struggling with her need to be defiant and her desire to comply. "Now, come to bed."

Two more dramatic huffs and she finally approached the edge of the mattress and climbed on top. The fact that it was no more than a double meant she didn't have much room to play with. No matter what she did or which way she turned, she could feel my body heat warming the sheets.

"And I'm sleeping on the bed because I want to sleep on the bed," she muttered under her breath after a few long moments of silence.

"Sure thing, baby girl," I said, turning on my side so that my front was to her back. Her shoulders were tense, her damp hair curling at the ends while her chest rose and fell in a way that told me she was too ramped up to sleep.

I reached out my left arm, grabbed her waist, and tugged her against my chest. She stiffened for a moment before relaxing into my hold, as I pressed my mouth to that spot just under her ear and nibbled and sucked a path along her neck. Down to her shoulder. The little moan she let out had my cock twitching against her ass cheeks, while the grinding of her hips had my precum marking her skin as mine.

I rolled over and pulled Dani under me, bracing myself just above her head. My arm was throbbing, but then again, so was my cock. And only one of those appendages mattered at the moment.

She was already so fucking wet for me. I could feel the slickness of her cunt as I pressed my tip against her entrance and glided my cock back and forth without thrusting forward. The stimulation had Dani's lips parting on a moan, and I used the opportunity to lower my mouth to hers. To fuck that mouth with my tongue.

At first, she fought me. Dani wanted to be fucked, not kissed. But my hand around her throat, holding her in place, had her jaw loosening and her mouth giving way to my intrusion. What she wanted and what she needed were two very different things. And sometimes my little control freak just *needed* to release those reins a tad bit.

It didn't take a genius to figure out her deal. My girl liked it fast and hard. So she didn't have to think about it. I liked it slow and deep so that she couldn't think about anything else.

I alternated between plunging my tongue down her throat and twirling it around the inside of her mouth, tasting everything she offered me. She was squirming beneath my grip, gyrating her hips so that my cock was gliding across her clit in a sensual back-and-forth motion. And it took every ounce of strength I had in my body to keep from thrusting forward. Couldn't explain what was holding me back. Sure as fuck wasn't the lack of protection —we'd already crossed that line.

If I had to take a guess, I'd say it had more to do with me not wanting this to end. For her to pull away. I enjoyed watching her squirm. Being needed by a woman who didn't need shit. It was rare and I wasn't ready to give it up just yet.

So I kissed a path from her lips to her jaw, then across to her ear before whispering, "Tell me you want me to fuck you, Dani. Tell me you need it."

She huffed her irritation, biting her bottom lip in open defiance. And I inched forward, only an inch, breaching her entrance just enough to be not nearly enough.

I groaned and she wrapped her thighs around my waist. But I wasn't moving. No matter how much we both wanted it.

"Tell me, Dani," I urged her. "Just a few words and I promise you'll feel a whole lot better."

Another inch had my thighs trembling and her cunt trying to suck me down.

"Say it, baby girl. I'm begging you to beg me." I pressed my lips against her ear and made that low growl in the back of my throat, the one I noticed seemed to get her going.

"Goddamn it!" She pounded a fist against the mattress

before finally giving me what we both needed. "I want you to fuck me, asshole. Now. And it better be good or I swear to —*fuck*!"

The threat died on her tongue the moment I dove in and buried myself to the hilt. And it was like the dam broke as I rested one of her legs on my shoulders and angled my cock just slightly to the left, hitting that spot that had her head thrown back and her hands grabbing the sheets.

I'd love to credit my stamina; though the fact I'd been able to keep myself from nutting had more to do with stubbornness than anything else.

But, hell, a win was a win. And fuck if I wasn't going for gold right now.

Dani was making those little whimpering sounds that told me she was close. Three more good thrusts and I had her nails in my back, her lips cursing my name, and a fresh wave of pussy juice drenching my cock.

I wanted nothing more on God's green earth than to say *fuck it,* coat her tight walls with my kids and pray that none of 'em stuck. Instead, my better judgment had me pulling out and marking her thighs with a hefty serving of my cum.

Dani glared at me, her expression curious and her eyes lust-heavy. Then, without saying a word, she rolled off the bed, the combination of bodily fluids running down her leg before plopping on the linoleum tiles as she stalked out of the room. And I craned my neck, watching her go with one thought on my mind.

Yup, definitely not lickable floors...

21

His eyes were the problem. The way he looked at me like... I don't know what. Gouge out the eyes and you might have just had yourself the perfect specimen of a man.

But something in the back of my mind told me Connor would need a little more convincing before he let me near his face with a blade.

I took a deep breath and tried to shake the crazy from my head. Which was easier said than done.

I didn't know what the fuck I was thinking. *I wasn't* and that was the problem. I was doing what Danica Rossi did best. Diving face-first into avoidance while using sex as an escape. But there was also more to it than that. Because the fucker was growing on me.

I liked the way he made me feel. Hated it too. But liked it in an odd way. Which brought me back to those eyes and the way they were looking at me right now.

"A little privacy, MacCullagh?" I grunted from where I was seated on the toilet—ya know, like a proper lady and all.

"Sure." He shrugged before closing himself inside the bathroom with me.

"Not what I meant."

"Then you should have been a little clearer with your instructions." He smirked.

"What do you want, Connor?" I tried again while wondering what the fuck I thought I saw in this fucker a few seconds ago. Because right now I wasn't seeing it.

"In life? I dunno—maybe a wife, a white-picket fence, a couple of kids who look a lot like you and me."

When I nearly choked on the air I was breathing, he rushed forward to pat me on the back.

"Fuck, Dani, I was just messing with ya. I might be a few gallons short of a full whiskey barrel, but even I know a guy has to nut inside a girl not *on* her if he's really looking to lock her down."

I lifted a questioning brow. "Meaning?"

"*Meaning,*" he stressed the singular word, "if I wanted your ass knocked up, future baby mama, you'd already be well on your way."

The wink he added was enough to have me risk pissing on myself as I pushed to my feet and reached out a hand to slap him upside the head. "Remind me to stock up on condoms whenever you insist on hanging around, instead of doing what's good for ya."

"One, that pussy is what's good for me—perfect really. And two, if that's your way of begging me to fuck you again, game on, baby girl. Just tell me where, when, and what position and I'm your guy."

Guess he needed a little more work than I thought. The vocal cords definitely had to go too...

22

"Dani... Dani... Dani! Watch out!"

I grabbed the steering wheel and jerked the car back onto the road, blinking my eyes twice before the air from the rolled-down window blasted me awake. Not a blackout. Those were different. I didn't feel the usual post-episode fog. No, must have been a quick adrenaline drop that had me dozing off.

Fuck!

"Pull over. Let me drive."

My eyes flicked to Connor. Hunched forward in the passenger seat, blood pooling from the hole in his gut and darkening the polyester interior. One of his palms was keeping his guts in place while the other was tracking red marks across the grab handle attached to the car's head lining.

"Pretty sure you need two hands to drive. So why don't you just sit pretty," I replied before returning my eyes to the road.

"Pretty sure you need two eyes too, so you might want to keep 'em open, baby girl," he grunted as a pothole sent him bouncing a little too high in his seat. "How much longer?"

"Not long."

This was what we did. Gave each other shit. It was becoming a habit of sorts. The more uncomfortable the situation, the heavier we dished it out. And, well, right now we were fucked. *Him* especially.

I needed to stay awake. It was just a few more miles before we reached the Renegades' compound outside the city limits. It wasn't the smartest move for me to be making at the moment, especially with a newcomer in tow. The boys loved fresh meat. And that wasn't a good thing. But I didn't have much of a choice, seeing as pretty boy was bleeding out from a knife wound he took for me. Not that I asked him to do it. But that was an argument for another day.

Point was we couldn't chance a hospital, not with those fuckers having every pig and their mother on the payroll. It was bad enough that I chanced stopping by my storage unit and grabbing my "go" bag and whatever spare clothes and cash I could carry. Dropping into a clinic now would be like waving a white flag and lying down on the floor till they got there.

So this was it. My Hail Mary move.

The Surgeon owed me a favor—several if I was being petty. Though I knew better than to try. Fingers crossed the sick bastard didn't suffer from a convenient bout of short-term memory. Because I was no Florence Nightingale. Sure, I could throw in a few stitches and do my best to stave off infection. But piecing together intestines was out of my league.

There was a real possibility he'd die. And I didn't know how to feel about that...

"Hey, dollface...?" Connor drew my attention away from those dark thoughts and back to him.

"Yeah?"

"Where we headed?"

The real question was if I was getting him help. He didn't want to ask it. But I could tell that's what was going through his head. Was I getting him help or just taking him somewhere to die...

Couldn't blame him. Roles reversed, I'd be wondering the same thing too.

"To see a friend..."

"Didn't think you had any." He forced a grin on his face. He was hurting, way more than he was letting on, and for some reason that bothered me.

"Yeah, well, stop thinking so hard and you might just live long enough for me to get us there."

Fifteen minutes and several broken speed limits later, we were pulling up to a nondescript brick building in the middle of nowhere. Anyone who didn't know better would assume it was an abandoned prison or maybe a former looney bin—*they wouldn't be far off.*

But the bars on the windows and electric fences were as much for keeping people out as they were for keeping 'em in. It all depended on the type you happened to be.

If only Connor MacCullagh knew the sort of business I really dealt in, the sort of men I called *friends*... 'Cause if he did, I was pretty certain he wouldn't be looking at me with those tiny green hearts in his eyes.

I jumped out of the car before it came to a full stop on the gravel driveway and rushed around the hood to the passenger side, tugging the door open and grabbing Connor by the shoulder. Almost like he was afraid I might break, he leaned more on the frame than on me as he slowly pushed to his feet. His white t-shirt was now stained a deep red, his hand still clutching the shredded meat of his abdomen tight against his body.

The longer I looked, the more I wondered how the fuck he hadn't passed out yet.

Two tentative steps brought us to the large double doors. I didn't bother knocking. There was no point. They already knew we were here. It was just a matter of if they would let us in or not. A quick scan of the doorframe had my glare narrowing in on the blinking light of the camera, making sure they got a clear view of my face.

When static crackled over the intercom, and a familiar voice came over, the hair on the back of my neck stood on end. "Danica Lynn Rossi, what brings a pretty little thing like you to our neck of the woods?"

Casper. At least that's what they called him. Fuck if I could tell you any of these bastards' real names as readily as they could list off mine.

"Don't really have time for your games right now, Cas. Get the Surgeon."

"*Tsk, tsk, tsk.* Thought you knew better than to come to our doorstep and make demands—no matter how great those tits are looking. They *are* looking great by the way."

Connor stiffened beside me, his jaw clenching in a way that told me it had nothing to do with the pain and everything to do with the guy on the other side of the microphone. Wasn't sure what kind of delusions he was suffering from. No one had a claim on me except me. But his misplaced jealousy could be addressed at a later date. His current blood loss? Not so much.

"Fuck this. Dani, let's go," Connor hissed under his breath as he tried to steer me back towards the car. But in his condition, he wasn't gonna make it far without me, so I dug a heel into the dirt and held my ground.

Then I glared up at the ass clown I now knew was watching me from his chair in a room full of military-style surveillance equipment. "Cas, open the goddamn door. We both know you owe me. Do this, and we can call it even. Maybe I'll even let ya'll call in a freebie. No strings attach—"

A loud buzzer cut me off and the metal doors swung open, welcoming us in like a haunted mansion in ona those horror flicks. Even though it had been a few years, I didn't expect any less. The Renegades were always a little over-the-top dramatic, a description that sounded a lot nicer than the men themselves. While I toed the line between right and wrong, depending on my mood, these guys jumped over the far end and landed on sick and twisted. But cash was cash, and something we had in common was our love for the green stuff.

It was an *I'll scratch your back if you scratch mine* sorta deal. Because, on occasion, it was nice to have a chick on the books... or so they liked to remind me. Couldn't tell you what they actually did in this compound of theirs, other than that you were probably better off not knowing about it and that it required them having a full-time surgeon under their employ. *Two*, if you counted Frankie for the light stuff —again not a real name. It was short for Frankenstein on account of how fucked his face was after some bike accident. The first time I saw it, I didn't ride for days.

Obviously I got over that quick.

I helped walk Connor into the open foyer before fixing my boots to the spot again. There were doors on all sides of us, so there wasn't much point in going farther. The building was like a maze, which meant we'd sooner get lost and die there than find the fucker we were looking for.

It was the middle of the night but these guys barely slept, and when they did, it was a hair trigger reaction for them to roll outta bed wide awake and ready to jump into action.

Don't ask me how I knew that. Other than a dick's a dick and sometimes the closest one would have to do. Though something told me pretty boy wouldn't appreciate that answer so much, even if I was hoping one of these fuckers would save his life.

"We're bleeding out over here!" I yelled into the cavernous room, only to have my own voice echo back at me.

I had no doubt the whole lot of them were hanging out somewhere watching me. Just because they let me past the door didn't mean they were agreeing to help. They got bored easily and some things they did just for the sick enjoyment of it. Like eating popcorn while someone's guts plopped down on their tiled floor. They'd probably even force me to clean it up.

I flicked my gaze into each darkened corner, more little red lights all flashing in my direction.

Yup, all eyes were on us. The bastards just hadn't decided what they wanted to do with us yet. Probably trying to figure out what Connor meant to me and if they could score themselves a better deal.

I was two seconds away from knocking down the first door, when Casper came strutting out like a rooster at daybreak. You could practically see the guy's cock swinging between his legs with the way he entered a room. Hands in his tactical pants, shoulders relaxed like he didn't have a care in the world. He probably didn't. You couldn't care when you didn't feel shit. Literally and figuratively. Saw him take a bullet square in the chest once. Didn't slow 'em down one bit. Sure, it was embedded in muscle and didn't hit any vital organs—the man wasn't a cyborg. He just didn't feel pain like the rest of us. Almost like he was immune to it.

Frankie mentioned how Casper suffered nerve damage or some shit at a young age. Regardless, the fucker wasn't normal. Then again, who was I to judge?

"Camera just didn't quite do ya justice, sweetheart." Casper grinned and Connor growled from somewhere deep in his throat. Or maybe it was a gurgling sound? He *was* losing a lot of blood.

"Enough with the small talk, Cas. Ya'll gonna stitch him up or not? Stop wasting my time or I'll have to send ya a bill."

His face went stone cold, the grin gone like it was never there. And his posture stiffened, almost as if we were seeing an entirely different version of the man. Then his lips curled around into a Joker-esque smirk, the Heath Ledger version, though somehow eerier. "Come on back, folks. The doctor will see you now..."

23

A FEW HOURS PRIOR

The sound of hushed voices outside the window had me shifting my body up and off the mattress, my eyes searching for the clock on my bedside table only to come up empty. It took me a moment to realize I was at my uncle's place and not holed up back at my and Zeke's apartment. Getting your brains fucked out of your head would do that to ya. Having you forgetting your name and zip code.

A smirk tipped up one side of my mouth, before the whispers turned to shouting, and my hand reached out to find the sheets tossed around and the other side of the bed lacking one very thick-skulled woman. My gaze bounced around the small room. Dani was nowhere in sight. While the noise of a few trash cans being knocked over told me where I'd most likely find her.

"Fuck." I pushed to my feet and scrambled to shove one leg through my jeans, then the other, as I rushed for the door, down the stairs, and out the back entrance. Stopping short when I rolled up on a scene like something from one of those dubbed ninja movies Zeke liked to watch every Monday night.

Dani had a hammer in one hand, her other gesturing forward in *a come and get me* motion, her brows creased in determination and her legs spread wide in a fighting stance. Two guys had positioned themselves in front of her, appearing ready to toss my girl over one shoulder and shove her into the trunk of the car I could see idling at the side of the street.

Honestly, I was surprised Benny didn't send more. I'd only known Dani for a few days in total and even I knew she could take these fuckers. Or at least give them a run for their money. I was bouncing on the balls of my feet, struggling to decide what was the best way to go about this, when the son of a bitch to my left lunged forward, the streetlamp above him catching the sheen of the blade he had clutched in a palm.

Before I could really think about what I was doing, and honestly how stupid it was to not have grabbed some sort of weapon on my way out here, I was jumping in front of Dani. Shoving her to one side while taking a blade to the gut.

That shit fucking hurt by the way. A sharp sting, followed by throbbing. Until the first wave of adrenaline kicked in—*thanks for nothing*—and I rolled backwards on the concrete, forced myself to one knee and up on my feet again. One hand trying to keep all the inside shit from coming outside. Pretty sure it wasn't meant to come outside. At least that's what I was told in that anatomy class I took back in high school.

Dani cursed under her breath, her glare flicking in my direction. Then she was flying through the air and on

Benny's guys like gravity didn't exist in her world. And maybe it didn't. That or I was already starting to hallucinate. I'd never been stabbed before, so couldn't tell you if seeing shit was normal or not.

Because what I was seeing was unhinged and oddly arousing. *At least my dick still worked.*

She held the hammer high above her head, bringing it down on the one fucker's skull and turning back to the second guy just in time to press her fingers somewhere near his shoulder. His arm went limp and the blade clattered to the ground, disappearing from my view during all the chaos.

I was slumped over in the middle of the sidewalk, though I didn't remember sitting here, with my back leaning against a telephone pole, one leg kicked out, and a hand still clutching my abdomen.

I was tired. So fucking tired. My eyes blinked closed a few times, only to shoot back open when I felt someone standing in front of me. Dani. Then her arms were reaching forward. Helping me back onto my feet and into a car. Not our car.

Whose car is this?

24

PRESENT

"So what happened to the Mick? Get a little handsy before ya had your morning coffee?" Casper quirked a brow while leaning a little too close for comfort. Worst part of it all? The guy liked to imply we had a long history of fucking. Which I wouldn't have had a problem with *if* it were true.

It wasn't.

Don't get me wrong, Cas was good looking and all. A jawline that could cut glass and lips that were made for sucking clit. But something about him unnerved me. And there weren't a lot of people who could do that. Nope, Casper hadn't been my flavor of choice back in the day— much to his displeasure.

Then again, I think the guy liked the chase more than anything else. If I were to give in, I had no doubt he'd run for the hills with his cock tucked between his legs.

"Nope, took a knife meant for my gut," I grunted in reply. Connor had been back with the Surgeon for the last hour and for all I knew the sick fuck could be saving his life or butchering him up like Sunday's roast. None of them would tell me either, not until someone revealed pretty boy's head to me under a serving dish and waited to see my reaction.

Like I said, we were out of options. These psychos or a shallow hole in the woods.

"Aw, so Danica Rossi went and got herself a Prince Charming?"

"Wouldn't say that either." I shrugged a single shoulder, my eyes flicking towards the door without me even meaning to do it. The not knowing was irking me. Almost as much as Casper's incessant chattering. "Guy's got a nice dick. You should know better than anyone else how hard those are to come by." I left my tone dry, sarcastic, while Cas barked out a laugh.

It wasn't true. It only took a glance south of his hard-pressed zipper to know Casper the not-so-friendly ghost was more than packing. But like I said, the kid got bored easy. He enjoyed a little dig now and then, seeing as most people were too afraid to try.

"Ah, sweetheart, we have missed ya 'round here. Frankie's got a stick up his ass half the time, holed up in that dungeon of his, and Surge wouldn't know fun if it bit him in the left nut. You should think about staying a while. Earn some real cash." Casper reached out a hand to tuck the loose strand of hair back behind my ear, and a chill traveled down my spine. And not the good kind. There was something dark beneath those light eyes. "Promise I'll make it worth your while." He winked, and I slid off the counter and onto my feet, watching his boots kick back and forth while dangling over the ledge. The fucker had this thing about appearing far more youthful than the deranged thoughts I had no doubt were festering in that twisted little brain of his.

"Thanks but no thanks. I like being a free agent. Some of us just don't work well with others. I'm sure someone like you can respect that, am I right?"

"Suit yourself." He sighed before jumping down to stand in front of me. "I got shit to do anyway. Catch ya on the other side of the law, Danica Lynn Rossi," he threw over his shoulder before stalking out the door in search of trouble. I was certain he'd find it too.

Boredom was dangerous with a man like that. Because there was no telling what he'd do to satisfy it.

Some unknown amount of time later, I could describe the shape of each crack in the drywall, point out every corner that needed dusting, and give ya a full rundown of how often and at what intervals the pipes creaked above my head. I didn't have a phone to pass the time—the guys would have confiscated it the moment I walked through the door anyway. The bare room was intended to drive you nuts, to make seconds feel like minutes. Minutes, hours.

Might as well have thrown me in a padded cell and called it a day. Being alone with nothing but your thoughts was slow torture for anyone. But especially for me.

"Danica," the Surgeon's deep baritone was startling after so much silence, his boots deliberately squeaking as he took a single step over the threshold to pin me with a set of near-black eyes. "It's been too long." He grinned, though that seemed too simple a word to describe the look he was giving me.

It was sinister. Calculated. Measured so that each slow curl of his lips held a hidden meaning. Leaving you feeling like you needed to pluck his words from the air and turn them over to fully understand what he was really saying.

"Has it? I hadn't noticed." I kept my own voice even. Level. The slightest hint of fear and these fuckers would eat it up until there was nothing left of you. Then they'd use your bones like a fucking toothpick.

He was wearing the usual light-blue surgical scrubs and a pair of black latex gloves, looking like he just stepped off the set of *Grey's Anatomy*. Though he was more prone to taking life than he was to saving it. He was also an expert in torture, knowing how and where to inflict the most pain while keeping someone alive enough to feel it. Each of the boys had a specialty and the human body was his.

"He still breathing?" I asked the question I knew Surge would refuse to answer until he got something out of me first. So why not get straight to the point?

"What's the guy mean to you, Danica?" He repeated my name on purpose. It was an interrogation tactic, meant to both unnerve and put you at ease. It was familiar and intimate, suggesting they knew you better than you knew yourself.

"I already told Ghostface at the door. One job, no questions asked. No favors in return. You won't get a better offer from me, Surge. You know that."

"Two," he countered, and I met his stone glare with one of my own.

"One."

He didn't reply, just snapped his gloves off and tossed them into the wastebasket to his left. Then he wiped a smearing of blood from his cheek and waited. He wanted me to agree before I even knew the outcome. Either way, I was stuck. In their debt for God only knew how long. Because they wouldn't call on me straightaway. No, that would be no fun. They liked the idea of having me on a short leash until the job was, for the lack of a better word, *interesting*.

I hesitated for a beat, the pounding of my heart growing louder in my ears the longer I stood my ground. I couldn't make it easy on them. Or they would see it as a sign of weakness. Use it to their advantage. And I meant what I said. I liked working on my own. I was no team player, especially when that team was made up of a buncha mask-wearing, gun-toting sociopaths.

"Two. Within two years or the deal is null and void." I crossed my arms over my chest—wrong move. It was defensive posturing but the air was intentionally running full blast and I'd raised them without thinking. "That's more than enough time for ya'll to cash in."

Surge nodded once. Then that grin of his reappeared. "Sure hope the boy's worth the trouble, Danica."

Yeah, you and me both.

25

I was no fan of drugs—alcohol was my poison of choice —but I tell you what... Whatever these fuckers had pumping through my veins, it was good shit. Couldn't feel my legs and honestly I was so high I didn't care if they were still attached or propped up on some freak's front lawn as this year's winning Halloween decoration.

There was a noticeable chill in the air while my body was burning up from the inside out. I couldn't open my eyes. It was like they were weighed down by a couple of cement blocks. Even when I felt a hand trail along my lower abs and rip the sheet from the makeshift hospital bed I had only a vague memory of being strapped down to, I couldn't do much more than lie here and take it.

Then a palm was gripping my cock at the base and tugging. And I felt an instant sense of relief, knowing at least one appendage appeared to be fully intact. A sense that was short-lived the moment I heard the voice belonging to that hand and it sure as fuck wasn't Dani's.

"It ain't that big..."

"To be fair, it ain't fully erect yet. May need a few more pumps to get the whole picture."

Also not Dani.

And there wasn't shit I could do about these fuckers groping me when my limbs refused to move. A couple more awkward jerks and I was waiting for one of them to pull out the measuring tape. I didn't know what the fuck was going on but this put a whole new spin on the term *aftercare.*

"See?" They were still fumbling around under the sheet. "Sorry, Cas, but as a neutral party, I have to tell ya the guy's a decent size."

"Doesn't mean he can do fuck all with it."

"Ain't that the truth, brother. It's all about the motion of the ocean." A loud, barking laugh was the last thing I heard before a fresh warmth shot through my veins and I was knocked the fuck out all over again.

Couldn't tell you what day it was. Barely knew my name when I woke up again. This time in an all-white room that had me wondering if I came out on the other side or was just waiting for my number to be called. The overhead lighting was blinding as I tried to keep my eyes open—*tried* the key word.

It took several minutes for me to get the job done and even then I couldn't tell if I was actually seeing something or merely looking at the underside of my lids. Until the sound of a door opening and a loud clattering had me shooting up in bed, before a sharp pain in my gut had me doubling over for a second time.

I thought I'd felt it all. Broken bones, bloodied knuckles, almost severed a finger as a kid but this... this was new. Nothing short of agony that radiated from my bones outward.

"Shouldn't try to get outta bed, Mr. MacCullagh. Surge doesn't take too kindly to patients who don't like to listen to doctor's orders." I didn't recognize the voice as belonging to one of the two fuckers from before. But this guy didn't seem any less hostile, especially when he stepped into the light and I realized that one side of his face was more jacked up than a stray hand falling into the butcher's meat grinder at the corner shop.

"Where's Dani?" I asked before I could stop myself.

Some part of me had been expecting her to be here when I woke up, while another part wondered if she planned to use my ill-timed injury as an excuse to make a run for it. Wouldn't blame her. I was dead weight and she was better off on her own than with my ass bleeding all over the interior of her newly stolen car. It wasn't like we could be inconspicuous, crossing state lines as I tried to hold the lower half of my body together with a spool of thread and some fish wire.

My last name was MacCullagh, not MacGyver.

"How the fuck should I know? Isn't that your job? To keep a leash on your bitch?" the fucker grunted while pulling an apple out of his black cargo pants and taking a bite.

"What the fuck did you just call her?" I ground my teeth, clutching a hand to my side as I attempted to throw my legs over the mattress and mow the bastard down. I didn't make it two steps before my knees gave way and I was meeting the shiny tile floor head-on.

I mean, might as well add a broken nose to the list while I was at it.

When I looked up again, the guy was gone and Dani was standing in his place. She came rushing forward, yanking me to my feet and guiding me back to the bed with an odd expression tugging her brows together. The girl was unreadable at the best of times, and stone-cold at the worst of them, especially when she was looking to hide something.

"Glad you're not dead," she muttered under her breath, and I could tell it killed her to admit as much. Danica Rossi saw emotions as a weakness, caring for someone else the most damning one out of the bunch.

"Could say the same about you, baby girl," I replied as I brought her hand to my lips and placed a kiss on her knuckles.

"You didn't have to take that knife, ya know." She pulled her arm free to pin me with a glare. Her posture defensive and her hackles raised. "I know what the fuck I'm doing. He never would have stuck me like he stuck you."

"Maybe, but how else is a guy meant to get your attention if not by nearly bleeding out all over your boots? Didn't think the usual flowers and chocolates would do the trick, dollface."

26

Two years at these fuckers' beck and call. Two fucking years of being collared by pretty boy's poor decision-making and my soft spot for his cock. And I still couldn't tell you why I did it. The last bastard I'd given a shit about sent a bullet flying towards my skull after fucking my literal brains out.

Then again, I wasn't the one left bleeding this time around. So I guess things were looking up. Sorta. They could be worse.

Connor was passed the fuck out, still feeling the effects of Surge's opiate cocktail, and I was left staring at the ceiling in the room the boys set up for us... after giving me shit for the last few hours about my choice in bedmates. But I didn't see any of them taking on the Mulligans without asking for something in return.

Sounded a little like jealousy to me. And not because they wanted me on their arm. More like they wanted to be me. Have someone who didn't want something from them for once. Even a cold-hearted bastard felt lonely now and then. And being holed up in this compound twelve months out of the year, except when they were working a job... yeah, something told me the isolation was getting to 'em more than they liked to let on. Probably why they let me through the door in the first place.

It was hard not to be bitter, to open myself up to whatever emotions this dumb fuck beside me was stirring up in my chest. But I had to admit—at least to my subconscious—that the idea of having him around was growing on me. Even now, as he slept, he had an arm slung around my waist. Like he was afraid I might run. Which meant he knew me better than most people. Because that's exactly what I wanted to do.

Avoidance was my favorite flavor. Self-destruction my usual mode of transportation. Sex and alcohol the accelerants that fueled the fire. I was a walking red flag that the poor son of a bitch had mistaken for a green light. And there was something both off-putting and appealing about that.

I gently nudged Connor's arm aside and swung my legs over the edge of the bed, and he was pulling me back down before I made it to my feet.

"Go to sleep, Dani," he muttered into the pillow, not bothering to look up to see what I was doing.

"Can't sleep," I huffed before flopping back down beside him. I should have been a tad more careful but the fact that he caught me was irritating.

"Happens a lot, doesn't it?" Connor's voice was weighed down by a mix of pills that sounded real good right about now, but it was clear none of it was gonna stop him from trying to dig deeper under my skin. "Normally, I'd be all about fucking you unconscious but even I have my limits. So why don't we try talking 'bout it for once, baby girl?"

"Talk about what, Chatty Cathy?"

"All that shit goin' on in that head of yours, Dani. Those weird trances you go under where the rest of the world seems to go on 'round you but you're miles away. The reason you showed up at Mollies that night. The reason we're both here. And I don't mean in this bed. I mean on the run. What's your history with the Mulligans?"

"That's a lot to unpack in one night, Connor. As for the Mulligans, you already know the history there." I sighed. "The Irish and Italians have been fightin' on those streets for ages, long before I came around. They don't hate me. Just my last name."

"Nope." He rolled onto his back, slowly, the whole ordeal painful to watch. I could only imagine how it felt.

"Nope?" I parroted.

"*Nope*," he repeated. "There's more to it than that. This is personal. Whatever's goin' on between ya. Junior especially. Were you two a thing or something? A breakup gone wrong."

This had me coughing out a laugh. "Me and Junior? Fuck no. I'd love to see that little prick even try to put his *little prick* anywhere near me. I'd cut it off, if that didn't mean I'd have to touch it first."

"Right, then, what is it?"

"A long fucking story is what it is, Connor."

I could make out the pearly white of his grin even in the pitch-blackness of the room. "Good thing I have all fucking night, baby girl."

27

"**C**aught your creepy little brother watching me again," I huffed the moment Leo pulled up on his bike.

He knocked the kickstand into place and removed his helmet while attempting to smooth things over with that panty-melting smirk of his. We both knew what he was doing, trying to disarm me with his cock magic, hoping I'd drop the subject and not make it a thing.

But fuck that.

"I'm not messin' around, Mulligan. I think the kid's seen something. And we both know he's desperate enough to use it against you. *Us.*" I crossed my arms over my chest, my hip set in a way that told him I was serious. "I don't know 'bout you, but I sure as fuck don't feel like cleanin' up the streets after the bloodbath my pops is sure to unleash if he gets wind of how you corrupted his perfect little girl."

Leo tilted his head to one side, observing me like some

sort of curiosity. Then he grinned, a sign that he must have liked whatever it was he saw. "*Me* corrupt *you*, babe? Pretty sure it was the other way around." He tucked his helmet under one arm before tugging me against his chest, gripping a handful of my hair and yanking my head back so that I was forced to look him in the eye.

"Maybe, but my old man won't see it that way." I shrugged. "And it will be your ass that's on the line. Shotgun wedding and all that. Probably kill you shortly after—it's much better to be a widow than a whore in my family."

"Wedding, ya say? Is that your way of askin' me to marry you, Rossi?"

"Fuck no," I grunted, shoving Leo back a step. The son of a bitch clearly needed air. Seemed the lack of oxygen was going to his head.

"Would it really be so bad?"

Scratch that. It was too late. His brain was fried and there was no coming back. It was time to pull the plug.

"Think about it, babe. We could finally put an end to this war. Do somethin' good for both sides. Is the idea of being with me that much of a hardship you'd rather risk sneaking around?"

"I *like* sneaking around, Leo," I reminded him. "And the way your cock springs up at the mention tells me you like it too."

He raked a hand through his hair, his leather jacket and longer-than-usual locks only adding to that bad boy look of his that got me goin'. "I do like sneaking around, fucking around, but I *love* you, Dani."

28

PRESENT

She was doing it again. Her mind somewhere else when I was right here in front of her. It was a real kick to the balls to lose your girl to her demons. Especially when she was lying in bed with you. But seeing as my flag was only flying at half-mast, I guess I had to give my cock a break. Wasn't much he or I could do once my guts had been Frankensteined back together. Talking it out seemed like the best option, until my questions had her curling in on herself again.

Whatever was going on in that head of hers... it had to be almost as bad as whatever those sick bastards were up to in this real-life house of horrors.

"Hey, baby girl." I reached out a hand to tilt her jaw in my direction. It was dark but light enough for me to make out the whites of her glassy eyes. Tears clinging to her lashes but refusing to fall. "Come here." I tucked her against my chest, ignoring the sharp pain that shot down my abdomen and pulsed in my toes before shooting back up again. "You can talk to me, ya know? Probably won't make it another week with the way bullets seem to come your way, so your secrets are safe."

This had her stifling a laugh as her shoulders finally relaxed, and she sank deeper into my hold.

"What's so funny?"

"The fact you actually think this room isn't bugged," she mumbled under her breath, and my eyes immediately flicked around.

"You're fucking with me, right?"

"What d'ya think, Connor?"

"I think you're just as fucked up as they are—so whatever you tell me it's a 50/50 shot if it's true or not."

"Guess you're smarter than you look, pretty boy." Dani's fingertips glided along my chest before trailing north as she guided my mouth down to meet hers.

It was the first time she'd been the one to initiate a kiss. And I wasn't so dumb as to think it wasn't being used as a means to distract me. Shut me up. But there was more to it than that. The shit she didn't say with words she more than conveyed with her body. I took notice of how she watched me when she didn't think I was looking. How much she cared about me despite trying so desperately not to.

The fact she brought me here? Yeah, that might as well have been her asking me to go steady. I knew it wasn't easy for her to bring me into her world. I also knew the heat she was catching because her... *associates* didn't think I was good enough for her. And they were probably right. But that didn't mean shit. Because I wasn't about to give her up either.

Something I think she needed more than she'd ever

admit. Someone who didn't give up on her. Run away at the first sign of crazy, which I was fully aware she unleashed on purpose.

Her tongue twisted against mine in an open invitation to plunge deeper. And fuck if I didn't want all of her. Every part of her she was willing to give. Even more so the parts she was holding back. I wanted to fuck the worries out of her head and then hold her till she was certain they were gone. I wanted her to fight me at every turn just to show her I didn't mind giving in. Because it didn't make me weak. It made me strong enough to take it.

She was moaning into my mouth, her pelvis grinding against my hip, while I was doing everything in my power not to let her know how much it fucking stung.

This was the last fucking thing we should be doing. Then again, so was most of the shit we did together.

Dani pushed upright, tugging the loose t-shirt over her head, before throwing a leg over my waist. She was wearing nothing but a tiny sliver of underwear as she straddled my thighs without putting pressure on my abdomen. Which I was grateful for. I didn't mind popping a stitch—it was a sacrifice I was willing to make for the greater good. The *greater good* meaning my girl's tight cunt wrapped around my cock. But something told me I wouldn't survive the additional blood loss.

But what a way to go, am I right?

Dani leaned forward, mindful of my injury, as she captured my mouth in another harsh kiss. It was her way of telling me she needed me. *This.* And hell if I didn't want to give it to her.

"Thought you said the place was bugged," I grunted against her lips, and she grinned.

"If they really wanna watch, might as well give 'em a

show…" She shrugged. But her hand was already gliding between us to slip under the waistband of my pants. When her warm palm wrapped around my cock, I jerked involuntarily and the sudden movement had me cursing under my breath.

Dani froze, her body going rigid. I already knew what she was gonna do. Say. How she felt. Her tells lighting up like the lightbulbs on a marquee. It was easier for her to run when she feared being rejected. Easier to assume rejection than to try to dig a little deeper. She'd run, and in this state, there was no way I'd catch her.

Her lips parted, some smart-mouthed comment likely dancing on her tongue. An insult meant to push me away so she could make a beeline for the door. But I cut her off before she could verbalize it.

"I'm gonna need you to do me a favor, baby girl," I said, one hand gripping her waist while the other cupped her wet cunt.

When she didn't answer, I took it as an open invitation to run a finger over her clit and watch her head dip back. Her thighs were trembling as she tried her best to bear her own weight without leaning on me.

"As much as I want to remember how good this pussy feels around my cock, I'm the first to admit I'm not up for the job—not yet. Something I will make up to you. Again." A quick twirl of my finger. "And again." Another. "And again." This time I made a full figure eight that had Dani moaning my name and grinding against my palm. "So what I'm gonna need you to do… is get that ass up here and ride my face. Use me, baby girl, like I'm your favorite fuck toy. Can you do that for me, Dani? Can you make yourself come on my face?"

She was too lost to the feel of my fingers playing her

cunt like she was an orchestra and I was her goddamn maestro to respond with anything other than a whimper.

"Come on, Dani, can't leave your friends waiting around with their dicks in their hands. Throw the fuckers a bone and show the pervs how pretty you are when you come on my face."

29

Ask me where I was, and I'd tell you I'd died and gone to heaven. Because the feel of Dani's thighs squeezing my head as she ground her drenched cunt back and forth over my tongue was otherworldly. A celestial experience. Spiritual ascension if I'd ever heard of it.

She was making those little sounds again. The ones that told me she didn't care who was listening. My eyes were drawn upwards to watch her. What I could see of her. One palm flat on the wall and bracing her upper body, her head tipped to the side, and her hair flowing freely down her back just begging to be pulled. I dug my fingers into the meat of her thighs, not caring whether or not this breath was my next or my last.

Either way, I was content with the fact that I'd lived a full life.

When her movements began to stagger, her rhythm uncoordinated, I growled deep in my throat. The vibration of my vocal cords traveling across the lips of her pretty pink pussy and sending my girl flying over that edge of bliss. Her body jerked with the shock waves and I took the opportunity to suck in a deep breath and lap my tongue along her swollen cunt. Drinking down everything Dani offered me on a pussy-flavored platter, while wrapping my lips around the ball of her clit piercing. I tugged just slightly on the jewelry with my teeth, enough to have her shuddering one more time before I was done with her.

"There's my good girl." I grinned while pulling her down next to me on the bed. Her chest was still heaving and she had that satisfied smirk on her face—the one that screamed *attaboy*. At least to me it did. "Feel better?" I asked as I wiped a hand across my cheeks before sucking my fingers clean.

Fuck if I'd waste a drop of that well-earned juice.

"Much." She sighed, her eyes glued to the ceiling and an arm draped over her face. The air smelled like sweat and sex—and maybe a little bit of blood—but I wouldn't change a thing about it.

"You really think they were watching?" I cocked an eyebrow and turned my head in her direction. My heart skipping a beat at just how perfect she looked at this moment.

"Probably." She laughed. "Why? Does it bother you?"

"Which part?" I grunted, shifting aside so that I could watch her, read her cues as she spoke.

"The fact that I fucked at least one of 'em before. The fact that at least one of 'em wants to fuck me? The fact I might let 'em."

She was baiting me. Testing me. Because taking that knife for her wasn't enough to prove I was in this with her for the long game. Nothing I'd done, said, shown her surpassed those doubts she had in that head of hers. And I couldn't be sure they ever would. This girl would back me up to the edge of an emotional cliff and shove me over before she'd ever admit she liked having me around. Something that would be a problem for a lesser man. With a smaller ego.

Lucky for the both of us, I wasn't that man. I wasn't fragile. And I didn't mind beating her down with my affections. I'd smother her if I had to. Fuck her when that wasn't good enough to make her stay. And tire her out till she was too exhausted to run. It was a hard job but someone had to do it. And I was more than happy to offer myself up as tribute.

I sucked in a breath before composing myself enough to respond—just because I knew what she was doing, it didn't mean it didn't get under my skin. The thought of her with someone else... The realization that she might just do it to push me away... And I'd have to either get over it or move on.

"Dani, your past is the fuckin' past. I don't care who you fucked before me. As for them wanting to fuck you? Can't do much about that either. Half the male population is right up there with them on that platform. Probably just as many females. And when it comes to you fucking anyone else in the near future? Ain't gonna happen, dollface. Not if I do my job and keep you plenty satisfied. Which..." I reached out a hand, tipping her face up and forcing her to look at me with hooded eyes. "I seem to be doing just fine, if I say so myself."

I watched her nostrils flare, her eyes narrow, and her jaw set tight. I'd hit a nerve. *Good.*

"Here's the thing, pretty boy. I'm gonna fuck who I want. When I want. How I want," she hissed.

I nodded. "And that's perfectly fine."

"Really?" she gritted out. I could hear the sarcasm dripping from the six-letter word.

"Yup." I popped my lips dramatically because. Just fucking because. "Who? Me. Over and over again. Until we're both too tired to move. When? A few seconds ago, and again very soon. Let me grab a glass of water and my tongue is yours for the taking. And how? Well, that's lady's choice, baby girl. Just tell me where you want me and I'm your guy."

30

I stomped down the hall, my boots clacking against the cement flooring with each step I took closer to my destination. My legs were bare, the t-shirt I'd borrowed ending just below my thighs and causing a chill to run up my spine and dissipate some of the rage boiling under my skin.

This was childish.

I didn't give a fuck.

I had something to prove. To myself if no one else. And I'd set the world alight if it meant being right. Fuck anyone who got in my way.

I turned the corner, down another long hall, glancing left then right before saying fuck it and going straight. Like I said, this place was a goddamn maze and I might as well have been a test rat trying to sniff out my cheese—which would be whoever the fuck I ran into first.

My eyes flitted over to the camera directly in front of me. "Bugs, Donnie, Casper… whoever the fuck is behind that lens right now, we need to have a fucking chat."

Surge didn't care much for technology, not unless it

involved sawing into bone, and Frankie was more than likely hunkered down underground with a goddamn bushel of apples—*don't bother asking because I didn't know the answer to that one.*

I was sure at least one of the fuckers was still watching me. No one roamed freely in the compound, not unless they were being chased. And right now, I was doing the chasing.

Two seconds and one eerie creak of a door later, and Ghostface himself stepped into view. His arms crossed over his chest like a disapproving father figure and his lips pursed into a fine line.

He wasn't happy. Which was just peachy fucking keen. Because I wasn't either.

"It's the middle of the night, sweetheart. Why all the yellin'?"

"Please, like any of you fuckers actually sleep," I grumbled, and he quirked a brow, waiting for me to answer his question. "Right, well, I'm gonna need you to put your money where your mouth is and fuck me, Cas," I told him matter-of-factly. And I couldn't deny how much I liked unnerving a man who was known for maintaining his composure.

"And why's that, Danica? That dick not as good as you thought it was? Or did you just finally come to your senses?"

"Where's your bunk these days? Or you wanna just press me up against the closest wall? I'm not picky."

"Clearly..." he grunted, and I wasn't sure if that was meant to be a dig at me or Connor.

"Need me to help you get it up first? Is that the problem?" I reached out a hand towards Casper's zipper and he slapped it away.

"Ain't no problem with me or my dick. The problem's

with you." He stalked forward until my back was forced against the closest surface. "I don't like my women willing, sweetheart. I like 'em kicking and screaming and fighting as I hold 'em down with a palm and fuck 'em into submission. Think you can do that? Or those balls of yours not as big as you like to believe they are?" He grinned, and the way his lips curled slung that familiar shiver up my spine. The kind that sent my central nervous system into overdrive as my body tried to decide between fight or flight.

When Casper snatched my wrists, one in each hand, *fight* won out as a knee shot up between his legs. He turned his hip, keeping me from making contact before he pressed his nose into my hair and took a deep breath.

"Do you know what fear smells like, Dani?" He didn't wait for a response; he didn't want one. "It smells like sweat, sounds like a heart beating out of your chest, and tastes like tears—salty and sinful—all rolled up in one."

31

uck. Me. That girl was quick. And I was bleeding, bogged down by the arm clutched to my abdomen and the trail of bodily fluids leaking behind me.

It was my fault. I'd spooked her. Come on a little too strong for her to handle. Don't get me wrong, Dani was a force to be reckoned with. As long as it didn't involve anything emotional. Because that shit was baby girl's Achilles' heel.

By the time I rounded the corner, following the sound of her irritated stomping, my heart was jumping in my throat and a couple of torn stitches turned to several as I rushed the fucker who had her wrists in one hand and his cock in the other. Didn't matter if she went looking for trouble or not, she'd found it and I'd found her.

I lunged forward and tackled the son of a bitch to the ground, landing one good blow to his jaw before he could stop me. Then it was game on as he smirked up at me between a set of bloodied teeth.

"You're dead and you don't even know it." He laughed. His arms thrown up and his palms tucked under his head as his eyes flicked from me to Dani. Just as quickly as the grin appeared, it was gone when he pinned me with a glare. "She begged me for it, in case you're wondering. Go on and ask her. Ain't my fault if a little mouse stumbles into my trap, then suddenly changes her mind about wanting to play the game. That's not how the world works, sweetheart." It was clear the last part was meant for Dani as the bastard's scowl landed on her this time.

"Guess your mama never taught you no means no," I spit in reply.

"Nah, because the woman knew her place was to service with the rest of 'em." He tossed his head back on a cackle as I slowly pushed to my feet, stumbled over to Dani, and grabbed her hand.

"We're getting the fuck out of here."

For once, she didn't argue with me as I dragged her back down the hallway, stopping by our room to grab our duffle bag and slinging it over my shoulder. I made two wrong turns before landing us in the same cavernous foyer where this shitshow all started.

"I'm driving," I grunted, half in annoyance and half in pain, as I guided her out the front door and jumped behind the wheel.

She stood silent for a minute, leaning a palm on the passenger side window without actually making a move to get in. I didn't have the energy to fight her on this but I would if I had to. 'Cause one thing was for certain. We'd spend the night locked in this car before stepping foot in that madhouse again.

I started counting to ten in my head. By the time I got to eight, the car door was opening and she was positioning herself on the blood-stained seat. I'd almost forgotten the crime scene I'd left behind less than twenty-four hours ago.

The interior smelled musky, metallic, rotten. But it sure beat whatever bullshit was going on a few feet away.

I turned the car around, continuing down the bumpy path of the hidden driveway as trees blurred by on each side of us. It was only a few hours till daylight, but I'd drive through the goddamn night if I had to. I was too ramped up to sleep at this point anyway. An irrational rage boiled beneath my surface, causing my blood pressure to spike and my jaw muscles to tighten. I wasn't an angry guy. Didn't really lose my temper. Right now I was fucking furious and I couldn't tell you if it was at the Joker we left cackling to himself on the floor, the eerily tight-lipped woman to my right, or worst of all... myself.

So much adrenaline was pumping through my system, I didn't even feel the pain anymore. Barely acknowledged the dampness of my own blood still seeping through my shirt. Or the feel of my foot pressing a little too hard on the accelerator. Not until Dani's hand was covering mine on the wheel.

"Ya need to slow the fuck down, Connor. Unless your goal is to get us pulled over in a car that looks like something out of Forensics Digest." Dani's tone was softer than it'd usually be. Especially considering she wasn't the one in control at the moment. "And I'll need to close those stitches you popped. Surge threw in a few sub-Qs, so your intestines shouldn't be falling out anytime soon. But if we don't close the top layer, you'll be down with infection before you get the chance to properly reprimand me like I know you're dyin' to do."

That last part had me side-eyeing her as my foot eased up on the gas just slightly. "I'm not gonna reprimand you, Dani. I'm not your father," I snapped.

"But you do wanna be my daddy, don't you, pretty

boy?" She batted those long lashes at me, and I shook my head.

"Now? Now, you have jokes?" I grumbled under my breath, pausing before asking the question that was still weighing heavily on my mind. "What did he mean back there? The whole *you're dead and you don't even know* it thing?"

She sucked in a deep breath, telling me I wasn't gonna like whatever it was she was about to say. Though that wasn't much different from the norm. "He was commenting on your technique. You left yourself vulnerable when you jumped him. Vital organs within reach. He was envisioning all the various ways he could have killed you in those few minutes. In his head, he'd already done it ten times over."

"Why the fuck not just do it then? Why not just kill me if he was so sure he could?" My jaw was clenching so tight my temples were pulsing.

"Honestly?"

"For fuck's sake, yes, *honestly*, Dani."

"Because it would have been too easy. And it was more fun for him to wind you up like this than it would have been to just kill you."

"Well, thank god for small fucking favors." It was good to know I was entertainment for a bunch of fuckers who were too old to be playing dress-up. "Who the fuck are those guys anyway and what do they have to do with you?"

"Connor, don't ask me shit you really don't wanna know," she huffed, her arms crossing over her chest and her eyes looking straight ahead again.

"I wouldn't ask you if I didn't wanna know, Dani." I slammed an open palm onto the steering wheel.

She was right about one thing. I was wound the fuck up.

More twisted than I ever remember being in my life. Two seconds later, and I would have walked in on them... doing whatever it was they were doing. And part of me didn't know if I'd saved her from something or interrupted her good time. With Dani, it could go either way.

"They call themselves the Renegades. Simply put, they're kinda like a gang if a gang were full of ex-military ops and straight-up psychopaths specializing in torture methods. As for what they have to do with me? I take on jobs for them every once in a while, whenever I'm short on cash or really just bored and looking to kill some time."

"Right, and what is it that you do again?" I lifted a curious brow. Truth was she never told me. Baby girl loved to dodge the subject almost as often as she dodged bullets.

Dani shrugged. "I'm self-employed. Some people might even call me an entrepreneur."

"Are these the same kinda people who consider glue a delicacy?"

"Maybe," she hummed. "Or maybe they're just the kinda people who know better than to jump in front of a blade that's got someone else's name on it."

32

The shitty, rundown motel was something straight out of *Hitchcock Presents,* but we were short on cash and even shorter on energy. At least I was. Dani seemed to be fueled by warm whiskey, the occasional cigarette, and a hefty dose of rage most days. I wasn't so lucky. I was starving. And for once, I wasn't thinking dirty. Other than the IV bags full of God knows what that had been run through my system, I couldn't tell you the last time I'd eaten.

I shoved a few bills in the vending machine three doors down and carried a couple of off-brand candy bars and colas back to our room.

Roach motel would have been putting it mildly. I was pretty sure nothing good happened on these beds, but it was a place to hunker down and regroup for a couple of hours. Especially since we'd been doing nothing more than winging it the last few days and it hadn't gotten us far.

I peeled my t-shirt from my abs, taking some skin and a shit-ton of dried blood with it as I tugged the material over my head and tossed it into the sink.

Dani was sitting cross-legged on the bed in her usual tank top and sleep shorts, her hair piled high on her head as she watched me. "Let me take a look," she said, jutting her chin towards the dozen or so stitches presently lining my lower abdomen.

It was the first real glimpse I'd gotten of the guy's threadwork, and it honestly wasn't half bad, especially when you took into account I hadn't exactly been easy on myself. The wound was oozing but I didn't see any sign of infection yet. It would be one hell of a gnarly scar though.

I took a tentative step towards Dani, standing just within reach. I wouldn't say that I was mad at her. More like irritated. Hangry. And probably a little hurt too. But that much I wasn't about to admit out loud. The woman knew how I felt about her, which meant she also knew exactly what she was doing when she'd left my bed in search of someone else's. Whether or not she'd planned to go through with it was beside the point.

She trailed a fingertip over the end knot, before flicking her eyes up to meet mine. "Surge went with an interrupted stitch." When I lifted a single brow in question, she added, "That's a good thing. Means the few you popped won't affect the overall healing process. I just need to wipe it down a bit and add a sterilized bandage. Then we'll switch between covering it up and airing it out."

"I think I got it, thanks," I grunted in reply and watched her expression morph. Into what? Couldn't tell you. She just wasn't used to me pushing her away like this. Truth be told, I didn't want to. I was just tired. And fucking hungry.

When I turned to step away, she tugged on the waistband of my sweats. "Connor, just stop."

"Stop what, Dani? What is it that you think I'm doing now?"

"I get it, okay? You're pissed off. But being stubborn ain't gonna help either of us keep your ass alive."

"Me? Stubborn?" I barked out a too-loud laugh, raking one hand through my hair before gesturing it between us. "Pot meet fucking kettle, baby girl. You were gonna fuck that guy or he was gonna fuck you—I honestly don't know anymore—just because you're *too fucking stubborn* to admit you like me, and you won't even tell me why? Why the fuck you're like this? What the fuck happened to you to make you like... *this?*"

"Like what, Connor? What am I like?"

Great, now she was the one irritated with me. How the fuck did she manage to turn the tables so quickly? It must have been witchcraft or some shit. My ma had a way of doing the same thing. Making me feel like a complete ass when she was the one in the wrong.

"Scared, Dani. You're fucking terrified. Of feeling something. Anything. And you're too fucking stubborn to help me *help* you. So, instead, you do everything in your fucking power to try to chase me off. The most fucked-up part about it all?" I towered over her, leaning forward so that she was forced to lean back against the mattress to look up at me. "The most fucked-up part is the fact that everything in you wants me to stay. To fight you for you. To prove that I ain't going anywhere, abandoning you no matter how much you hurt me."

"I..."

I brushed the back of my broken knuckles across her too-soft skin. "Don't bother arguing with me, baby girl. Because I know the truth. Nothing you say is gonna change that. And tomorrow I'll go on fighting you, but right now, I'm fucking exhausted. So eat your goddamn chocolate bar and go the fuck to bed, Dani." I pushed back off the mattress, turned on my heel, and walked into the bathroom before I did or said something stupid.

Stupider? More stupid?

Fuck if I knew.

33

I could hear the world around me long before I regained the ability to open my eyes. At first it was the beeping sounds, the machines, so loud that I could have sworn I'd died and all the noise was meant to slowly drive me mad. Then it was my sense of smell. A hint of gunpowder that would never quite leave my nostrils—the docs would later tell me it was psychosomatic. Almost like a phantom limb.

But what the fuck did they know? From what I would come to see over the years, the medical field was made up of a whole lotta guess work and not so much actual knowledge. Just one of many reasons I would never again step foot in a hospital.

Touch and taste took a bit longer to come around. But when they did, it was like being hit by a semi-truck. The pounding in my head and the rotten flavor of the tubing shoved down my throat, all while I couldn't say a word. Couldn't do much else but listen to them talk about me like

I wasn't there. When I was. *I was there.* I just needed them to shut up long enough for someone to notice.

None of them had much hope. The docs, my friends, even my family. And soon the voices stopped coming. Stopped talking. About me, to me, over me. To the point where I wasn't sure if I'd ever heard them to begin with.

Maybe this was what hell was like? All the chatter followed by silence.

Until one day the harsh hospital lighting felt especially bright, irritating, and my eyes blinked open as if they'd always had the ability and just never felt the need to move before then.

I would love to say this was the point where I shot up outta bed, pulled the feeding tube from my throat, and immediately sought revenge against the Mulligans. And if anyone were to ask, that's exactly how it happened. I went in guns blazing and killed off every last one of 'em.

In truth, I lay there for hours before someone noticed me, days before I could piss in a toilet, my vocal cords restrained and my legs of no real use. It was worse than being dead, having your mind trapped inside its own body. Feeling completely helpless, dependent on the people who'd already checked you off as not being worth their time.

I was nineteen years old, though I'd never remember or regain the months that had passed, which included my birthday and five funerals—there was already a headstone with my name on it. Just waiting for me to join my parents and brother.

That was the world I woke up to, a world where my family hadn't abandoned me in life; instead, they were waiting for me in death.

The streets were still stained red with blood from both

sides. Though the scales were definitely tipping in the Mulligan Gang's direction. My pop had killed their eldest son, their heir. An eye for an eye, I was certain he'd say. In turn, it earned him, my ma, and brother matching bullets to the back of their heads. And that was it. The Rossi line ended there. With me.

Except it didn't. Because I wasn't dead.

But I *was* over it. The whole mafia thing. Not so much the violence—I'd been born with a thirst for the stuff. No, it was the rules that irritated me. Being caged in by my last name and the expectation that I would step in and take over what was left of my inheritance. Or at least what hadn't been plundered by the men within my father's ranks during all that time I'd been... *incapacitated.*

I visited Leo's gravesite exactly once, immediately after I'd been discharged from the hospital. Besides the gunpowder, I could smell the rain that was about to come heavy in the air. Feel the slight chill on my skin with the breeze. As my eyes landed on the words embedded in stone.

León Arthur Mulligan, beloved son

The last part gave me pause. *Beloved.* What the fuck did that even mean? If they knew anything about the guy, they'd know he hated his full name. Almost as much as he hated *them*. His parents. The lineage that haunted us. That killed both of us in one way or another. Because he was entombed in the casket under my feet, and I was restrained by a feeling of betrayal I could never quite shake.

Then again, I guess I hadn't known him either. If I had, I never would have turned my back and allowed him to put that bullet in my head. Something I wouldn't forget. I couldn't forget because I could still feel it there. Like an itch I couldn't scratch. Just beyond my skull's surface. Deep enough to keep me in a coma but not to kill me.

It was weird, waking up in what felt like an alternate universe, where I was an orphan and the man I thought I loved was dead. My fingers twitched with the urge to grab a shovel and dig him up. Because none of it felt real. It was like blinking my eyes and everyone was gone. Hard to believe when I hadn't seen it happen myself.

I mean, for all I knew, it could be any old corpse decaying beneath the fresh layer of tilled dirt. There was no proof it was Leo's. At the same time, I could feel it. Somewhere in that soul I didn't know I had. Almost like another part of me sensed it the moment he was gone.

A thought that would go with me to my actual deathbed, because there was no fucking way I could admit it to anyone aloud. It was my secret to keep. Along with the fact I loved the same man who tried to kill me.

"*Vaffanculo, León,*" I hissed before spitting on his grave and walking away. "*Vedo l'ora di vedere le margherite mettere radici.*"

It was an idle threat. Something I would come to realize later in life. Because I never returned to see those daisies take root. Instead, I left my past to rot in the ground with what remained of the memories of the last fucker who was slick enough to ease his way under my skin.

34

PRESENT

At first, I thought I was imagining it. Dreaming up the incessant ringing that had me swatting the air and looking for the source. I peeked a single eye open to find Dani still knocked the fuck out, her soft snoring bringing a curl to my lips as I took a moment to watch her before the noise started up again. We'd both ditched our cells days ago. So it took me more than a few minutes to realize the ringing was coming from beyond the door.

I quietly slid off the mattress, careful not to wake my girl, then closed the short distance that had me resting a palm on the handle and slipping outside while Dani remained none the wiser.

The cool night air was like a slap to the face, and if I wasn't awake before, I sure was now. The ringing continued as my glare honed in on one of those pay-by-the-minute phones.

Of course the creepy-ass Bates Motel would have a payphone. Because why the fuck not?

If you asked me, I wouldn't have an answer for you, but for some god-forsaken reason, I was compelled to pick it up. While knowing this was something straight out of a teen horror flick and I was more than likely Leatherface's next, well, *face.* But it was another one of those impulses I just couldn't resist.

My fingertips rested on the cool plastic before I swiped the handset from the receiver and placed it against my ear. Now, I half-expected the voice on the other end to start asking me about my favorite scary movie. But what I heard sent a different kind of chill down my spine.

"Conny?"

"Ma...? Is that you?" I raked a tired hand through my hair. "How'd you get this number? You okay? It's the middle of the night..." All valid questions on their own but not nearly as important as the fact that she was calling me on a payphone at some no-name motel. My eyes bounced around, from shadow to shadow, as if I could pinpoint someone watching me. There was nothing outside of the occasional chirping of crickets and rustling of branches. Yet the hair on my arms was standing on end.

"Conny, some men are 'ere. Started bangin' on the door. Nearly gave your da a heart attack." She was whispering, one hand more than likely locked around the receiver as she sighed into the phone. Though I couldn't tell if she was more disappointed or frightened at this point.

Knowing my ma, it was the former.

"What kinda men, Ma?" I asked her. But I already knew the answer to that one too.

"The sort I warned you not to hang 'bout." Yup, disappointment it was. Should have known nothing scared my ma. "They gave me this number. Told me to call ya to come home. Said ya would know what that meant. What'd you get yerself twisted up in, Conny? Is it because of that girl ya told me about? You know your da always said not to mess around with—"

I clicked the handset back onto the cradle before she finished that thought. I was well aware of how my father felt about Italian women, but they weren't the ones hunting us down right now. No, it was my *kin*—another thing he liked to remind me. How we were all kinfolk. Maybe back on the island, but here in the States, the only blood these bastards cared about was the sort you spilled for them to line their pockets.

I didn't know how the Mulligans found us. But their message was clear. They knew exactly where we were. More than that, they were using my parents as bait. If I didn't convince Dani to head back into the city, it wouldn't be fists knocking on my ma's door. It would be boots kicking it in.

"Fuck," I grunted, toeing a loose stone across the empty parking lot before stalking towards room 707.

Lucky number, my ass.

The moment I slipped through the door and crept towards the figure on the bed, I was being grabbed from behind. A small, toned arm wrapping around my throat in a headlock... and the blade of a knife staring me in the face. Instinct had me wanting to flip my attacker over my shoulders and onto their back, while common sense told me one of two things would happen. I'd either end up needing another set of stitches or severely hurt the girl I wanted to love.

Yeah, the fucking word gave me pause but I ignored that too. I'd joked about it a lot but now I was certain shit was real. And there were only so many revelations I could deal with on three hours of sleep.

"Dani, it's just me," I grunted through my constricted airway. Then I tapped her wrist, signaling for her to loosen up before I passed the fuck out and we had bigger problems than the Mulligans' bullshit game of Ding-Dong Ditch.

She dropped her arms and jumped off my back, tucking the blade into her waistband as she flicked on the dodgy motel room lights. They blinked twice, like the bulbs were on the verge of giving up before deciding to stay on a bit longer. And I was confident no one would be replacing them anytime soon.

"What the fuck were you doin' out there? I thought— you know what? Doesn't matter what I thought." She shook her head, and something hinted that I was witnessing a rare moment of vulnerability. I'd pegged her right after all. Baby girl had abandonment issues. She thought I'd run out on her in the middle of the night.

"You thought what, Dani?" I found myself asking before my brain could stop me. I took a tentative step forward and she took one back. Mirroring my stance.

"I already told ya it didn't matter. Now, are you gonna answer my question or not?"

"If you answer mine, dollface." I gestured a hand between us. "I'm equal opportunity. Ya know, quid pro quo."

She crossed her arms over her chest, drawing my attention to the way her breasts rose with each exaggerated breath she took.

I know what you're thinking. This wasn't the time or the place. But men were simple creatures. Easily distracted. A fault I wore like a badge of honor.

"Fine. I thought you skipped out. Is that what you

wanted to hear?" she hissed, and I tugged her into my arms, ignoring the throbbing in my gut—as well as the one in my pants.

"No, Dani, that's not what I want to hear. Because you should know me better by now. Between the two of us, I ain't the one skipping out," I reminded her, before tipping her chin up and forcing her to look me in the eye. "Next time you get stuck in that head of yours, I want you to remember something. You do the runnin'. I do the chasin', baby girl."

35

"We need to go. Get out on the road. Now." Connor was trying to play it cool, but the deep stress lines extending across his forehead told me *trying* was all he was doing. The man was wound tighter than the tension spring on my forty-two—before I had it modified.

"What do you mean get out on the road? We just got here and you need to rest or that wound's never gonna heal right."

He started pacing, which was amusing to watch in a room no bigger than two hundred square feet, including furniture. "That's not really an option anymore, Dani. They got to my ma," he said while combing a hand through his hair for the millionth time. I watched a stray lock drop over his eye, only to get quickly brushed aside again before his words finally sank in.

"Who? How?" Not that it mattered. Just because I didn't have any family left, it didn't mean I couldn't empathize.

"Who do you think? As for how, good fucking question. I have no fucking clue. But they know where we are. That we're here. They had her call the payphone. That's what I was doin'. It wouldn't stop ringin' so I went to check it out."

We were being tracked. That much was clear. Though for the life of me, I couldn't figure out the method. We'd tossed our cells before we left the city, stolen a nondescript car after we lost our tail, and hadn't reached out to anyone other than...

"What about those friends of yours?" Connor grunted as if reading my mind. "Don't seem all that loyal if you ask me."

"Yeah? And what about Mr. T?" I countered.

"Who?"

"That fucker still workin' for Benny?"

"Zeke? Ain't even a question. Grumpy bastard is like a brother to me."

"Yeah, well, the guys wouldn't play ball with a cock-sucker like Mulligan on principle alone. Besides, I owe them now. They won't do anything that would keep me from making good on our deal."

That had Connor stopping in his tracks, his glare landing on me in a way that had my skin burning. I reached up a hand to rub at the phantom pain.

"What deal? What did you promise them?" He cursed under his breath. "Fuck, Dani, what did you promise them you'd do in exchange for fixin' me up?"

I rolled my eyes. "Nothin' I wouldn't have done anyway. Can we leave it at that?"

Was I being stubborn? Abso-fucking-lutely.

Could I have made up some bullshit lie? Sure could.

Did I want to? Not a chance in hell.

The man needed to learn this was my life. I did what I had to do to survive. Apparently so my self-proclaimed bodyguard would survive too. And if Connor was so insistent on hanging around, it was something he had to accept. Or move the fuck on. I wasn't gonna stand here and feel judged. Apologize for taking the path less traveled.

I mean, at the end of the day, I got results, didn't I?

"No, we can't fucking leave it at that, Dani. If they're making you do something... something... I don't know... Because of me—*fuck*."

My dark laugh had his eyebrows knitting together as he peered over at me a little too innocently. "No one makes me do shit, Connor. And it's just a couple of jobs. Which I was more than happy to take on for the right price. They just didn't need to know that at the time. It's called leverage."

"Dani—" he tried and I raised a hand to stop him.

"Nope, I'm not done yet." It was those damn eyes again. The way he looked at me with a tenderness I wasn't used to having aimed in my direction. If this was all a game to him, he was sure good at pretending. "I like what I do, Connor. I fucking live it. Breathe it. I could have had it all, you know? Married myself off and spent my days in a shiny fucking tower in any city of my choosing. Could have had the designer clothes, the fancy cars, more cash than I could count. And all I would have had to do was tolerate my husband, perform my wifely duties a couple times a year, pop out a few kids. I would have had my pick with my last name alone." I spun on my heel.

Yeah, now I was the one pacing. I saw the irony. I just wasn't about to acknowledge it.

"The last Rossi. Do you have any idea what that meant? What that still means? There are fuckers out there who would kill for my bloodline, the power that comes with it even now. I am mafia fucking royalty, Connor."

"Why didn't you?" He tilted his head as he continued to

look at me, and I could have sworn he was searching for something. What it was? I couldn't tell you.

"Why didn't I what?"

"Take the out? The way you describe it, you'd be crazy not to want all those luxuries. Instead, you're here, in a shit motel, with me. So, yeah, I'm askin' you why?"

"Because it wasn't the way out of anything. It was the way in. Willingly stepping into a cage and slapping a cuff on your wrist disguised as a wedding ring. That life got my family killed, Connor, put a ransom on my head, and—" I stopped myself short before I offered up more than I should.

"And? And what, Dani?" He was already closing the distance, once again trying to comfort me when all I wanted was space. Or maybe I did want the comfort and just didn't want to admit it. Either way, I felt like I was crawling out of my skin.

"And it doesn't matter. We both know you're too clean for this life, pretty boy." I stepped back as far as I could get without falling onto the mattress.

"That's where you're wrong, dollface. I can be as dirty as you want me to be." Connor's lips tipped up at one side and it was hard not to play into his charms.

"I'm being serious, MacCullagh. This is still an adrenaline rush for you. Your dopamine levels are all over the place. But once the high wears off and you realize this is my day-to-day... my reality... That I'm not gonna stop just because some guy with a decent cock decided he likes me... Once that happens, you're gonna run. And I'm not gonna stop you. I'll be that girl you used to fuck before you met your nice little perfect Irish wife and had your 2.5 kids. And you'll be the fucker whose dick I think about every now and then. That's all we are to each other, Connor. Soon-to-be memories. Maybe not even that." I didn't know where any of this came from. I just knew it felt both lighter and heavier to say. I also knew it was the truth. Every word of it.

I didn't believe in fantasies, in pretending I was someone different from the image the harsh world made me out to be. Sure, I didn't mind getting lost to the sex, alcohol, drugs. But right now, I was too stone-cold sober to escape the truth of our situation. Connor and I, we were temporary.

"Well, you got one part right. I do have a decent cock. But the rest of it? Yeah, it's all bullshit, Dani. All assumptions you're making on my behalf. Insecurities you're manifesting in your head and deflecting onto me."

"I'm not—"

"You are." In place of the softness, Connor's expression was set hard. Determined. And I had to admit I admired his ability to transition between the two so freely. It was much more difficult for me to let down those walls. Took much more time and effort. "But that's okay. Because I think I'm beginning to understand you a little better now. And all that's doin' is making me fall for you quicker, Dani. Deeper."

Before I had a moment to think, to realize what he was telling me, Connor was leaning forward, one palm pressed to the side of my face as he lowered his mouth to my lips in a kiss that was meant to silence me. And it worked. I was struck dumb.

"Now, let's go see my ma."

36

It was the most freeing feeling in the world. Like stripping bare and running naked through a field. You get the visual. Though it wasn't something I recommended. No one warned you about all the insects biting your ass, the vegetation chaffing you in parts you shouldn't be chaffing, your balls bouncing in a way that was unnatural. But that was beside the point. For the first five minutes, it was fucking liberating.

And that was me. In this moment. Right now. With the realization that I was falling for this girl. Maybe I was already there. Who the fuck knew?

It was like a weight was lifted off my shoulders as soon as it occurred to me that that's what it was. Yeah, I'd been coming on strong since day one. Was drawn to her in a way I didn't quite understand from the moment her knuckles made contact with my jaw. But when did that infatuation turn to more? Couldn't tell you. It was both gradual and all at once.

We were driving into the unknown together, one hand on the steering wheel and another on her thigh. My muscles ached, my gut was still on fire and fucking itchy as hell, and a bunch of Irish mob bosses were waiting to do God knows what to us in the city. And I couldn't be more at ease, as I hummed along to the song on the radio and tapped my free hand to the beat, my eyes laser-focused on the empty road ahead of us.

"You're gonna have to let me take the lead on this one. You know that, right?" Dani asked from where she was positioned on the passenger seat, her tone like a bucket of ice water on my good mood. "I've been dealing with Benny my whole life. I know how the fucker works. How our world works. They'll just see you as an outsider, Connor. You have to trust me on this."

"Trust you with my fuckin' life, baby girl. Them, not so much." I shifted my hand from her thigh back onto the steering wheel, clutching the faux leather until my knuckles turned white.

"Good. 'Cause you shouldn't trust them. This is some sort of game and I need to figure out their next move."

"And if you don't?" I quirked a brow.

"You trying to imply they're smarter than me, pretty boy? It took those fuckers six years to find one *wee lass* living a few blocks down the street from them. And only because she willingly walked into their club. More than once."

"Look at that. We might just make a proper Irish girl outta you yet." I grinned, glancing in her direction before returning my gaze to the road.

"Not a chance in hell, Connor. But grease back that hair of yours and throw on a leather jacket and you might be able to hang in my neck of the woods."

"Anything for you, dollface."

"Something tells me you actually mean that."

"'Cause I do. There isn't anything I wouldn't do for

you, Dani," I told her honestly, chancing a glance her way while waiting for the aftermath.

"Why?"

Well, that wasn't the reaction I was expecting. No, what I was expecting was a smart-mouthed comment or a too-hard jab to the arm.

But progress was fucking progress and I'd take it. I just needed to tread carefully or risk having her backpedal.

"Because you're my girl. Because when you care about someone, you wanna make them happy. Because makin' them happy makes you happy too. It's simple as that."

"Nothin' you just said is simple, Connor." She sighed. "I'm not who you think I am. Whoever you made up in that head of yours and think you like. Once all those chemicals in your brain wear off, you'll see that's all it was. A lust-fueled few weeks of really great sex. A good time, sure. But, at the end of the day, we're all out for ourselves, and anyone who thinks otherwise will learn that shit the hard way."

"Why do I get the feelin' you aren't talking about me anymore, Dani?" My eyes bounced between her face and out the windshield as I tried to read her expression, what she was telling me without telling me. Because I was certain something more was there. Like she was speaking from experience.

My girl had a broken heart under all those layers of pent-up emotions, compounded by years of avoidance and self-medicating.

She remained tight-lipped, staring out the window with a far-off look on her face.

"You never did tell me, ya know?"

"Tell you what?" she asked with that distant voice of hers. The one that meant she was pushing me away again.

"Well, a lot of things. But in this instance, I mean about those weird blackouts you have."

"Women don't like it when you call them weird, Connor."

"And men don't like it when you deflect their questions, Danica."

Her lip twitched. Just slightly. Enough to tell me she was loosening up a bit again. "Truth is I don't fuckin' know for sure, but could have something to do with the bullet that one of the Mulligans put in my skull six years ago."

"The what?" I turned my head to look at her, turning back just in time to see the car that was coming at us head-on drift into our lane. My foot slammed on the brakes, even knowing that it shouldn't. But it was instinct. And I couldn't stop myself.

The tires screeched, the vehicle lost traction, and we spun out towards the concrete divider. I closed one eye and braced for impact, flinging an arm out across Dani's lap. Like a few pounds of meat could do what a seat belt couldn't. But fuck it, I'd lose a limb if it meant a little extra padding for her.

Before I could apologize, tell her I was sorry for putting her in danger, for whatever damage we were about to incur, Dani shoved at my arm with an odd expression on her face. It wasn't fear. No, it was more like acceptance. Like part of her wanted this. Because my broken girl didn't care if she lived or died.

37

I could feel the music vibrating through the leather of the seat, thumping with the rapid beating of my heart. I was several drinks too deep to be driving, my fingers loose around the wheel, my inhibitions looser as I pressed down on the accelerator and ignored every posted speed sign as they blurred by.

My red sports car was like a beacon for the coppers to find me, while the guys on my old man's payroll knew better than to even try. Yeah, everything screamed *dumbass* rather than a hint of common sense. But I was still at that point in my life where I felt invincible. Like death couldn't touch me or anyone around me.

Until my dulled senses reacted a few seconds too late, the semi-truck headed in my direction unable to do much else but lay on his foghorn. I knew slamming on the brakes was exactly the wrong decision to make, while my delayed cognitive abilities couldn't quite figure out the right one. So I froze, my lungs expanding as I sucked in a breath and prepared for whatever new hell would greet me on the other side.

I mean, it was no secret that I liked sinning too much to ever make it to those pearly gates.

But instead of the crunching of metal and bloodcurdling screams, I was met by the sound of Leo's soft chuckles. I prized my lashes open to see his hands on the steering wheel, a cocky smirk playing on his lips, and an arrogant glint in his eye.

"Maybe you should let me drive, Rossi?"

"Maybe you should suck my dick," I grunted in reply.

"Nice try, but I've spent more time between your legs than anywhere else. If ya had a dick, I woulda found it by now."

"Ya sure? Ya might wanna take another look." I lifted a challenging brow, my heart rate returning to normal before speeding up again when Leo guided us to the side of the road, and I impaled myself on his cock. For the third time that day.

38

PRESENT

Scratch that. That look wasn't acceptance. It was arrogance.

Baby girl was full of herself as she grabbed the steering wheel, adjusting my overcorrection and setting us back on the road like our little brush with death was an everyday occurrence. Then again, considering the woman walked a thin tightrope that teetered between getting taken out by a barrage of bullets and getting kidnapped in the middle of the night, it wasn't hard to understand why.

I took a deep breath and swallowed down my churned-up guts, which were presently lodged in my throat, while Dani pinned me with another one of her horror movie grins.

"Maybe ya should let me drive. At least until your balls drop back into your pants again." She laughed, while I couldn't help but reach a hand between my thighs to make sure those fuckers were still there.

They were—*ya know, in case you were wondering.*

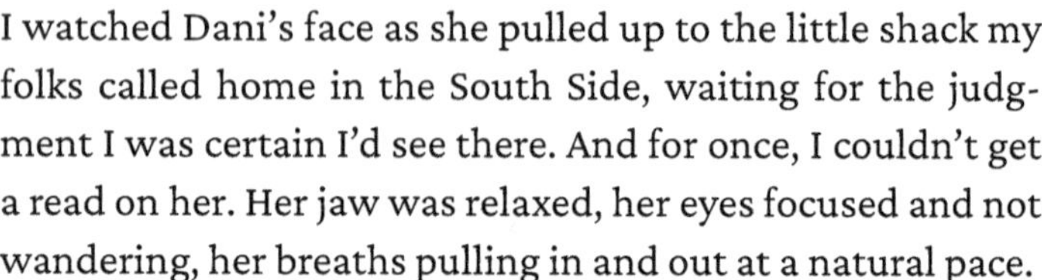

I watched Dani's face as she pulled up to the little shack my folks called home in the South Side, waiting for the judgment I was certain I'd see there. And for once, I couldn't get a read on her. Her jaw was relaxed, her eyes focused and not wandering, her breaths pulling in and out at a natural pace.

I'd worked at Mollies long enough to know the mob life meant mob money. Even if she didn't have it now, her family had it at some point. Which meant our upbringings were worlds apart. Mine more cabbage and potatoes, and hers more prosciutto and truffle oil.

I wasn't embarrassed. What I didn't have in my pockets, I made up for with the package between them. I was more *aware* than anything else of what this place might look like to someone who was used to the finer things in life.

Dani maneuvered us into the small spot left by my neighbors, killing the engine on our stolen car and pivoting her body in my direction. And I shuffled myself out of the passenger seat, rounding the hood with a slight limp in my step and opening her door before she could think up another aptly timed escape plan. Because if there was one thing I knew for sure it was the fact Danica Rossi didn't like the idea of being brought home to meet the parents.

If the realization hadn't sunken in yet, it would soon. And I didn't have it in me to force my reluctant girlfriend through the front door with my guts five seconds from plopping out onto the concrete between us.

I grabbed her hand and guided her up the steps the best I could while clutching the rail and sucking in a sharp breath. I was never much for pill popping, but right now, I'd sell my left nut for a swig of smooth whiskey and a fistful of those circular tabs Benny liked to stash in the back room of the club.

Before my knuckles could make contact with the door, it was swinging open and my ma was pulling me in for a hug. Pushing me back and staring at me with a scrutinizing eye.

"What d'ya do, boy?" She shoved an accusatory finger in my direction, then behind me when her glare landed over my shoulder. "That her?"

I grinned without bothering to turn around. I could already feel Dani's eyes boring into my back. "Yup, that's her, Ma."

"Conny…" My mother started, and I cut her off at the pass.

"Ma, we have a guest."

"Ye've got something all right," she grumbled under her breath, pivoted in the small entryway, and reached inside the hall table. Pulling out a card and slamming it into my palm. "Those men, they left that for ya."

I flipped the simple white rectangle over and then back again. There was nothing but a phone number embossed across the front.

"They say anything else?" Dani asked while snaking an arm around me to grab the card from my hand. I quickly tugged it out of her reach. I already knew what my girl was thinking, and I wasn't about to let her go after those fuckers on her own.

"Just that ye were trouble. But I gathered as much by lookin' at ye." Ma pursed up her lips, her eyes narrowed in that way that would have most grown men shifting on their feet.

But not Dani. She just returned my ma's scathing look with a grin. "If only some of that sense rubbed off on your son."

And I saw it. The moment my ma's tough shell cracked just enough to let my girl worm her way inside. The woman did that to ya. Got under your skin without you realizing it was even happening. And my mother was no exception when it came to Dani's—let's call it—*charisma*.

"If only..." Ma waved us into the house. Though I didn't miss the way her eyes hooked on the blood seeping through my shirt before dropping again when she directed us over to the kitchen table. "Fill yer bellies before goin' off to do something ye shouldn't."

39

My eyes dropped to the bowl of stew plopped in front of me. Accompanied by a look that said refusing wasn't an option. Couldn't tell ya what kind of meat it was, just that it was brown. Definitely not pork or chicken. And surprisingly delicious. Much better than the slop they served up at the local pub I would hit up most nights. Or anything I could dish up myself. Never really took to the whole being domesticated thing.

Who woulda guessed?

Pretty boy's mother was warming up to me. I could tell from the way her scathing glare had simmered to something resembling slight distaste. Though something told me the man of the house would be a little more difficult to win over. Not that I cared if Connor's parents liked me or not. I mean, Leo's family had wanted me dead almost as much as he did.

Shit, six years later, and the fuckers were still coming at me hard. If anything, I should have been proud of that one.

"So, Dani, what do yer parents think about whatever's goin' on between ye and Conny here?" Mrs. MacCullagh was eyeing us from across the tiny kitchen table, her elbows planted wide in front of her and her time-weathered fingers clasped together.

The woman was a hair shorter than I was, her back slightly hunched—suggesting she was bent over a stove most of her life—and her tight bun peppered gray. Though none of it made her look any less formidable. Sixteen or sixty, I had no doubt she'd throw ya over a knee all the same.

"Not much, seeing as they're dead." I shrugged before shoveling another spoonful of mushy vegetables into my mouth. If I expected her to be shocked, it was clear she wasn't.

"I had a feelin' ye'd say that. Name's not all that common 'round here no more." She drew in a long breath and let it out on a sigh. "It's a shame what happened to 'em, ye know. And that boy. Your brother, I'm assumin'."

"Yup, Anthony. He was four." My voice sounded dry even to my own ears. I could hear it. But when death surrounded you, you learned to become numb to it. Or else grief would find a way to pull you under and keep you there. Drowning you in shit you couldn't change. I could also feel Connor's eyes on me, watching my face, then flicking back to his mother's.

"How come I never heard about this?"

She lifted a finger in her son's direction. "Because ye ears are always clogged with nonsense and ye never listen, Conny."

"Ain't that the truth," I muttered into my bowl as I lifted it to my face and drank down what was left of the broth.

A girl could get used to this. Couldn't tell ya the last time I had something resembling a home-cooked meal. I pushed up from my chair, walked over, and rinsed out my bowl before setting it in the sink. While Connor continued to watch me the entire time.

"Ya wouldn't have heard about it. At least ya shouldn't have. Unless one of the families wants ya to. None of it makes the news. And on the rare occasion that it does, it's always listed as something else. A house fire, a car accident, maybe a mugging if someone is feeling froggy." I lifted a shoulder in a half shrug. "But never murder, never homicide. Never the truth about what it really is."

I hated the way he was looking at me right now. Like I was lost and broken. Like I needed taking care of when I didn't. Like I needed saving and he was the one to do it.

I crossed my arms over my chest and leaned back against the countertop, daring the fucker to say something stupid. The fact that his mama was present wouldn't stop me from dropping his ass to the kitchen floor.

I could only assume my expression told him as much when his gaze left mine and shifted to his mother instead. "Then how'd you hear about it?"

"Not me. Yer da." She pressed a palm to her chest with the slight raise of a thin brow. "The boys at the factory like to drink. And when they drink, they like ta talk. Then yer da comes home and tells me all about it. Most of it's nonsense. Some of it's not. Only takes a wee bit of yer brain to know the difference."

Connor closed the door to his childhood bedroom, barely waiting for it to click into the frame before he was pivoting in my direction.

I quirked a brow as a slow smirk crept across his face. "Thought your mama told your ass to sleep on the couch?"

He rolled on the balls of his feet, his hands tucked into the pockets of his sweatpants and that boyish charm of his reaching panty-melting levels. "She also told me not to be messin' around with them unruly Italian girls, yet here I am and there you are."

He stepped forward, and I stepped back, the underside of my thighs hitting the metal of the tiny bedframe.

"You really need to change those bandages." I gestured a hand towards his exposed abdomen, my eyes glued to the deep V that defined the muscles there.

"Mmhmm." Another predatory step, and I had nowhere left to go.

"Your mother's gonna be pissed as hell if she finds your dumb ass bleeding out on her carpet in the morning."

"Yup." His mouth was on the side of my neck. Sucking, licking, biting. And my head tipped back to let him do it, my teeth sinking down into the meat of his shoulder to muffle the sounds of my moans, as his hand reached under the hem of my loose t-shirt in search of my clit.

The streetlamp was shining in through the small breach in the thin curtains, the light dancing across Connor's face. The cocky bastard even smirked in his sleep. Though a few good orgasms would do that to you.

I should know.

My lips were curling a bit on their own, as I carefully slid off the tiny twin-sized mattress and lowered my bare feet onto the pleasantly plush carpeting. Each step I took felt louder than the last, though I was certain they were soundless, as I tiptoed towards the door. My eyes skimming over the various family photos and childhood knickknacks strewn across the walls and propped up on shelves.

When my left foot brushed something soft, I reached down and swiped up Connor's discarded sweatpants before rooting around his pockets and finding exactly what I was looking for. A little white calling card. That might as well have had "it's a trap" scrawled across the top.

Pretty boy thought his coming up here would keep me from skipping out on him, when all it really did was offer me an opportunity to put his ass to bed. Sex was just as good as any tranquilizer I was looking to use. Sometimes it was better. More predictable.

The stairs creaked as I shifted my weight from one to the next, holding my breath as I eyed the front door, which felt much farther away than I was certain it measured. Only to choke down a gasp when I saw a figure turn the corner and stare back at me from the lower landing.

"Sure ye don't wanna put some pants on first?" Mrs. MacCullagh crossed her arms over her chest, the whites of her eyes glowing in the darkness of the entryway like something out of my nightmares. Not much sent a chill down my spine anymore. But this mousey Irishwoman?

Yeah, she just made the list of things that went bump in the night.

40

I t was one thing to wake up and find out that the woman you'd spent the night with had skipped out. It was another altogether to realize your mother had taken her place. And not in the way you're thinking.

Get your mind out of the gutter.

My ma wasn't *in bed* with me. But she *was* in my bed. With me. Her nightcap on and her ankles kicked up and crossed over the footboard, to alleviate the swelling she was prone to have after spending all day on her feet. My gaze flicked to her arms, which were set over her chest as if she were waiting for the Grim Reaper to snatch her up and drop her off at her own wake.

Like I said, us Irish were a weird lot.

I scrambled off the bed, clutching the sheet to my waist, as I did my best to put distance between my mother and my cock in such tight quarters. Pretty sure the big guy woulda crawled up inside me if he could.

"Ma, what the fuck are you doin' here?" My eyes scanned the room as if my girl might just materialize from one of the walls. "And where's Dani?"

"I live 'ere or don't ye remember?" My mother waved a dismissive hand before throwing her legs over the side of the mattress and onto the floor. Standing to her full height, which wasn't much, so that she could close the distance and point a finger in my direction. "Ye musta forgot. 'Cause me Conny wouldn't be dumb enough to be sinnin' under his da's roof."

"Ma..."

"Don't *Ma* me, boy." She shot me a glare that had flashbacks of my teenage years flooding my brain, and threw an arm out towards the bed. "Now sit. Yer gettin' blood all over me sheets."

My eyes dropped down to the red splotches seeping through the white, semi-translucent fabric, then back up to my mother again as my mouth spread into a sheepish grin. "Sorry. But I really do need to find Dani." I raked a hand through my hair as my thoughts went a mile per minute. "I'm worried she's out there doin' something stupid."

My ma didn't bother to look at me as she started rooting through the drawers, finding and pulling out an old first aid kit before wadding up some gauze. I used to bleed a lot as a kid too. So this shit was nothing new to her. "Girl's got enough sense to sneak out on ye in the middle of the night. I'm sure she'll be just fine."

"You saw her leave?"

"Mhmm," my mother hummed as she removed the tape from between her teeth and sealed the gauze in place.

"And you didn't try to stop her?"

"Ain't no stoppin' a woman who's got 'er mind set on something, Conny. You'd do well enough to remember that."

I pushed back up from the mattress, took a few steps, dropped the sheet, and bared my ass to my ma for as long as it took me to tug on my discarded sweats. Without thought, I slipped my hands into my pockets, turning them inside out only to find them empty.

"Son of a bitch," I hissed under my breath, and my mother climbed up on a chair to slap me upside the back of the head. "Sorry—hey, Ma, can I use the house phone?"

She studied my face for a second, then dipped her chin in a curt nod. "Make it quick, and keep yer voice down. Yer da is still sleepin'." Then my ma pushed open the bedroom door, stopping on the threshold to peer over at me. "I'm supposed ta tell ye not to follow 'er by the way. That's what she said. But we both know I'm better off tryin' to blow hot air into a cup and call it whiskey."

The morning air nipped at the back of my neck as I stood outside my folks' place, waiting for Zeke to pick me up. I shoved my hands into my pockets, my hood pulled over my head and my weight shifting from one foot to the other. Trying to keep the chill from creeping up my spine.

I knew if I called, he'd answer. And there really wasn't anyone else I could count on at the moment. Not anyone who would indulge my stupidity as much as he would, while also ensuring I didn't fly off the rails. There was balance there. And right now, I needed fucking balance. I was going out of my mind thinking up all the worst-case scenarios. All of which ended with Dani dead, me single, or a fucked-up mix of the two.

I could hear the rumble of the engine before the fucker

even rounded the corner. And I was jumping off the sidewalk and into the middle of the street by the time the dark-blue paint job on Zeke's decades-old Civic came into view.

41

"Danica Rossi," Junior hummed my name, his leather shoes scuffing across the concrete flooring as he pivoted on his heel to face me again. "Why do I feel like we've been here before?" His grin curled the thin mustache on his upper lip, giving him that iconic villain in a silent movie look.

"How the fuck should I know?" I shrugged, dropping my eyes to my cuticles while wondering if it was blood or dirt staining my skin. "Can't say that I recall ever being this close to your creepy ass..."

"Yeah, but there's a lot you don't recall, isn't there?"

Now he had my attention. Whether I wanted to admit it or not. Sure, the bastard could be fishin' but at the same time there was history there. Things I was pretty certain he knew. But couldn't prove.

"What do you want, Junior? You sure went to a lot of trouble. Hunting us down at the hotel, threatening Connor's parents, leaving that cryptic business card with a number that directed me here, so why don't ya just cut to the chase and tell me?"

"Us? I couldn't give two shits about your fuck toy, Dani. Though he does remind me of someone…"

There it was. The past coming to haunt me. But I couldn't drop my guard, couldn't let this little prick know his words had an effect on me.

"He'd be turning twenty-five this month, ya know? If your dad hadn't put him in the ground on account of you."

"Seeing as my old man is right there with him, along with my mother and brother—who were both innocent, mind you—I don't understand all the bad blood. Or your obsession with hunting me down…" I shrugged before pushing off the wall to stand toe-to-toe with the little Irish shit. "Do you have a crush on me, Junior? Is that it? Because I can't think of another reason for you to be so up my ass after all these years." I watched his face, waiting for the discomfort to set in, for the look of disgust I was expecting. And found… nothing.

"Funny you should mention that. Why don't we share a drink and then we can talk business?" Junior gestured to the door, guiding me out of his makeshift interrogation room and into a sparsely decorated office.

Other than four bare walls, there was a desk, a few chairs, a minibar, and not much else. It reminded me of a frat house more than a grown-ass man's supposed working space. Which was fitting for an adult male still going by Junior. Add in the fact he got the nickname because he was his brother's shadow (and not because he was named after anyone) and it was just pathetic.

He gestured towards the leather chair in front of the desk and I lowered myself onto the stiff material, which had clearly seen better days. A shiver ran down my spine as I did my best to not focus on the origin of the white stains. I took a steadying breath, returning my attention to Junior as he positioned himself across from me. It didn't escape my notice how his chair was slightly raised. Allowing him to look down at me while encouraging me to look up at him. It was a move often used by men in power, meant to intimidate whoever was in the respective hot seat, give the other player a facade of authority. Leverage.

But I didn't scare so easy. The higher up you were, the harder you fell. Every fighter knew that real leverage was found at ground level. I'd sit on the floor crisscross applesauce if it meant giving this fucker a false sense of security.

"I wasn't aware we had business, Junior." I lifted one leg over a knee and placed my hands on my lap like a proper lady while his eyes followed my movements, leering on my chest much longer than was appropriate.

"We've always had business, Dani. You just never stick around long enough for us to discuss it."

"Hard to do when you have a bounty on my head and my face plastered all over your club like wanted posters. None of that is all that inviting."

"That's not me. That's my uncle. Old Ben has never had an eye for the future. Growth. He insists we do things the way we've always done them."

"And you don't?" I lifted a questioning brow.

"I'm a forward thinker, Dani. Have a real gift for seeing potential before it's fully... *matured*."

"A real renaissance man, huh?"

Junior slapped a hand on his desk. "Yes, exactly. See? You get it, babe. You understand me."

I didn't understand shit. I was merely feeding his ego, telling him what he wanted to hear so he'd drop his guard and hopefully let something slip. Though the way he was eyeing my chest again told me he was getting a little too comfortable. Enough to call me *babe* at least.

"I think I do. But just to make sure, why don't you tell me what you're getting at, Junior?" I leaned forward, feigning interest while giving him a direct view down my shirt.

"You and me are a lot alike is all I'm sayin'."

"And how's that?" Now I was truly curious.

"Always goin' against the grain. Willing to do whatever it takes to break through the roles given to us at birth. To take what we want instead of what the world is lookin' to hand us. It's not easy, you know. 'Least your folks are dead. Mine are still hangin' around, constantly on my ass, wanting me to be more like León."

"Right. My parents are dead... lucky me." It was hard to keep from rolling my eyes. This fucker wasn't just fucked in the head; he was full-on delusional. Which made him dangerous too. Because he honestly believed everything he was saying.

"Exactly." He grinned. "But you're lucky in more ways than one." He pushed up from his chair, maneuvering around the desk to stand in front of me while leaning his ass on the ledge. Then he reached out and used a dainty hand to lift my chin and force me to look at him. "You're lucky that brother of mine is outta the picture, and I'm lucky that bullet I put in your skull didn't actually kill you."

42

SIX YEARS PRIOR

If you were to ask me what it was about her that first caught my attention, I would have had to say it was her fucking smile.

Yeah, I know. Corny as fuck.

But there was just something about the way Dani looked at you, that mischievous glint in her eyes drawing you in, while those lips of hers were what finally set the trap. Ensnared your ass. Made it so that you didn't know what was up and what was down. Blurred the lines of right and wrong until all you saw was this girl and that smile. And somehow you knew it was meant only for you.

I was sure most of the guys in the pool hall that night felt the same. But I knew. I fucking knew it was directed at me.

Don't bother asking me to explain. I didn't have a reason that made sense. I hadn't even spoken two words to the girl. A girl I knew shouldn't be here, on my family's territory. Not with eyes like those, and skin like that. But like I said, what I knew flew out the fucking window as soon as she smiled at me.

I didn't know I was moving until my feet stopped in front of her and my palm landed on the wall, pressed just above her head so there was nowhere for her to go, nowhere for her to look except at me. Her palm was wrapped around the pool cue, stroking it up and down in a way that I was certain was intentional as she peered at me with lashes too long to be legal.

"Wanna get outta here?" My lips curled into a smirk that I was more than aware would highlight the dimple in my left cheek. I watched her face, waiting for a reaction. For some sense of whether she was intrigued or appalled by the suggestion.

And the girl didn't flinch, didn't appear the least bit offended or shocked. "Depends," she hummed, as if she could taste the word with those supple lips of hers. Just a few inches more and I could lower my head and try 'em for myself.

"On?" I could feel my heart beating in my chest as I asked the question. Like nothing mattered except what she had to say.

"Whether you can keep it up long enough for me to slap a condom on ya."

That was Dani. Forward as fuck. Told ya exactly what was on her mind. And not afraid of anything. Least of all me and my last name. Whether she recognized it that first night, I could only guess. Either way, I doubted it would have stopped her from taking me up on my offer. Or *me* from making her one to begin with.

For a nineteen-year-old girl, Dani could fuck. And being a nineteen-year-old guy, I couldn't get enough of it. Or her.

That first night turned into two. Two turned into a

week. A week into months. Spent sneaking around and fucking like rabbits. We both knew the danger involved, the war we'd cause if either of us were caught. We both didn't care, fueled by hormones and the thrill of the forbidden.

But there was also more to it than that. At least for me there was... Dani was a harder egg to crack.

"Where ya goin'?" My eyes followed the outline of her body as she shimmied back into her jeans before throwing her t-shirt over her head.

"Home. Where d'ya think, Mulligan? I got thirty minutes before curfew and my pops starts painting the streets red looking for me."

I hated this part of the evening. The part where it felt like just an exchange of bodily fluids and a quick "good game" before she sauntered out without so much as a backwards glance. I knew Dani felt something for me. Like I said, there were just certain things I knew about this woman, whether or not she told them to me herself. I also knew she put on a good front. It was only to be expected when you were born into the life. Showing weakness was like putting a target on your back. Giving the enemy ammunition to use against you. And no matter how much I didn't wanna see it that way... I understood I was the enemy.

"What if I asked you to stay? Could you make up an excuse? Just for tonight?" I pushed myself up on an elbow, continuing to watch her collect the various articles of clothing we'd tossed across my room. We had been a little too preoccupied with the heat between our legs to pay attention to what we were doing when we first crept up here.

Now, the first wave of post-nut clarity was setting in and I realized more than anything I didn't want her to leave.

Dani tucked her phone into her back pocket, leaning forward over the mattress to press her lips to mine before pulling away again. "Are you asking me, Mulligan? Or are you still going with the whole *what if* bullshit?"

"I'm asking you, Dani. Stay the night. I'll drop you off as close to home as I can in the morning. So what d'ya say?"

She grinned and my heart did that thing where it beat faster whenever she looked at me like that. "I say... you better not hog the covers, or I'll kick your ass outta bed. I don't give a fuck if it's your room or not."

Couldn't tell you what she told her dad that night or why he didn't come knocking on our front door. What I could tell you was that I was more sure than ever that I wanted to marry this girl. No matter what the consequences would be for us later. I just had to get her onboard with the idea first...

I'd gotten my nan to give me her wedding ring, had the thing burning a hole in my pocket for days now, while trying to ease Dani into the topic of settling down. Though that was the wrong way to put it. I didn't want her to settle for anything. I wanted us to share in the chaos together. And a proper union between our two feuding families would do that. It wasn't unheard of. Was common practice even. It was just usually done within the branches, not outside them.

Nan's first question had been about the nice Irish girl who caught my eye, what her name was, who her family knew. And I did my best to not lie, without revealing the truth either.

It all seemed so simple at my age. Like if I wanted it bad enough, I could get it. I just had to try harder, impose my will, and all that bad blood would go away and everything I wanted would be at my fingertips.

By the time I realized how wrong I'd been, it was too late. Because I was staring down the barrel of my twelve-year-old brother's nine, watching him turn it from me to the girl I loved.

I had two seconds to breathe, less than that to act, as I drew my handgun from my nightstand and aimed it in his direction. I had to choose my family or my future. And in that moment, I chose Dani. It was a gut reaction. What I felt was right without having to think about it.

But my arm was trembling a little too much with the adrenaline rush. I missed Junior's hand but did a good job at scaring him enough to fuck up his aim. My bullet hit the wall next to the window Dani was propped up on, to the right of my little brother, and his bullet hit her off center above her left ear when she turned around to look at me.

And I saw it. I saw it in her eyes. The betrayal staring back at me. She didn't understand. She didn't see him. Neither of us had. Until it didn't matter anymore.

Then I watched her topple backwards, out the window and onto the front lawn. As the pounding in my heart stopped and jumped into my throat.

43

PRESENT

That bullet I put through your skull...

I could hear the blood rushing to my head, feel the familiar pulsing in my temples while the pounding in my ears was so loud that everything he said from then on was nothing more than white noise. A whooshing sound, like the spinning of a metal fan blade or the static through an old CB radio.

My chest was constricting at the same time my heart was beating against my rib cage, and something told me if it tried hard enough, it could break free and splatter on the floor between my feet.

That bullet I put through your skull...

A handful of words that changed everything I thought I knew about my life until now.

Connor had been right. I didn't see this move coming. There was no way I could have planned for it. And if I didn't stop myself from spiraling, I was two seconds away from a blackout.

For the first time, I could sense it. The haze creeping over my peripheral vision, the light-headedness that was sure to follow, the weakness in my limbs that was the precursor to the inevitable memory loss.

Focus, Dani. You're better than this...

I cracked my neck from side to side, hoping it was enough to shock my system into compliance. When I looked up again, Junior was staring at me with that shit-eating grin on his face and suddenly he was that same twelve-year-old kid. The one leering at me from across the room, watching me when he didn't think I could sense him watching. Plotting while his brother and I were oblivious to his schemes.

Couldn't tell you how I hadn't seen it before, how I hadn't connected the dots that all led back to one name. And it wasn't the one on that grave I cursed all those years ago...

"It's okay, babe. Breathe." Junior crouched down in front of me, his too-soft fingertips reaching out to stroke my cheek. "I know it's a lot to take in. Everything I did for you. For us. For this moment."

"Us?" I choked out the word, stifling a humorless laugh as I rested my neck on the back of the chair and peered up at the ceiling. Once I'd managed to compose myself, I dropped my chin and pinned him with a glare. "You think there's an us? If the fact I hate your guts didn't tell you that was never gonna happen, the little tidbit about you shooting me in the head sure as fuck should have."

I watched Junior's jaw clench as he pushed to his feet, returning to his assumed position of power with his arms firmly crossed over his chest. Ironically enough, it was a sign he didn't have power at all.

No, the guy in charge always maintained a relaxed,

open posture. While a submissive personality closed in on themselves, protected their vital organs without realizing what they were doing.

"You're still in shock. I get it. But I've waited a long time for you to come to your senses, Dani. And I ain't about to wait around forever."

"Your brother had a nice dick, ya know." I tilted my head to the side, eyeing his reaction like it was a curiosity in one of those carny sideshows that popped into town every now and then. "Was that it? You had a thing for watching us? Did you like the way I used to ride his cock all over that fancy-ass mansion of yours while your pops was none the wiser?" I leaned forward and Junior leaned back, as far as he could go with the desk behind him. "Did ya used to think about me when you'd touch yourself, all curled up in your red race car bed with those Looney Tunes sheets?"

"Space Jam…"

My lips curled into a grin. "What was that? Can't hear ya when you're mumbling. Use your big boy voice, Junior."

"Space Jam," he hissed. "They were retro-style Space Jam sheets. Special ordered, with a super high thread count."

"Riiight, excuse my oversight." I walked my fingers over his still-crossed arms, as the light hair on his wrists appeared to stand on end and a chill traveled up his spine. "So, you saw something you wanted… and decided to go for it. Take out whoever was in your way, is that what your sayin'?"

I could see the wet spot already forming on the left side of his pants, just a few little drops that told me Junior here had a degradation kink.

A bit on the nose but I could work with that.

"Exactly. He didn't deserve you. Leo was weak. Given

everything the world had to offer just because of birth order. Because his sperm happened to get to the egg first."

"Mmm, I see..." When my hand reached his chest, I honed in on his nipple and pinched. Junior tipped his head back on a groan while one of his palms slammed flat on the desk. "But if Leo was the problem, why shoot me?"

He wasn't paying attention now, too lost to the feel of my hand playing him like a goddamn fiddle as I waited for my little piggy to squeal.

"Tell me, Junior. Tell me why and I'll make all those sick fantasies of yours come true. Bet your into some real fucked-up shit, aren't you?"

I took the incoherent grunting sound he made when my fingertips traveled south as both agreement and confirmation that I hit the nail on the head.

"I didn't get it at first... didn't realize that he was making you do all that stuff—*ngh...*" Once again, his words died off into a strangled sound in the back of his throat. The bastard was nearly coming in his pants and I hadn't even reached his waistband yet.

I mean, great for me. Bad for every woman he tried to please in the sack. *Tried* being the key word there.

"Go on, Junior. We're both so close to getting what we want..." I urged him, my voice dipping an octave as I lightly brushed along the sensitive skin just above his pubic area. Men had so many nerve endings if you just knew how to find 'em and use 'em to your advantage.

"I was pissed off that everything was so easy for him. Just had to look at something and it was his, so I thought *not this time.* He couldn't get the girl too. Which worked out better than I thought. I got to keep you, Leo took the blame, and your old man did what I should have done in the first place."

I thought hearing the truth would bring me some sort of peace, that knowing the *why* would somehow put my mind at ease and diminish this weight on my chest. But all it did was make me angrier. To know that at the end of the day it had all been by chance...

One little shift in time, a centimeter here, a millisecond there and I'd be the one dead. Or maybe I would have seen it coming, did something to stop it, killed the fucker so that Leo...

Fuck, Leo... I'd focused so much energy on hating him... for what?

But none of that mattered right now. Not when I had a prick and a pecker to deal with. And not necessarily in that order.

"Oh, Junior, you stupid little cunt..."

44

proper jab to the femoral artery and a fucker could bleed out in seconds. Frankie would have told me the correct term was exsanguination. Draining of an essential bodily fluid. The color was a bright red. Like a fire hydrant. Oxygenated and prime for the taking, only a little over an inch below the skin's surface in that sensitive area next to the groin. A spot men were all too willing to offer up to you on a silver fucking platter whenever their cocks did the thinking for them. Which was more often than not.

And Junior was no different. If anything, the son of a bitch was easy pickings. Not worth the effort. Something that was equal parts infuriating and mind-numbingly dull.

By the time his pants were yanked down around his ankles, his less-than-impressive cock on display (apparently some things didn't run in the family or maybe Leo had been the outlier) and Junior's hands were white-knuckling the desk as he awaited what he assumed would be a life-altering experience, my Kershaw was already two inches deep in his thigh. Probably more than the fucker would have given me if I let ' em.

He wasn't wrong though. This was *life-altering*. For him. Me? Not so much.

There was something freeing about the feel of a knife slicing through the first few layers of flesh, subcutaneous fat, ligament, and finally a nice juicy vein. Picture a slab of meat not quite raw but not medium rare either. Now imagine that meat has a turkey baster shoved through the middle and as soon as you cut into it, someone on the other end squeezes, sending a heavy dose of slightly warm gravy raining down in your direction.

Yeah, that's about as close to this moment as you'll get if killin' a man isn't your thing.

Not that it was my *thing*. I didn't get off on it or nothing. My panties were dryer than a properly poured glass of Assyrtiko. I just didn't mind getting my hands dirty whenever it was necessary. And right now, it was more than necessary. It was well-deserved. A longtime coming.

It was also the only thing *coming*, much to this fucker's dismay.

I pushed to my feet, looking Junior in his eyes as recognition slowly colored, then drained from this face with the rest of his blood. Seconds, remember? That's all it took. All the time I had to enjoy the way his arms flailed about like the wings of a recently plucked chicken, the panic unwittingly increasing his blood flow and quickening his death as his skin turned the clammy color of a fresh corpse. His heart was pumping faster, his innate survival instinct the same thing that would help kill him in the end.

The weirdest part of the whole ordeal? The fucker never lost his erection. If anything, it appeared a bit... *stiffer* (no pun intended) as he slowly sank to his knees before I shoved him onto the floor.

I shouldn't have done it. I knew that. It wasn't well thought out or executed in a manner that meant I could get away scot-free. Not here, on enemy territory. But the fucker admitted to shooting me in the head. He was lucky all I did was send him off with a bad case of blue balls. If I had time, proper planning, I would have been a tad bit more creative and shoved them down his throat. Watched him choke on his own testicles with a bowl of popcorn in one hand and a recording device in the other. So I could hit playback whenever I was feeling a little... *nostalgic*.

As much as I wanted to bask in the grotesque for a few minutes longer, I needed to think. Plan. Plot.

There were a dozen or so of Junior's goons hanging around at any given time, so slinking out wasn't an option. Not without spilling a lot more blood in a very short timeframe. Sure, I could do it. I was quick with more than a knife. But that would be sloppy. And I knew better than to be sloppy. Usually. When my temper didn't get in the way.

But if there was one thing I could count on, it was the fact that men like Junior liked to talk. More than that, they liked to brag. Self-inflate their own egos. Live in the fantasy world they created in their heads, because reality wasn't what it was cracked up to be. Think of it like a veteran with all the war stories—that guy? Yeah, he didn't do shit. But the quiet fucker sitting in the corner? He was the one to keep your eye on. The same applied to dick size and bedroom skills. The more someone had to say, the less they could actually do.

It was a known fact. And one I would use to my advantage right now.

Junior took me in here for a reason. He called it business, but it was very much leaning towards the pleasure side of things. And I'd bet the fucker's left nut that he preened all about it to anyone who'd listen. Meaning I had a solid five minutes—five being generous—before these dumb fucks realized something went wrong.

My lips twisted into what I could only assume was one helluva fucked-up smirk, as an idea came to mind and my hands rooted through Junior's left pocket. Then his right. My grin widened when my fingertips brushed over the slick case of his oversized cell phone. Might as well have been a brick... the fucker was so heavy.

Compensating much?

Two seconds and a quick swipe of a dead man's thumb later, and I was scrolling through Junior's very active Pornhub account, while trying to select a clip with the most realistic audio. No easy feat, by the way. None of the girls on the first few pages of results were Oscar-worthy when it came to faking it. Then again, that might have been my best bet if I was aiming for authenticity.

Here's to hoping we picked a winner, CumPrincess247.

45

While CumPrincess was doing her thing, her thing being a fairly impressive ten-inch cock attached to a fairly *un*impressive torso, I was trying my best to wipe a good bit of arterial splatter from my face and hands.

Thank fuck for black clothing.

I slammed a hip against Junior's desk a few times, scraping the furniture along the floor in a back-and-forth motion, and knocked the occasional trinket across the room. I waited until Princess's "stepbrother" reached his moment of peak performance. Which included pulling out to jiz all over her chest. His awful grunting noises more than enough to make my uterus shrivel up and die. Before closing out of the video, tearing one sleeve of my tank top, and ruffling my hair until I looked properly fucked. Or just fucked enough to accept disappointment.

This had to be believable after all.

Then I walked to the door, took a deep breath, and wrenched it open. The hall was empty but I knew it wouldn't be for long. Princess and I put on quite the show, and I knew Junior's men were holed up in some darkened corner listening. Maybe closing their eyes and participating in a less-than-gratifying circle jerk. The fact no one came running after I stabbed the bastard told me he wasn't smart enough to have the room wired. That or he didn't want anyone else knowing what he was up to in there.

Probably a little bit of both, if I'm honest.

I could hear the shuffling of boots and tried to embody my inner porn star—that part wasn't all that hard. I loved sex. Didn't mind the camera either. It was my choice of partner I was a tad more picky about. And no amount of cash could tempt me into faking it. If you didn't hit the right spot, I sure as fuck was gonna tell you about it.

Otherwise, don't waste my fucking time. Wonder if there was a niche for that? Ya know, if this whole bounty hunter shit didn't work out in the end?

Two of Junior's men approached me with equally wicked grins. If they had a brain cell between the pair of 'em, they'd be able to smell the blood drying on my clothes. Lucky for me, the Mulligans didn't choose their men based on IQ level.

"Hey, boys." I grinned while gesturing a thumb behind me. "Seems I tuckered out your boss back there. Poor guy is sleepin' like a baby. Think ya can help a girl out and show me to the door? Junior mentioned something about stopping at my place to pick up a few things. Didn't exactly plan for an extended stay and all. And what's a girl to do without her curling iron..." I lifted a hand and began counting off on my fingers. "Oh! And I need my makeup bag... and don't forget tampons... Nothin's worse than a heavy flow day without—"

"Okay!" The brute with the pierced eyebrow looked like he was gonna be sick at just the thought of female menstruation. "Shut up and I'll lead ya out for fuck's sake."

Guess the big galoot never earned his red wings. Pity too. Nothing was more of a turn-on than a guy who didn't give a fuck what time of the month it was. Find me that guy, and I might have just reconsidered my thoughts on marriage.

Kidding, of course. But you catch my drift.

I followed Thing One and Thing Two past a few more doors, cataloguing every detail as we went—how many cameras, rooms, and men were hanging around, all the possible exits and so on—before they froze in their tracks and turned around to glare at me.

"Don't we know you from somewhere?" Justin Bieber's overstuffed clone asked while quirking his jewelry at me. "Can't put my finger on it but something about you seems familiar…" he grunted.

"CumPrincess247? Maybe you've heard of me?" I smirked.

I KNOW! Dumb move. But fucking hell, Connor's smart-ass attitude was rubbing off on me in all the wrong ways and I just couldn't help myself.

I watched as confusion settled over JB's face, maybe a hint of recognition too, before something had him reaching a hand towards his hip. His silent counterpart clearly didn't get the hint until I kneed the fucker in the balls and tugged his forty-five free. Stupid fucks should really have invested in some ALS guards if they didn't want their own weapons pulled on 'em.

Firing would be another dumb move and send the—by my count—twenty or so of them my way with maybe thirty rounds between me and Thing One, if their mags were fully loaded. But I was also never someone to turn down a chance for a good fight. So I put a slug between each of the fucker's eyes before JB's thumb even danced over his trigger. And spun on my heel, waiting for the ensuing bloodbath to begin.

In three, two, one...

46

"Fuck!" I sent my knuckles through the first thing within reach, staring at the fist-sized crater I left behind as white dust filled the air and dotted my black shirt. The drywall in our apartment had seen better days anyway. So what was one more glob of plaster in the grand scheme of things?

Doubt the landlord would even notice. The place was a shithole, but it was all Zeke and I could afford at the moment. Four walls and a roof over your head was a hot commodity in this area and the real estate owners knew it. Used it to their advantage.

"Feel better?" Zeke lifted a single brow in my direction while I continued to pace back and forth in front of the door.

"Not in the slightest." I spun on my boot to look him in that smug-ass face of his. He was enjoying watching me unravel. It was different from the cool, calm demeanor he was used to seeing. The guy who never took shit serious. Who could make a joke out of anything and would, whether or not it was appropriate.

Yeah, I was wondering where that guy was too, brother.

"She shouldn't be doing this shit alone. You know what the fuck these fuckers are like. Fuck!"

"Yeah, think you have enough *fucks* in there? Might wanna try one more for good measure." Zeke grinned.

"Fuck you. How's that?" I grunted, and his grin widened.

"Look, something tells me the girl can handle her shit. I mean, she's not the one bleeding all over the fuckin' place right now."

I glanced down and eyed the red droplets dotting my movements across the room, before rubbing the closest one into the carpet with the tip of my boot. Probably not the worst thing staining these floors. My eyes flicked around the cramped space. All that was missing was one of them chalk outlines you see on all those crime shows, and I was sure we could find a few if we looked hard enough.

"Would ya let Annie go in there on her own? Bet she thought she could handle herself too."

Zeke's head snapped up at the mention of his sister's name. "Fuck no."

"Yeah, that's what I thought," I grumbled under my breath, resuming my back-and-forth movements while raking an exasperated hand through my sweat-drenched hair. It was October and cold as fuck for the season. Still, the stress had me sweating like a pig.

"But Annie's different," he said, and I paused to glare at him. "You know I'm right. She doesn't have street smarts. Not like your girl. And she's always looking for trouble, putting her nose in shit she has no business putting her nose in. Doesn't know how to keep her mouth shut either."

"Yeah, well, sounds a lot like Dani. Except her kinda

trouble includes a buncha masked military operatives with a thing for comparing dick size."

"What?"

"Nothing. That's not the point." I reached out an arm and snatched the lukewarm beer from Zeke's hand before chugging what was left of the contents. Which wasn't much besides some spit at the bottom. I needed the burn. Not whatever the fuck this was.

I glanced around the room again. There wasn't a bottle of liquor in sight.

"Fuck," I grunted for the millionth time, and Zeke laughed.

"If you're so goddamn impatient, why don't you go find her? Wait outside the building or some shit if it'll make you feel better?"

"You're the one who fucking told me to stay put?"

"Yeah, that was when I thought you were gonna be chill about it. Not have a coronary. I've never seen your ass this worked up."

I didn't wait for him to say more before I was turning my back and grabbing his keys off the hook. My Buick was still fucked.

"Hey! Be careful with my car!" Zeke called after me, as I slammed the door shut on whatever he was gonna cry about next.

If they weren't at the club, there was only one other place Benny would take her. The unofficial Mulligan head-quarters, located across town. The Ice Cream Shop. Which had nothing to do with frozen desserts and everything to do with the little white crystals those fuckers like to deal to kids. It was why Zeke and I got stuck in this shit in the first place. Annie got hooked, borrowed more than she could pay back to feed her habit, and now her brother and I were working off her debt. And I'd do it all over again if it meant keeping her off the streets and getting the kid back in school.

She was doing well for the last few months. But the threat was always there. Lingering above our heads. She could relapse at any moment. Or, worse yet, Benny and his crowd could lure her back in. The fucker threatened as much whenever we didn't want to pick up an extra shift or stay longer than we were scheduled. Our hands were fucking tied.

Which was just another reason I had a sick feeling in my gut, knowing that Dani was confronting these guys on her own. It didn't matter how well she could fight, shoot, and do whatever else she could do. It was still a five-foot-nothing girl against a small army. An army that had no qualms when it came to beating and raping women and children.

Like I said, I knew the kinda men I worked for. Didn't say I felt good about it. I just didn't have much of a choice in the matter. I wasn't about to let my brother from another mother make a deal with the devil on his own.

Forty minutes in city traffic had me pulling up to the back of the Ice Cream Shop, which was really nothing more than an old warehouse with a cute street name. And not long after that, I watched a side door swing open and Dani come rushing out. Covered in blood. From head to fucking toe. Looking like something straight out of the movie *Carrie*.

"Fuck, Zeke is gonna fucking kill me," I grunted before flashing the headlights in her direction.

47

*I*t all happened in slow motion. *Like time stopped. As if the world around ya was playing out on a film reel.*

It was always some variation or another. I called bullshit.

There was nothing slow about it. At least not for me. If anything, I moved at double speed. My hands working on muscle memory, as though the guns in each palm were extensions of my arms. Bodies dropping and blood splattering like one of those action flicks where you didn't know one face from another because everything flashed so quick your eyes didn't have time to focus.

Don't get me wrong, half the shots I took with my left side were off center, some missing their targets completely, but none of that mattered as long as I eventually took the fuckers down without getting grazed myself.

At the same time, I wasn't looking to try my luck. With seven men out by my count, and several more on their way, I swiped Thing One's badge over the panel by the door and slipped into the blackness of a side alley. Only to stop in my tracks when I spotted a dark-blue Civic blinking its lights. Instinct immediately had me raising my arm and taking aim as I waited for the driver to come into focus. To take my shot and jack the fucker's car. Until two steps forward had me both wanting to drop the forty-five and fire it just as fucking much.

"I told you not to follow me," I hissed the moment pretty boy was within earshot, jumping into the passenger seat, as he shifted the car into reverse and sped in the opposite direction towards the main road. We could lose a possible tail in the city traffic.

"Didn't follow ya, baby girl. Just had a pretty good idea as to where you'd be." He grinned, and I had never been more glad and more annoyed to see someone in my life. The rush was wearing off and I was fighting back all those emotions I didn't want to deal with. Not now. Not fucking ever if I had a choice in the matter.

What I needed more than anything else was to forget. To forget everything Junior told me and cling to the lies I'd believed for the last six years. I needed oblivion. Feeding my blood lust wasn't enough tonight. It didn't stop my skin from crawling or my mind from racing.

A good dicking should do it. Should help calm the growing tension in my head. At least for a few hours. And if Connor wasn't up for the challenge, I would find someone who was. But this? This ache in my chest?

Yeah, fuck this.

I flicked my eyes in his direction, watching the way his jaw was set tight. His eyebrows knit together and his shoulders pulled back a little too straight.

Bet he could do with blowing off some steam himself.

He was annoyed with me again. Or something having to

do with me. I could tell. The guy was an open book, wore his emotions on his sleeve, waved them around like a white flag on the battlefield. And I was here to accept his slow surrender.

I reached out a hand, curling my palm around the noticeable bulge in his pants. Connor grunted, shifting in his seat before trying to swat my arm away. But I was too entranced by the way the blood on my skin soaked into the material of his jeans. There was something erotic about tainting something clean. Couldn't tell you what it was. Just that I liked it.

"Dani..." he ground my name between his teeth. "I'm tryin' to focus on not getting' us killed. Or, ya know, pulled the fuck over, looking like ya stepped straight out of a slaughterhouse."

Instead of stopping, I doubled down, gliding my hand over the length of him while enjoying the way the muscles hardened beneath my fingertips. "Pull over."

"Dani..." he repeated, but I could hear the dip in his voice. The one that told me he was warring with himself.

This was the opposite of what we should be doing for a multitude of reasons. One being the fact I'd just taken out a shit-ton of Benny's men, including his nephew. And two being Connor was still fresh out of surgery with more than a few popped stitches.

I didn't give a fuck. A couple of strokes and pretty boy wouldn't care none either.

I grabbed the wheel with my free hand, urging him to pull to the side again without having to say the words. Connor quickly turned off the street and parked under a flyover while the sound of passing vehicles echoed around us, traffic breezing by so quickly the Civic shook with the force.

I leaned across the console and tugged the lever next to the door, sending the driver's seat flying back before shimmying out of my blood-drenched pants. Connor watched on, dumbstruck or maybe a little in awe, as I flicked his top button open and made quick work of his fly. I grabbed his cock in my right palm, enjoying the weight of it as I threw one leg over his outer thigh and sank down. Then I braced my hands on the ceiling and began to grind my hips. Slowly at first. Teasing myself as the pressure gradually built up in my lower stomach while the fog in my head momentarily cleared, so that nothing mattered but what I was feeling right now.

Full. Numb. And so fucking good.

Maybe it was the angle. Maybe it was the mixture of girth and length. Maybe the bastard really did have some form of cock magic at his disposal. Fuck if I knew. But I wasn't about to question a gift dick in the mouth.

His hands gripped my waist, pulling me up and forcing me back down when my pace wasn't quick enough to get him there. And I leaned back towards the windshield, allowing gravity to do the work for me as I arched my spine and hummed along to the rhythm of the car bouncing.

Connor slid down in his seat, slapping a palm on the glass by my head while he thrusted up into me, the new position sending him deeper than before. It ached in the most delicious way. Like I could feel him rearranging my organs, adding to the pressure, the buildup until his fingers reaching out and rubbing against my clit sent me flying over that edge, my pleasure-induced moans accompanied by a guttural sound in the back of his throat.

He was hurting. I could hear the strain in his voice but he was too far gone to give a fuck as he came deep inside me. Something that would be a problem for another day.

Right now, I just needed to soak in the temporary bliss, feed off it so that I could function. Continue to do everything that had to be done. Bury the past and focus on the present. Whatever that meant now that I knew the truth. At least until I could figure out a way to ignore that too.

48

Your life flashes before your eyes.

That's what's supposed to happen when you're close to death, right? But for me, that's what happened the first time I came inside a woman so hard I was seeing fucking stars. The first time I fucked a girl without pulling out or using protection. The first time Dani's cunt took my cock so good I was left coating her walls with my future kids.

It felt fan-fucking-tastic.

Until reality set in and my lust-addled mind realized what my cock had done. What was far too late to take back. All while some primal part of me got off on the idea of my cum dripping out of her still-clenched pussy.

It was probably that same innate part of the male brain that was driven to procreate. Carry on the species and all that jazz. The part that hadn't caught up with common sense and logic. And the very real fact that we were now both covered in blood, in my best friend's car, on the side of the road. In plain view for anyone looking. The part that was ready for another go-around if I were dumb enough to risk it. Again.

A few more minutes and I just might have been...

"Fuck..." Yeah, I knew I needed to expand my vocabulary. But that was all I had at the moment.

"Fuck is right," Dani huffed, her chest heaving up and down in a way that had drool pooling in my mouth.

If I had more of a blood kink, I'd be reaching out to suck one of those tits between my teeth. Fuck my cum deeper into her cunt until even Plan B wouldn't help her. Didn't care if that wasn't anatomically correct. I was no doctor and it sounded like a good idea in my head. For right now at least. I'm sure tomorrow it would be a different story. I just couldn't help the way my body reacted to hers. Even when my skin crawled at the thought of all that gore clinging to her face and clothes.

I mean, *her* blood wouldn't have stopped me. But I knew better. None of that shit belonged to Dani. Of that much, I was certain. Which I was more than a little bit relieved to know.

Should I have been worried? Probably, especially when it came to pissing her off.

But something told me this woman liked having me around more than she was willing to admit. Too much to kill me at least. For the time being.

My lips curled into a grin. Dani was falling for me. She just didn't know it yet. I had to ease her into the idea. Of me and her. And us being a very real thing.

I flicked my eyes in her direction as she shifted her clothes back into place and repositioned herself on the passenger seat. "Know a good detailer? 'Cause Zeke is gonna have my head for this." I gestured to the blood-splattered interior.

"As long as I get to keep your dick, I don't see the problem." She shrugged before lifting a curious brow. "Why you still smiling?"

"Because you just admitted to wanting to keep me."

"Not you. Your dick," she grunted, and I grinned wider.

"Same thing, baby girl." I eased the car into traffic, my glare bouncing between the road in front of us and the rearview. "So, what now? Should I even ask what went down back there? Not that I'm complaining if it has you riding my cock like that when you're done..."

"Nothin' you have to worry about." She was staring out the windshield, in that way she would whenever she was avoiding something, and déjà vu was reaching out a hand to slap me across the face. I thought we were making progress but here we were again. On the Island of Avoidance without a paddle in sight.

"Right, 'cause the best way to get someone not to worry is to tell them not to worry." I didn't know where we were headed but I'd drive all fucking night if it kept her talking. I had a full tank of gas and nowhere to be. And Zeke? Well, the neat freak would sooner take the bus than see his car looking like Dahmer's Death Wagon.

"It's not your problem, MacCullagh." Dani tapped her nails against the glass, and I wasn't sure if it was meant to calm her or irritate me. Either way, it didn't seem to have the desired effect.

"I feel like I've heard this script before and I didn't much like the original, so let's skip the sequel, Dani, and roll right into the credits. You don't have to tell me what happened if you'd rather keep those cards close to your chest. But you can tell me something. Whatever it is you're thinking, whatever bullshit is coming our way, so we can prepare for it together."

There was a long pause, to the point I didn't think a response was coming until she finally opened her mouth. Her words soft, dry, robotic. "War... war is coming our way, Connor. And not the shit you see in the movies. Not the shit you hear about on the streets. This is a full-blown, old-school *mafia* war. The kinda thing the city hasn't seen in years. And you've chosen the losing side. Because they have the resources, the contacts. And I have me... My entire fucking family is dead. No one's loyal to the name anymore. Not unless I'm looking to marry ona their limp-dicked sons. So that's what's coming *our* way, what I'm preparing for," she said in one, long, exasperated sigh as my knuckles tightened around the steering wheel.

"Yeah, not gonna happen while I'm still breathing."

"Hang around and you won't be. Just ask Leo..."

I would... if I knew who the fuck that was and what had her sounding so despondent at the thought of him. But my gut told me I was better off holding my tongue and figuring out the rest later.

49

It wasn't a lie. It just wasn't the entire truth. I had contacts too. Men worse than the fuckers I was up against. A lot of 'em. But they all came with a price, a deal, a little tit for tat. And the thought of being on a short leash with a bunch of two-faced gangsters all out for themselves was not my idea of a good time. It was exactly the sort of life I was running from. The life I left behind to set out on my own. And I couldn't go back there. I refused to go back there.

But it didn't seem like I had much of a choice to stay here either.

Way to go, Dani. You've done it again.

Part of me wanted to curl up on myself, mourn the girl I was before that bullet shattered more than my skull. And part of me wanted to mourn Leo too. But that wasn't me, not back then and not now. I needed to screw my head on straight, get over this weight bearing down on my chest, and act.

I had my fun, six years of it. Six years of doing things on my terms. And a few weeks of doing Connor. It would be selfish to want more of either. It was time to grow the fuck up and embrace the Rossi blood running through my veins.

Pretty boy was tapping his hands on the steering wheel, and the sound had my eyes focusing out the windshield. Once again, I didn't know where the fuck we were headed. The post-orgasm bliss both cleared and fogged my brain in the *best* worst way.

"Ya know..." he hummed. "You could be knocked up with my kid already."

I choked on air, my neck snapping in his direction so fast I was at risk of whiplash. "That's not how biology works, Connor," I ground my teeth with the words.

"Still, think we should get hitched. Just in case."

"Are you fuckin' insane? All that blood that rushed to your cock not quite return to your head yet?" Delusional wasn't a strong enough word for this man right now. Nope, the fucker was certifiable. And that was coming from the same person who just gutted a mafia heir and left the body to rot inside his home office like a neon sign asking his associates to come find her.

"I'm just sayin'... I adore you. You tolerate me. I've seen plenty of marriages start out a lot worse. And then, you won't have to worry about all them limp-dicked sons you don't seem too keen on. Nothin' limp going on here, baby girl. Or do ya need another reminder?"

My lips curled into a smirk before I could stop them. "Is that what this is about? You seeing green, MacCullagh."

"I'm Irish, Rossi. I'm always seeing green." He shrugged. "But if you're askin' if I have a jealous streak, you bet your pretty little ass I do. You know that. Else you wouldn't have pulled that stunt at Freddy's Funhouse."

"Freddy's Funhouse?" I quirked a questioning brow.

"Yeah, ya know, 'cause those fuckers think Halloween is an all-year event."

I smiled wider, and Connor knew it too. If nothing else, the guy had a talent for loosening me up. In more ways than one. And I hated to admit that it was refreshing to not feel so tightly wound all the time. Wasn't about to tell him that, though.

Leo would have hated him. My parents? They would be rolling over in their graves, if they weren't turned ass-up already. And I think that's what I liked about the guy.

Yeah, I know. Issues with authority. There was no surprise there.

It had always been a thing with me, since my pops tried enrolling me in that fancy private school. Only for me to get expelled six months later. But there was more to it than that too. I hated expectations. It was one of the greatest weapons I had in my arsenal. Someone thinking you were gonna zig, allowing you to throw 'em off with a zag. And vice versa.

"So, speaking of...?" I could see the wheels turning in Connor's head. And, not for the first time, I didn't know where this conversation was going. The man spewed nonsense like he worked for the Sunday rag. "This Leo guy, who is he?"

Right, he was still stuck on that whole jealousy thing. He might have just been harder to shake than I thought. Which was an oddly comforting feeling.

Don't get soft on me now, Rossi.

"Was. Who *was* he," I was quick to correct. "And he was Junior's older brother. Also my ex."

50

I guess you could say part of me always knew it would come to this, the blood still tainting the streets serving as a constant reminder that we shared a long, dark history. A mutual hatred between families. Another part of me hoped that Dani and I would be the exception. While the gun presently pressed to my forehead told me just how naïve *that* part had been.

"Look, Mr. R—"

"Shut your fuckin' mouth, boy."

Spittle bounced off Salvatore Rossi's lips and splattered across my face with each ragged breath he took. My hands were bound behind my back, my feet chained to the floor so there wasn't anything I could do to wipe it off.

Truth of the matter was I didn't want to. I didn't much care about anything anymore. Not with Dani laid up in some hospital bed, her skull pieced together with nothing more than cadaver bone and prayers. But it was better than watching her bleed out on my front lawn. Even when I knew what bringing her here—home, *her* home—would mean for me. I guess I never realized how little life meant without her until I was faced with that very real possibility.

Her father didn't often get his hands dirty, not when he had guys to do that for him. But I was the exception. I was the one who brought his baby girl... what was left of her. To his doorstep. In a goddamn body bag.

Yeah, I knew what it looked like. I knew what he saw when he opened his front door. I recognized the horror in his eyes. The rage too. But I also knew it was the only chance she had for survival. Told my family I'd handle the cleanup. It was my mess, after all. And I couldn't just drop her off at any bullshit city hospital. She needed the best. My girl deserved the best. And her old man was the only one who could get that for her. So I said *fuck it*. I did what I had to do, knowing the consequences.

And those consequences were staring me in the face. In the form of a two-hundred pound, six-foot-something, Italian Don who ate *Irish pricks like me* for breakfast, then used what was left of our ring fingers for toothpicks. His tailored Brioni suit was already mottled red with the blood from my broken nose, and my thumb was twisted so far back it was useless.

He'd stopped asking questions hours ago. I could only assume he realized I didn't have the answers to give 'em. Right now, it was his grief that was driving the blows to my jaw, gut, and groin—whenever he was feeling particularly vicious. Though I could tell he was growing tired, fueled by rage and not much food or water shared between us.

I got it. I really fucking did. Because I hated me too. She told me to be careful. Stressed what a risk this was. Warned me about Junior...

And I never really took any of it serious.

You're a dreamer, Leo. That's what she would say. Dani was one too. She had a lot of dreams. Fantasies about leaving this life of ours behind. Even when she didn't want to admit it, I saw the side of her she hid from the rest of the world.

Salvatore was running out of steam. I could feel it in the weight of his blows. They weren't landing right. I could also see it in the laziness of his gait. He was tired and sloppy. Then there was the tightness of his jaw. The guy was grinding his teeth down to nothing, trying to force himself to expend energy he didn't have anymore. So it didn't surprise me when he lifted the barrel to the center of my forehead again. The steel, cold and welcoming against the heat of my bruised skin.

No one really ever talked about the smell of a freshly fired forty-five, how the chemical odor of the nitrate ate up the little hairs in your nostrils. Burned to the point of discomfort. All of which told me this man wouldn't sit behind his desk and let someone else have the pleasure of pulling the trigger.

"Just tell Dani I lov—"

51

PRESENT

I was watching Dani walk back and forth in front of me, her words spitting out a mile a minute as she tried to explain this whole "mafia war" thing to Zeke. Sounded more like some sort of video game than anything you'd experience in real life... if ya asked me.

I glanced in Zeke's direction. His face was a shade of green I'd never seen on someone breathing before and his lips were pinched like he was two quick seconds away from losing his lunch and going *Exorcist* on our asses.

Funniest part was I couldn't tell you what bothered him the most. The prospect of the upcoming bloodbath, the bodily fluids sticking to my girlfriend's skin like she just spent the evening cracking some fucker's head open and fingerpainting with whatever she found inside, or the current state of his car. Which honestly wasn't much better.

We were holed up in another little no-name motel where they didn't ask questions and only accepted cash. A spot that reeked of hepatitis and desperation. I'd gotten my folks out of town, sent them down to my aunt's house in Florida. Though I wasn't sure they were better off with the gators. And none of us had much in the bank to do this shit long term.

My da was a warehouse employee, my ma a home-maker. They had three bucks between 'em. And didn't know the meaning of the word vacation. Which meant we had a week to sort this shit out. Max. Before the stubborn bastards were back within the city limits and the Mulligans were using them for target practice all over again.

"So, basically, what you're telling us is that it's a fucking game of Battleship? Take a shot in the dark and hope for the best? Pray that the other guy is sinking without a raft?" I quirked a brow, and Dani paused in her tracks to shake her head at me.

"I mean, no. But kinda. I guess." She huffed, her irritation cuter by the minute. "It's more nuance than that. Think Sun Tzu instead of Hasbro. *The Art of War*, not Monopoly."

"Right. Well, I call first dibs on the racecar." I grinned, and Dani sent me a glare that had nothing on Cyclops. Swear I could feel the heat of her eyes down to my bones.

Zeke seemed not all that amused either. Fucker needed to get his panties straightened out. Being so wound up wasn't gonna get any of us outta this situation sooner. Especially if he didn't calm the fuck down before reaching out to his baby sister. If Annie sniffed trouble in the air, the girl would be foaming out the mouth instead of lying low. She had a taste for the dramatics, even when we were kids. So it was no surprise to me when she found herself in knee-deep shit with the mob.

"This ain't nothing to joke about, MacCullagh," Dani hissed, and Zeke grinned from where he was standing behind her. "We need guns. A lot of 'em. Whatever fire-power we can get on short notice or we're all as good as dead."

"Yeah, well, something tells me you already got an idea in mind." I lifted a questioning brow. I knew better than to let her threats get under my skin. My girl didn't do anything without a plan in mind. Even when she was acting on impulse. Some part of her was already scheming, plotting her next move before she had to make it. And this time was no different.

"I do, but you're not gonna like it." She shrugged, her arms folding over her chest while she popped out a single hip in obvious defiance.

"If it has anything to do with those masked fuckers—" I started, and she quickly cut me off.

"How much do you know about the Bratva?" Dani's lips were curling into a grin while mine were pressed thin and tight.

"The Russian mob?" Zeke choked out while I responded with, "Are you fuckin' kiddin' me?"

52

Nikolai Volkov. *The Russian Wolf.* Heard my pops mention the name more than once. The current leader of the Bratva. A man known for his ruthlessness and loyalty to no one but himself, *his* people, *his* bloodline. And certainly not the Italians.

Yeah, I was desperate. But the fucker had the sort of weaponry I needed. Handguns, long-range rifles, explosives. No, no one had that shit on such short notice. No one but the Russians. Export laws were much more lenient in their parts. Fuckers didn't have to deal with all the red tape neither.

Guy didn't know me. But he knew my last name and I knew he was champing at the bit to get his hooks in Chicago. A fact I planned to use to my advantage.

Truth was, the coasts were owned by the Italians while the midlands bounced between Irish hands ever since my father was decommissioned. A nice way of saying dead and buried. Which meant my support meant something. Not much but something. It was all I had to give at the moment.

And it was enough to get my foot in the door. Schedule me a little face-to-face with the guy behind all those threats my pops liked to dish out about marrying me off to the Russians, *if I didn't start behaving real soon.* Like that'd ever happen.

Wasn't sure the meeting would get me much else. Didn't hurt to try though, and the Bratva just happened to be local right now, likely sniffing out a weak spot before deciding if they wanted to make a move against the competition.

I flicked my gaze to the figure cursing under his breath beside me. Connor was radiating nervous energy, and I was instantly reminded how much he didn't belong in this world.

It was his fault. Pretty boy insisted on tagging along. Normally I would have argued but it didn't look good to come alone. The Russians were old school, even more than the Italians, so women weren't worth more than the cunt between their legs. A wrong I would right when things settled down a bit. Until then, I needed to play the game. Pretend I had a man at my side. And it didn't hurt that this particular man was an Irish nobody. Someone no one would recognize. Harsh but true. If Connor kept his mouth shut, we might have actually had a real chance at making a decent deal.

Knowing him, though, it was a big fucking *if.*

"Let me do the talkin'." I lowered my voice to a stern whisper as we were guided through the first set of doors, only to be stopped and searched before being escorted inside. Security was tight. Much fucking tighter than what I was used to with the Mulligans.

Connor growled when I was patted down, while I was just thankful that the Russian fucks missed the blade concealed by the underwire of my bra. Served them right for underestimating me.

Then again, I knew better than to bring a knife to a gunfight. My Kershaw wasn't much more than a security blanket if push came to shove.

But I'd at least make someone bleed before I went down.

That thought had my top lip twitching when the man of the hour entered the high-end office space several minutes later. Nikolai Volkov was better looking than I would have imagined but I guess that was part of his charm. Pretty packaging that hid the monster lurking beneath. However, when his gaze skimmed my body from bottom to top, I couldn't mask the shiver that traveled along with it.

There was something about his eyes, black not brown, that was unnerving. Like there was nothing behind them. No humanity. No soul. Just darkness.

I recognized darkness.

"Danica Rossi," he hummed my name, tasted it, as a slow smirk curled his mouth at one side. "Let's not waste time with pleasantries. We both know why you're here. So why don't you just tell me what the Bratva can do for you today?"

It wouldn't be that easy. I knew that. And The Wolf knew I knew that. But these interactions were like a dance, a game of chess, and I only had one piece left on the board to play around with.

He sat. I remained standing. "Weapons, preferably heavy-duty artillery or explosives. Whatever you're able to part with on short notice."

I watched him watching me. Trying to figure me out without needing to do much else but look at me. "I can part with all of it. Or none of it. That's all up to you, *kotenok.*"

I crossed my arms over my chest, more out of habit than

intimidation, and flicked my eyes around the room. Looking at everything and nothing. There was no point in trying to pretend I had the upper hand when it was clear to everyone I didn't.

"Somehow I doubt that, Mr. Volkov." I pivoted on my heel to pin him with a glare.

"Please, call me Nikolai." Even his voice was wolf-like in tone. How? I couldn't explain it. But if you heard it, you'd know what I meant. It sank under your skin, crawled up your spine and sat there. Pinching the back of your neck like a mother chastising an unruly pup.

Connor remained tight-lipped but I noted the way his posture stiffened, his jaw set tight as his eyes flicked between me and the only other predator in the room.

"Okay, Nikolai, keeping with the theme of not wasting time, what is it that you want? And before you ask, I'm a little short on cash at the moment."

The Russian waved a dismissive hand. "Does it look like I need cash, Danica?"

I quirked a curious brow, a clear sign I wasn't impressed, and urged him to get on with it. This slow dance was turning into a tango and I was ready for something a little more heart-thumping. "Enough with the subtext. What do you want?"

"I mean, I am a businessman and you're no charity case. Which means I can't just give you something for nothing. That being said, not every exchange needs to be monetary..."

Connor stalked forward, and I flung out an arm to stop him. He was wasting his energy and coming off as more of a hothead than a tangible threat. Neither was a good look when we were knee-deep in negotiations. I shoved him down into the closest chair and propped my ass up on his thigh. To keep him in place, not to appease his misplaced sense of ownership. But pretty boy didn't need to know that.

Nikolai's eyes followed my every movement, his hands steepled and a single dimple punctuating his slow grin. "Guard dogs aren't of much use when they don't know when to yield."

I could feel Connor tense beneath me. So I quickly reached a hand just under his kneecap and pressed a thumb into his femoral nerve, causing his leg to go limp before he could think about getting up again.

"Sit," I hissed, and Nikolai barked out a laugh. I flicked my glare from Connor back to the man in front of me. "Something funny?"

"*Nyat.* You just remind me of someone." He shrugged, his posture much more relaxed than it was moments ago.

"Right, well, I'm all for being nostalgic but can we get on with it? What sort of *exchange* did ya have in mind?"

The Wolf pushed back in his chair, his thumb and forefinger rubbing against his stubbled chin, as he eyed me from across the large desk presently separating a predator from his intended prey. I could see the gears turning in his head. The plotting. As I held my breath and waited for the first designer shoe to drop.

"Do you know how important blood is, Danica," Nikolai said more than asked, and I could already tell where this shit was going. "I'd do anything for my family. For my blood."

"No offense, but you're a little old for my taste."

"Not me." He shook his head. "I have a nephew though. A good-looking kid with a strange..." He waved a hand as if trying to find the right words. "...*affliction* for Italian women. I never could understand the appeal but—"

53

"No." I threw the idea out the window before the fucker could finish his thought. And had to admit I was more than a little surprised when Dani didn't make a move to stop me. Even as my arm wrapped around her waist and my hand clamped over her mouth.

She could shake me off if she really wanted to do it—I wasn't putting all that much pressure on her face—but baby girl was looking to avoid causing more of a scene. Though that didn't keep her teeth from digging into the meat of my palm vicious enough to draw blood.

"No?" The fucker in front of us tilted his head to one side, eyeing me like a curiosity rather than a threat. Like he found me fucking hilarious or some shit. And I was dying to throw my fist through his too-perfect teeth. Ya know, show him how *fucking funny* I could be.

"No," I repeated, since it was clear the bastard didn't hear me the first time.

This had Dani elbowing me in the rib, forcing my arm to drop back into my lap and my hand to latch on to her thigh.

She was about to interject when the Russian lifted a palm to stop her. "*Nyat.* Let the pup speak." His nostrils flared as his lips pulled into something resembling a tight smirk. But not quite. "And why the fuck not, guard dog?"

I laughed. Because it was fucking funny in an awkward sort of way. Like someone tripping at a funeral. I could hear his teeth grinding with my lack of a response. It was clear the guy was used to people asking *how high* as soon as he barked at them to jump.

"Go on, boy. You look like ya had something to say. Suddenly the cat got your tongue?"

"Oh, something's got it for sure. But it's more pussy than cat." I grinned, only to widen it when Dani knocked me upside the head, and the Russian finally had the decency to drop that smug-as-shit smirk of his. Not so amusing, now is it?

Welcome to the club, buddy.

He flicked his wrist in my direction, like someone swats at a fly buzzing a little too close to their ear, before slowly returning his focus to my girl. "Who you fuck is of little importance. A discussion to be had after the marriage contract has been agreed upon and signed. So what do you say, Danica? Do we have a deal? Your choice of weaponry, whatever you can carry as an act of good faith." He lifted a single shoulder in a half shrug while leaning back in his seat as though the guy were looking to audition for the role of villain in a Bond movie. "Think of it as a wedding gift for my future niece?"

"What part of *no* don't ya understand?" I snapped, despite the weight of Dani's scathing glare boring through the side of my face. "Is it the N or the O that was lost in fucking translation?"

"It's the part where this is none of your fuckin' business," he growled, appearing much more animalistic and far less suit and tie.

"Pretty sure it's entirely my business, seeing as you're tryin' to marry my wife off to some prick who ain't even here to speak for himself."

The Russian balked while Dani nearly choked on air, hissing my name under her breath a little too late for me to care. I might not have been married to the woman just yet but I sure as fuck would be the moment we stepped out of this office and found ourselves a priest. I wasn't about to let her be used like some bargaining chip between a bunch of thugs who didn't give two shits about her as a person.

"Well, this is news to me." He made a sound low in his throat. Like a hum but not nearly as appealing to the ear. "I don't recall getting an invitation?"

"No shit? Musta gotten lost in the mail. Sent it by carrier pigeon and everything."

Dani's eyes flicked between me and the Russian before finally settling on him. "Yeah, well, I never was one for tradition. Kept things intimate," she grunted, and I grinned like the fucking cat who ate the goddamn canary. It might not have been my ideal proposal but the fact she wasn't making me out to be a liar was as good as a *yes* to my ears.

"A shame. Really would have been a mutually beneficial solution to both our problems." His words were calm, measured. His demeanor was not. The fucker was pissed.

Good. He and his nephew could both go fuck themselves up the ass with the vodka bottle they rode in on.

He pushed up from his desk in a movement that told us this meeting was over without ever having to say the words. Which was no skin off my back. I'd heard about enough of what the fucker had to offer.

I grabbed Dani's hand, prepared to tug her out the door

behind me, when she dug her heels into the carpet, causing us both to turn and look at her. "I thought wolves were supposed to be clever," she mused, and he lifted a single brow as if daring her to say otherwise.

"The same could be said for you, *kotenok*." His palms landed flat on the desk in front of him with so much force there should have been an audible thud, but somehow the fucker's precision had him stopping short as his fingertips barely brushed the surface. "But I am curious as to what's churning in that shattered little mind of yours."

I was vibrating in my skin, itching to do something stupid, while Dani's hand on my wrist begged me to do nothing at all.

"Marriage ain't the only thing I have to offer. At least not my own." Her voice was dry, emotionless, and I didn't like the sound of it. "I heard you were the type of man who saw the bigger picture. Played the long game." She shrugged. "But if I'm wrong, that's on me. I'll just have to find someone with a little more... tact."

His glare dropped to her stomach before trailing back up to her face. All the while his lips curled into a slow grin. "How far along?"

My head snapped in Dani's direction. She dug her nails deeper into my wrist. "I'm not," she huffed. "Not yet. But I will be. Soon."

The Russian clapped his hands together with a curt nod. "*Pozdravleniya!* Your firstborn daughter to my firstborn son—"

"No!" Dani was quick to interject, and I felt like I could finally breathe again before she added, "Son. My firstborn son to your daughter."

"*Soglasen.* Done."

54

The weird thing about lying was when you started to believe it yourself. The idea that I was selling children that would never exist didn't sit well with me. Though I had yet to figure out what was leaving me with this fucked-up hole in the pit of my stomach. Like I ate something sour and it was ready to travel back the way it came.

I wasn't motherly material. Never had been. I didn't ask for dolls or Barbies as a kid. Never cared much for playing house neither. I just didn't have it in me. Long before everything that happened with Leo, I knew the Rossi line would end this go-around... unless my baby brother didn't keep his little prick in check.

But that lie was tomorrow's problem. The Russian bastard couldn't fault me for being barren. And I'd make sure it looked that way. At the very least I'd buy myself a few years. Earn myself a few more favors with the right people that would hopefully come in handy when The Wolf came looking to collect. That was assuming he ever had kids himself. At the end of the day, we were negotiating with lives that didn't exist. On either side.

"What the fuck was that about?" Connor hissed the moment we were behind closed doors with a shit-ton of heavy artillery in tow. "Did you really just sell off our future kids like they were nothin'?"

I pivoted on my heel to face him, the barrel of the empty nine aimed at his forehead. Because why the fuck not? It had been one fuck of a day, and I was over dealing with another man with *another* fucked opinion about what I should do with myself and my body.

"Not kids. Kid. My kid. Not yours," I ground out between clenched teeth. "A bouncing baby boy who has no chance of ever existing in the first place."

His eyes flicked downward before meeting my face again. The cocky son of a bitch really thought his swimmers were Olympic level or somethin'.

"*Our* kid, dollface. And why a son versus a daughter? What's the difference? Either way shit's just fucked." He raked a hand through his hair.

It was evident the *make-believe* was getting a little too real, weighing heavy on the Bible-thumping morality that was so ingrained in him the fucker was sweating. And for some reason, the muzzle I had trained in his direction had nothing to do with it.

Which was just another kick to the lady balls.

I tucked the nine into the waistband of my jeans, then dropped the gym bag loaded with ammo and a couple of cases of hand grenades onto the small table in the corner. "Because women get fucked enough as it is. Wasn't 'bout to trade my imaginary daughter like livestock."

"The same rules don't apply for *his* daughter I'm guessing?"

"Nope." I popped my lips with the word. "Sounds like a Russian problem to me."

"You do know none of that makes sense, right? Your logic's fuckin' flawed, Dani." Connor sighed, and I shrugged a single shoulder in his direction.

Never said it had to work for anyone but me.

"Doesn't matter. I traded a whole lotta nothing for a fuck-ton of something."

He stalked forward, grabbing me by the waist and tugging me to him. Forcing my chin to tip up in order to level my gaze with his. "I thought I already told you our future kids ain't nothing, baby girl."

"And I told you our future kids ain't a thing at all, pretty boy. That much I can guarantee."

He searched my face, as if looking for the lie and coming up empty. "You don't know that."

"'Cept I do, MacCullagh." I pressed my lips together and watched his eyebrows furrow. "Having a bunch of Irish brats ain't in the cards for me. I don't want 'em, even if they were. I'm sorry if that bursts that little fantasy of yours. But it's better that you know now."

His chest rose and fell with a few quick breaths. Disappointment maybe? Fuck if I knew when it came to this man and the wild ideas he had in that head of his. Then his lips tipped up into a slight smirk. "Guess I'll have to settle for just wifing you up, fuckin' you till you forget what it is you want anymore."

"Yeah, 'bout that. You need to stop fuckin' saying crazy shit. Especially when people can hear you. Things could have really gotten fucked in there."

"Why? One day it'll be the truth. I'm just getting ya used to the idea until it is."

"I already told you I'm not having your kids. So what makes you think we're getting married?"

"Give me one good reason we shouldn't. I'll even take your last name. Heard being a Rossi comes with its perks." He grinned.

"What it comes with is a death sentence, Connor."

55

Have you ever had a cunt strangle your cock so good you forgot how to move? Breathe? Do much else besides exist?

Oh, right. Unless you're a dude, you probably have no idea what I'm talking about...

Well, to put it mildly, it was the best fucking thing since God created pussy. Since the first man had the bright idea of sticking his dick inside it. Or how ever the fuck the Bible said this shit came to be.

Guess I should have paid more attention in Sunday school. Not that my Catholic upbringing mattered all that much now, outside the fact I was seeing fucking stars. Those goddamn pearly gates. *Heaven.*

For someone who claimed she didn't want my kids, baby girl sure as fuck liked the feel of them inside her. The feel of *me* inside her. Pounding away until my muscles gave out and she was fucking breathless. I was addicted. And self-aware enough to realize it. But so was she. Dani didn't even try to hide it anymore. How much she wanted me. How much she enjoyed it too.

She was riding my cock, her head thrown back and her palms flat against my thighs as she positioned her body in a way that sent me deeper with each back-and-forth thrust of her hips. She liked the control. And I *loved* watching her take it. The bounce of her heavy tits as they landed a second or two after she did. The way she lost herself to the rhythm. How beautiful she looked bare-ass and impaled on a cock like my favorite porn star. Only better because this chick was real. And right in front of me. It was hypnotic.

Awe-inspiring really. My lips curled with the thought.

At first, the position was just practical. The best option to avoid pulling a stitch, but now it was more about the view. And I sure as fuck enjoyed the view.

Dani was close. I could tell by the way her face scrunched up, her eyebrows folding towards each other and her lower lip pulled tight between her teeth. I was *closer* just looking at her. And that was a problem. At least for me it was.

I flipped her over onto her back, ignoring the sounds of her protests as I tugged her ass in the air and rested each of her thighs over one of my shoulders. Taking a deep breath before diving into her cunt face-first. The moment my tongue stroked down that pretty pink center, Dani groaned and clawed at my head. Her nails digging into my scalp and holding me in place. Another few laps, and she was setting the rhythm again, angling my chin so that it rubbed against her cunt while I sucked at her clit.

She hummed my name, followed by a few choice expletives as I brought her to new heights. That edge that had her thighs shaking and her toes curling against my back. She locked her ankles and tugged me closer, the sloppy sounds mixed with her erotic moans having me so worked up I was two good yanks from coming on the sheets. And I wasn't too proud to admit it. This woman did things to me, things that could turn a pious man into a sinner.

And I was a far cry from either.

When her pussy started quivering in that way that told me her orgasm was one quick lick from bubbling to the surface, I crawled up and plunged back inside her, driving forward until the aftershocks had her thighs butterflying open and her arms dropping to the mattress. I leaned one palm on the headboard, the other flat on the bed as I continued to enjoy the feel of her wet cunt sloshing with each thrust of my hips.

I grinned as I felt that tingle in my spine, my balls drawing up with that familiar warm pressure that's usually a sign to pull out before it's too late. Except that was the last thing I wanted to do right now. Which was exactly when Dani slapped at my chest, shoved me onto my back, and closed her lips around my cock, my load shooting down her throat without my girl even having to move. My neck twitched and my body went as limp as the rest of me.

When I finally had enough energy to look up, baby girl was pinning me with a seething glare.

"Why d'ya do that?" It was more of a thought than a question meant to be spoken out loud, but I was still waiting for all the blood to return to my brain. Ya know, so I could start thinking with that part of me again.

"Because clearly I can't trust ya to keep your sperm to yourself," she grunted, and I grinned wider.

She was right, after all. No point denying it now. I wasn't caught up in the moment, lost to another good fuck-ing. That shit was as deliberate as it came.

No pun intended.

"Might wanna lose the smirk, pretty boy. Keep it up and

I'll trade your ass in for a boyfriend of the vibrating persuasion."

"So you admit it then?" I lifted my arms over my head and locked them behind the back of my neck, taking a deep breath as I waited and watched for her reaction.

"Admit what, MacCullagh?" She pushed off the bed and stalked towards the bathroom, my eyes glued to the sway of her perfect ass cheeks as she closed the distance between herself and the door.

"That I'm your boyfriend."

Dani glanced at me from over one shoulder, her lashes darker and thicker somehow as she eyed me from beneath the slight shadow they cast along the dip of her nose. "You're something all right. I just don't know what it is yet."

"Love you too, dollface," I called out as she slammed the door. A reaction I was guessing had just as much to do with a handful of unwanted words as it did a *cunt*ful of unwelcomed sperm.

56

"If you two could stop fucking for two fucking seconds and tell me what the fucking plan is that'd be great," Zeke ground out, appearing less than pleased with the lot of us.

"Nah, I don't think we will. I like the *fucking* part too much." I smirked and tugged Dani's back to my front, grinding my dick against her for emphasis. All baby girl had to do was say the word and I'd be ready for round... fuck if I knew. I'd lost count hours ago.

She reached a hand behind her and began rubbing up and down the length of me. I groaned against the feel of her palm, even with layers of clothing still separating us.

"My plan?" she hummed, her eyes fixed on Zeke and her grip fixed on me, though I was only half-listening by this point. "Didn't ya know my family started the original fires?"

"Is that true?" He quirked an incredulous brow, and Dani forced out a laugh.

"Nope. But better believe that's what we'll be known for when I'm done with this city."

Her declaration should have been alarming, and it was clear to Zeke it was. We had friends here, family, but I was too lost to the feel of my girl's hand to pay much attention to the words coming out of her mouth.

Call me cunt-struck. Didn't much matter to me when my balls were being emptied on a regular basis. Sex and sandwiches were the only daily requirements to make the list. And I'd gladly give up one for the other.

I'll leave it to you to guess which one.

Yeah, I knew we had an audience. But I was too far gone to care if Zeke was watching. Who knows? Maybe the fucker could learn a thing or two. Getting laid might lighten him up a bit. Sure as fuck did wonders when it came to putting *me* in a better mood.

I was a few short seconds away from bending Dani over the nearest piece of furniture when she pulled away, dropped her weight, and grabbed my wrist, twisting and tugging my arm behind my back before using the heel of her boot to nudge me forward. I was always much more into knocking boots than licking them. But if anyone could change my mind, it'd be this girl.

"You need a cold shower," she whispered next to my ear, while I remained bent over at the middle, just enough to remind me of the internal throbbing in my abdomen. "And I need to build a few bombs."

"Bombs?" Zeke choked out. I hadn't even noticed that he'd crossed the room, likely trying to distance himself before he became a casualty of our fucking *or* our fighting.

Let's be honest. With Dani, it could go either way.

"What? Did you think I was joking?" Baby girl loosened her grip on my arm and shoved me forward a step.

I shook out my wrist and plopped my ass into the chair opposite her, the smirk on my face wider and the fit of my pants a bit more... *snug*. I pulled at the fabric to give myself the extra room my cock needed. She could manhandle me any day. There was just something about a short girl with a filthy mouth that could bring a man to his knees. Get him hard in all the right places.

I could feel Zeke's eyes on me, his glare boring a hole into the middle of my forehead. His jaw was set tight and his nostrils were flaring in that way they did whenever he was being pushed to his limits. Which was his way of telling me if I didn't say something, he would. And neither of us would like it.

My eyes bounced from him to Dani, who was laying out and lining up ammunition on the motel room floor like a preschooler looking to build the newest five-thousand piece Lego set.

"We can't just go blowing up the city, dollface."

"No, we can't." She peered up at me through those thick lashes again, her voice too sweet to be anything but intentional. "But *I* can."

"Dani..."

She blinked. Once. Twice. Three times before huffing out a breath. "Don't get your panties in a twist, MacCullagh." She shook her head. "Never said I was blowin' up the entire city... just certain parts."

"And what parts are those?" Zeke cut in before I could stop him.

"Okay, just one part." She grinned. "Mollies."

57

Since I was tall enough to reach my pops's knee, I enjoyed watching the man work. Dish out orders and command the room. I may have never been interested in the life, leading the family, but that didn't mean I wasn't interested in the violence that came with it. The destruction. Ya see, I was fucked in the head long before I was *fucked* in the head.

While other kids my age were learning how to color inside the lines, I was learning how to load my mother's pearl-grip revolver, where the extra bullets were stored, and to always aim for the head. Or the dick. My old man said either one would do the trick, and he was right. Watching some fucker bleed out while scrambling to piece his balls back together was as close to nirvana for me as life could get.

So rigging a few homemade pipe bombs was literal child's play to me. The extra grenades and additional firearms I'd grab from the Russian's stock house more for my amusement than anything else. After all, the fucker said whatever I could carry. So you bet your sweet ass I was slinging a half dozen long-range rifles over one shoulder while scooping up an armful of frags.

The boys were none too happy with me at the moment. At least Zeke wasn't. Connor was much easier to win over. A couple strokes of my hand and I'd have pretty boy's frown turned upside down. But I'd let him stew for a bit longer first. I liked watching him squirm, his arms crossed and his brow creased as he eyed me like I'd pissed in his Cheerios.

If he kept up his pouting, I just might.

"Ya know we work there, right?" he grumbled, and I tilted my head to one side, my eyes flicking upwards while my hands remained on task. *My hands always remained on task.* "Like that's how we get our paychecks. What we live off?"

"Ya don't say?" I feigned shock, tapping a palm to my chest and quickly dropping it. "And here I thought ya just liked smelling like stale cigarettes and bad decisions." Then I lifted one shoulder in a half shrug. "My advice? Ya both might want to get your resumes together, find something less *blown to bits* and more *four walls and a roof*. Besides, I hardly think you'll have a job to return to, *Mac*. Not after they saw you leave with me."

"There's more to it than that, and you know it, Dani. So stop playin' coy," he grunted.

"Who's playin'?" I pushed up on one knee, then the other, shoving the various wires and timing mechanisms aside and crawling forward, before squeezing myself between Connor's already spread thighs.

I could hear Zeke behind us, huffing and groaning, as I rested my palms painfully close to pretty boy's sweet spot. His cock instantly rising to the occasion. No matter how determined he was to be angry with me, there was one part of him that couldn't resist succumbing to my... *charms.*

"I know what you're doing, baby girl. And it ain't gonna work."

"Oh, it'll work." My eyes flicked downwards, telling me I was right, before I returned them to Connor's face as my lips curled into a satisfied smirk. "But you have no idea what I'm doing."

He lifted a curious brow, urging me to continue, while Zeke's grumbling told me that was the last thing *he* wanted at the moment. The guy definitely wasn't into watching.

His loss. I could put on one helluva show.

"The only way out of this is for us to hit Benny where it hurts. And take him down when we do. Or else the fucker will just keep coming. He ain't gonna let this shit go. Not now. Not ten years from now." I lifted a hand and gestured to my chest. "Case in point."

Connor grabbed my wrists, his grip tight but not painful, as he tugged me up off my knees and onto his lap. "Look, I get it. I get there are things I don't understand when it comes to you and how you handle shit. We ain't stupid." He glanced in Zeke's direction, then back to me. "I also know better than to ask questions I really don't want you to answer. But ya can't just go in and blow up an entire club full of people. Innocent people. People who have nothing to do with the bad blood between Benny and you. Him and *us*."

"See? That's where you're wrong. I most definitely can—"

"Dani—"

I pressed a finger to his lips, pushing down and slipping it between his too-plump pout while watching the digit disappear into the warm wetness of his mouth. I quickly cleared my throat, and Connor grinned.

Yeah, we both had it bad. One of the very few downsides to good sex was the constant need for more. The inability to resist, accompanied by the reluctance to do so even if you could.

"*But* I never said that's what I was planning."

"I don't understand…"

"And ya don't need to. This is my game, my nature, one I've been suppressing for a very long time. But that doesn't mean I don't know how to win."

"Meaning?"

"Meaning nobody's gonna be in that building except Benny and his top guys. Anyone looking to take the fucker's place as soon as he's outta the way. I'll get rid of 'em all, then leave the Russians and Italians to fight over what's left of the territory."

"And you can do that? Make sure no one gets hurt who shouldn't be gettin' hurt?"

"There's a lot you don't know about me, pretty boy. A lot I can do if you'd just shut up and let me do it."

I could read the uncertainty all over Connor's face. And once again, I was reminded of all the reasons we shouldn't work… *couldn't* work. All that *ride or die* bullshit only lasted until I made a move he didn't agree with, until I crossed that line between hero and villain I walked so finely no one knew exactly which side I was standing on at any given time.

The answer was still neither. It would always be neither.

He would realize it soon enough. See all the ugliest parts of me I didn't bother to hide. He'd see them and that's when he'd go running. And I wouldn't stop him. Though there was something inside me that hoped I was wrong.

58

She was somewhere else, even when she was in the same bed with me. In a much different way than when she was suffering from one of her episodes. This was much more intentional.

Dani was distancing herself, closing off her emotions while doing her best to keep me at arm's length. I'd always been good at reading people. It came with the job, with working in a nightclub where you were surrounded by hundreds of drunk idiots at any given time. You had to know how to feel out the room, tell who was on the verge of going nuclear, who was one shot away from throwing a fist, who was too far gone to go home alone—or with one of the predators just waiting to pounce as soon as someone tried.

But when it came to reading Dani, I wasn't just good. I was close to expert level. More acquainted with her mood swings than I was with the birthmark on the left side of my dick. And I'd been staring at that fucker since I was old enough to piss standing up.

It had to be that way. I didn't have a choice. It wasn't like the woman was gonna tell me what she was thinking.

Nope, that was the last thing my girl wanted to do. And I didn't mind the challenge. If anything, some deranged part of me liked it. Liked her fight. Her resistance. The chase. How her mouth could insist she didn't want me at the same time her body was begging for it. For me.

Yeah, I could live with her hate. Because that shit was so close to love it was borderline amusing. Because it meant she felt something. But this... coldness? Indifference? It fucking hurt. Worse than the jab to my balls she offered me when I tried to tug her back over to my side of the bed.

We were fighting. One of us was fighting? Though I couldn't tell you what the fuck it was about. Just that my girlfriend was very *unimpressed* with me at the moment.

I finally willed myself to sleep, only to wake to the sound of harsh murmuring, the words inaudible but the intent clear. I didn't have to look next to me to know that Dani wouldn't be there. The near-shouting disguised as whispers coming from outside the motel room door clued me in as to where I'd find her.

I rubbed a palm against my eye, trying to alleviate some of the pressure building in my head before forcing my feet to the ground. So that I could cross the room and peer out the window to see what the fuck was going on. Sure enough, baby girl was throwing her arms around wildly— which was better than throwing fists—as she argued with someone in front of her. Someone very familiar.

I tapped on the glass, my quirked brow asking what my mouth didn't. Dani and Zeke blew back into the room, bringing a shitstorm of tension with 'em. Instead of telling me what the fuck was going on between my best friend and my girl, Zeke shoved his phone into my face, a picture of his baby sister hogging up most of the screen.

"They got to her," he hissed. And it took a minute for

the words to sink in and their meaning to land like a punch to my already tender gut. "That's why she hasn't been answering our calls. They have her, Mac. They've been shootin' her up with God knows what and they're refusin' to let her go unless we give 'em something in return."

"We don't have nothin'. What the fuck more could they possibly want?" If my brain were working on anything more than three hours of sleep and half the number of brain cells, I wouldn't have asked such a stupid question. But that shit was out of my mouth before I could stop it.

"What the fuck do you think they want?" he ground out between clenched teeth, one arm flailing out towards Dani while the other snatched his phone outta my hands. "They want a fucking one-for-one exchange. Your girl for my sister."

"Ain't happening." I crossed my arms over my chest, my glare more pointed than I'd normally aim it at my best friend. "There has to be another way."

"Another way? Are you listening to yourself right now? This is Annie I'm talkin' about. For fuck's sake, you're the one always claiming she's like a sister to you. *Family.* And you're willing to put her life in jeopardy for some girl ya hardly know? Is the pussy really that good it knocked the sense outta ya?"

Wish I could say I thought about it. But I didn't. My arm was reaching out and slamming Zeke against the closest wall, one palm pressed up under his chin and squeezing while my free hand was pulled back and ready to strike. Long before any thought crossed my mind.

"Watch your fuckin' mouth. Ya don't wanna go there, *brother*." I could feel Dani on my shoulder, but I refused to loosen my grip until I was sure Zeke got his head on straight. "All I'm sayin' is that we take a minute to sit the fuck down and talk this out. Come up with a plan that doesn't involve using someone as bait for a sick bastard like Benny fucking Mulligan."

The fucker shoved at my chest, and I let him, before he positioned himself on the other side of the room. "Yeah, I think we've done enough talkin' already. And I've heard everything you've said loud and fuckin' clear. You stay here and get your cock wet. I got this one. Don't you worry 'bout me, *brother*." Zeke didn't wait for a response as he shoved his way past Dani, one hand yanking the door open then quickly slamming it shut behind him.

59

"You can't go in there all half-cocked, MacCullagh," I grunted as a slow grin curled his lips. This plan was shot to hell and back if I didn't get the smug son of a bitch under control.

"Fully cocked. Got it. Shouldn't be a problem."

At the same time, trying to control Connor could be like trying to rein in the sun with a piece of rope and a whole lotta patience. And right now, I didn't have either.

"I'm being fuckin' serious." I returned my glare to the mess of metal pipes and wires in front of me, piecing together my last bomb for the night. "One wrong move, one fuckin' slip of a finger and your ass will be blowing us all to bits. And I don't know about you, but I like my bits still attached to my body and not spread out all over the sidewalk." I could feel Connor's hands coming up behind me to grab my waist. I quickly shucked them off.

"And what about Annie?" he asked with way more optimism than was good for a person to possess at any given time.

"Not my problem. Your friend was more than fucking

happy to shove an apple in my mouth and hand me over on a silver platter, like he was serving Benny Easter fuckin' roast." All the yapping was getting on my last nerve. I needed to focus, to keep the migraine at bay and to stay in the present. Or we were all more fucked than a hooker standing out on MLK Blvd.

"She's his fuckin' sister—"

"Yup, and not fuckin' mine. The girl's nothin' to me."

"But she's somethin' to me. Which I hoped was enough to make her somethin' to you too."

"Well, hope is a son of a bitch, ain't he?" I ground out between clenched teeth as I turned the last bolt clockwise and accidentally stripped the nut, cursing under my breath before I tossed the driver to the other side of the room. And watched it embed in the thin layer of drywall. "Get out!"

"Dani…"

"Connor, I said get the fuck out. I need to concentrate and I can't do that with you fuckin' buzzin' in my ear." I expected to hear heavy footsteps stomp in the opposite direction, followed by the slamming of a door.

Instead, there was silence. I couldn't even make out the sound of the bastard breathing but I could feel his eyes on me. The intensity of his glare. His nearness. And it was goddamn unnerving. Suffocating.

I knew I wasn't being fair to him. But life wasn't fair to me either. And it was time the poor fucker learned this world was no box of Lucky Charms. You didn't get to toss out the marshmallows you didn't like. And shit didn't work out just because you wanted it to.

You woulda thought his mama would have taught him as much. The woman was no dummy. One night under her roof was evidence of that. But even a sharply delivered lesson ain't enough to pierce a thick skull, and that was no one's fault but his.

"I ain't leaving you here." He sighed, and I recognized the emotions deepening his voice. Connor was desperate. To do what was best for his friend. And for me. Hurt by my constant need to drive him away. And probably a little pissed off by the same thing.

But then again, so was I.

"I'm not askin' you to leave forever. Just give me a few fucking minutes to breathe. Climb the fuck off my dick and let me work," I huffed. When he didn't immediately respond, I added, "Can ya at least go grab me another bag of 3/8ths, so I can finish up here and get a few hours of shut-eye? Ya know, before I have to run in and save the day?" I bit the inside of my cheek, forcing my composure while ensuring my voice was honey-sweet. "Please?"

"Fine. I'll go, but I'm calling Zeke to keep an eye on you."

"Good luck with that," I muttered, my glare honed in on my chewed-up nail beds and the blood pooling beneath the surface. Makeup and manicures were part of a life I didn't belong to anymore. Nowadays I felt naked without grease on my palms and knives in my pockets.

"No luck required. He just had to blow off some steam. Needed a little time to come to his senses. I meant it when I said we're family. And soon enough the stubborn bastard'll realize that shit includes my girlfriend."

"I'm not your girlfriend," I was quick to remind him. But the dumb fuck was already out the door, the added skip in his step telling me he was doing a piss-poor job of pretending not to hear me.

60

The moment I pushed my way back inside the motel room, the door bouncing off the little stopper thing some half-assed handyman glued to the wall, I should have known something was wrong. But the alarm bells in my head weren't going off. That feeling you get in the pit of your stomach telling you shit wasn't right?

Yeah, it was missing. And so was Dani.

For whatever reason, that reality didn't sink in. It wouldn't. Like some part of me thought if I looked hard enough, I'd find her under the bed or in the bathroom. Tucked up in a corner or hiding behind the dingy shower curtain that was no better than a flimsy piece of plastic. Pretty sure that shit was supposed to be see-through. It was definitely more of a brown color now.

My eyes flicked down to the mess of wires left sprawled out on the floor, then back up to the open door and the parking spot where Zeke's car should have been.

And wasn't. 'Cause he was gone too.

That was when every muscle in my body tensed, and

my sense of fight or flight chose freeze instead. My boots sticking themselves to the carpet and my feet feeling as though I couldn't move them if I tried. As though cement blocks were weighing them down and holding them in place as my thoughts went into overdrive.

My hand instinctively dipped back into my pocket and closed around the keys to the Mulligan's stolen car, as my brain finally forced my limbs to move. And then I was rushing off. Back towards the lot. Jumping behind the wheel and slamming the gears into reverse. My mind set on one thing. Getting to Mollies with a shit-ton of homemade bombs and dynamite holed up in the trunk. Because something in my gut—that same something that wasn't working when I first walked through the door—told me that was where I'd find 'em.

The place was a fucking ghost town. Just like Dani said it would be. Only it seemed this shit was going down a few hours earlier than anticipated. And with one less bomb in position.

What was it people liked to say?

Even the best laid plans went up in smoke. Or some bullshit like that. Whatever it was, we had to make do with the hand we were dealt. And my hand involved a girlfriend who didn't know what was best for her when *the best* was staring her in the face.

I spotted Zeke's car pulled off to the side of the lot. And jogged towards the employee entrance in the alley just behind Mollies while doing my damnedest to keep from shoving my hand in my pocket and fiddling with the keys. The whole time, Dani's words kept playing on repeat in my head.

One fuckin' slip of a finger and your ass will be blowing us all to bits.

She was right after all. I did like her bits attached to her body. And not raining down all over the goddamn sidewalk.

As I reached out an arm to tug open the door, it was already flying forward in my direction. Zeke and Annie pushing their way through with Benny and a team of his goons standing behind them. My eyes flicked to my best friend's face and the guilt that was waving at me so freely it's next stop shoulda been the closest speedway. Then dropped to his sister, who was clutching on to his shirt like it was the only thing holding her upright. Her pupils glassy and her movements stunted. And finally swept back up to meet Benny's glare. Accompanied by a wolfish smirk that curled his lips into a grotesque version of what I could only assume was meant to be a smile.

"What the fuck?" I hissed out. The question aimed at everyone and no one all at once as I waited for someone to give me a straight answer. "Where's Dani?"

Benny shrugged. "Ask your friend here. He's the one who called me in the middle of the night. Begged me to come and make a deal."

My head pivoted towards Zeke. The guilt was gone and in its place was something I didn't recognize. *Someone* I didn't recognize. Whoever this was, his spine was steeled, his chin jutting forward.

"I told you I'd fuckin' handle it. This was the only option you left me to work with," he grunted.

"You..." I couldn't say the words. They wouldn't travel up my throat or form in my mouth. None of this shit made sense. He wouldn't. I refused to believe it. "You really stabbed me in the fuckin' back...?"

"Nah, you did that to yourself, brother. When you chose loose Italian pussy over *family*."

Benny slapped a hand over Zeke's shoulder before the man I thought was my brother pushed years of friendship aside to walk past me, guiding his sister towards his dark-blue Civic without so much as a glance in my direction... at the same time my former boss shoved the door closed in my face.

Good thing I had enough explosives in the trunk to make my own.

61

SIX YEARS PRIOR

"Who the fuck is that?" I asked while peering through a crack in the bedroom door, my daggered gaze honed in on the two guys presently arguing in the hall. One of 'em I recognized as Patrick Mulligan, Leo's old man.

The other fucker? Couldn't say I'd ever seen him before.

Leo rushed up behind me and quickly pressed a finger to my lips. "That's my Uncle Benny. My dad's brother. And not someone you should be looking to piss off, Rossi."

I flicked my eyes over to the Irishman with a waistline that told me he was the sort to never turn down seconds before landing my glare back on Leo. "Pretty certain I can take 'em."

"In a fair fight, sure. But that fucker don't play fair. And ya can't trust a word that comes outta his mouth neither."

"Yeah, same goes for the lot of you, or so I'm told." I shrugged a shoulder, my mouth already tipping up into a grin.

Leo grabbed my waist and pivoted me to face him, clicking the door closed in the process. One arm propped up on the frame, the other locking me in place. "Stop looking for trouble, Dani. 'Cause one of these days you're gonna find it."

"Thought I already did," I countered, my fingers wrapping around each side of his unbuttoned dress shirt and tugging him forward. "Think you can fuck me against this wall without them hearing ya?"

"It's not me I'm worried about them hearing, babe," Leo grunted, and forced himself back a step while reaching up a hand to comb his fingers through his hair. Like he always did whenever shit was bothering him.

"What's wrong? Why d'ya look worried?"

"Ain't nothin' wrong, Dani. I mean, nothin' other than the fact we're playin' with fire here." Leo huffed, and I quirked a questioning brow.

"I thought you liked the heat, Mulligan? But, ya know, if it's too much for ya, I can leave."

"That's not what I'm sayin' and you know it, *Rossi*."

I popped a hip and pressed my lips into a thin line. "*I don't know,* 'cause ya won't tell me shit."

Leo watched me for a moment, those too-pretty for a boy lashes fanning his eyes and refusing to flutter. To blink. What he was looking for I couldn't tell ya. Didn't even know if he'd found it or not, but something had him shaking his head and dropping his guard at the same time.

"Him being here... it ain't right. Don't know what it is. Call it a feelin'. I don't fuckin' know. But whenever that slimy bastard gets his claws in shit, things go south fast. Worse is the fact that Junior idolizes the prick. Follows 'em like the guy's got whiskey-scented wind comin' out his ass."

"Yeah, well, your brother ain't the brightest marsh-mallow in this bowl of Lucky Charms."

"Dani, I'm bein' serious." Leo stalked as far away from me as he could get, perching his ass up on the sill of his bedroom window. "You asked me what the fuck was wrong. I try to talk to ya about this shit. And all I get is more jokes."

"What ya get, Mulligan, is all I'm willin' to give ya. A good sense of humor and a great set of tits. Never promised ya more than that." I didn't bother moving or lowering my voice, even as I noted how Leo's eyes zeroed in on the door as if the damn thing could remove itself from its hinges and come after him. "Ya want your cock sucked? I'm your girl. You want a wife? Find yourself one of those prep school princesses always following ya around."

"Ya mean the girls who wear those teeny-tiny uniforms that look an awful lot like the one you left on my floor that first night?"

"Yeah, but less flexible and more desperate."

The words weren't even outta my mouth before Leo was closing the distance, much quicker than he'd created it, and pinning me to the wall again. His fingers pinching my cheeks and prying my chin upward and his glare now perfectly level with my face.

"Drop the act, babe," he whispered in a way that didn't sound much like a whisper at all.

"What act?" I grunted in reply, my tone less threatening when pressed out through puckered lips.

Leo dropped his hold on my cheeks. "The one where you pretend like you don't love me."

"I—" I started to say, and my argument quickly died on my tongue the moment his was shoved inside my mouth. Three quick twists of that nimble appendage and Leo was pulling back with a cocky-ass grin. "Fine. Tell me what the fuck crawled up your ass and put ya in a sour mood."

"Ya really know how to sweet talk a guy, Rossi."

"What can I say? In this day and age, a girl's gotta have many talents." I shrugged.

Leo flopped himself onto his bed, his hands bracing the back of his neck and his eyes focused straight ahead. He patted the spot beside him, and it took all my willpower to keep from mouthing off again. Just because I could.

The problem was, the fucker was right. I did feel... something for him. Nothing I was willing to put a name on at the time. But definitely something more than *like*.

I stomped over in full brat mode before reluctantly accepting the arm he lifted, then used to tuck me against his side.

He propped his chin up on my head and sucked in a deep breath. "I think he's doin' somethin' behind my dad's back. My Uncle Benny, I mean."

I raised a shoulder in a half shrug. "Backroom deals happen all the time. That shit's par for the course. Someone's always lookin' to skim a little off the top."

"Nah, that's not the kinda thing I'm talkin' about. I think it's somethin' much bigger. Like he wants to take control of the businesses. Cut my old man out entirely."

"What makes ya say that?" I pushed up on my elbows to look Leo in the eye.

"Like I said, it's just a gut feelin'." He shook his head, then grabbed one of my wrists and tugged me on top of him, his cock already trying to pierce me through the fabric of his jeans. "But right now, I'd rather be feelin' your guts, *prep school princess*."

62

PRESENT

"So, Leo was right," I hummed, crossing an ankle over a knee in a very unladylike manner. My wrists twisted behind my back in a pair of standard-issue hinged cuffs, and my shoulders secured to a metal chair.

There was a man positioned in each corner of the room. Nine guns in total, counting their backups as well as the one tucked into Mulligan's overstuffed waistband.

"'Bout what? 'Cause it sure as fuck wasn't you, princess." Benny waddled in front of me, his suit jacket far too tight and his lips far too loose for a supposed mob boss. My old man would have known better than to take the bait.

You always commanded the room. You sure as fuck didn't let the hostage do it for ya. It was like Mafia 101 or some shit.

"Oh, he was right about that too. I can suck cock like a champ." I quirked a challenging brow. "Want the family discount? I'd love nothing more than to lock my jaw around that toothpick between your thighs and tug it loose."

The fucker's face blanched before turning a shade of red that'd put a firetruck to shame, while his men did their best to stifle the sound of their chuckles.

"I should cut that tongue outta that filthy mouth of yours, girl," Benny hissed, saliva peppering the air when the bastard spoke.

"Why?" I cast my eyes down over the buttons that were straining across Benny's gut, pausing where a cock should have been before flicking 'em up again. "I promise ya there's plenty of room for both." Then I lifted a shoulder in a noncommittal shrug. "But that's not what I'm talking about."

Benny leaned an arm on the desk, supporting his weight while urging me to continue with a dramatic wave of his hand.

"He suspected you were snaking your way into the businesses, lookin' to replace his pops. Get 'em outta the picture. I mean, that's why you're here, isn't it? You ran 'em outta town."

"That wasn't me." Benny's grin was something sinister, like the cat who ate the canary. Then spit it out and used a scalpel to see what was on the inside. It was the grin of a fucking psychopath. "That was all you, Ms. Rossi. The grief, the loss of his firstborn son. Ya see, that's what really did my brother in. Not me." He glanced down at his polished shoes before looking back in my direction again. "Thanks by the way. Saved me the work of havin' to do it myself."

"Ain't nothin' new," I grunted. "Us girls are always havin' to carry the load of lesser men. In some fucked-up form or another. Ya gonna have your mama take care of me for ya too? Clean up another mess you've gone and made for yourself?"

"Oh, no. That pleasure's all mine." Benny's jaw tensed,

like he was chewing on ice cubes and grinding them between his teeth. His nostrils flared and his chest heaving. Though that last one could have had more to do with being out of shape than the rage boiling beneath the puffed-up leprechaun's surface. "Your only saving grace over the years was my nephew's obsession with the cunt between your legs. And what did it get 'em? Ya gutted the kid like a pig and left the poor boy to bleed out on the floor."

"See, that's where you're wrong, Uncle Ben—love your rice by the way." I tilted my head and offered the fucker a grin that rivaled his level of crazy. "I didn't leave until *after* he bled out on the floor. Stayed long enough to watch the life drain from the bastard's eyes." I flexed my thighs in my seat, rocking the legs back and forth a few times before shifting to move 'em from side to side. A smart man would have bolted down the chair. "Don't know what sort of trainin' you had, but my pops taught me to always make sure they're dead. Never abandon a body before you know for certain. Then again, I guess that's why we're here, ain't it? Because someone forgot to check if the corpse they left behind was still breathing?"

Benny opened his mouth, his lips curled in a way that told me it would be scathing too. 'Cept the fucker never got the chance. 'Cause he was far too distracted by the rumble of an explosion that sent his men running out the door in search of the source.

"Ain't it a bitch when things don't work out the way you thought they would?" I hummed, my voice lulling Benny's head back in my direction. Just in time for me to finish sawing through the rope and pop my dislocated thumbs back into place. It was a little parlor trick I learned as a kid and definitely something that'd come in handy over the years.

"Wha—?"

Benny's words were cut off by the sick sloshing sound of the letter opener on his desk piercing his cornea and sinking into the white meat of his eyeball. The circular organ plopping out on the other end like a dead fish on a spear.

"It's smaller than I'd thought it'd be," I commented before flicking the little bundle of nerves off the tip of my makeshift weapon. I paused to watch his eyeball fly across the room. It landed with a sticky-sounding splat against the far wall and quickly tumbled to the ground, leaving a trail of gore in its wake. Then I turned back to Benny, a smirk tipping up one side of my mouth. "Though I bet that's not the first time you've heard that, am I right, Benny Boy?"

His shrill screams were piercing through my eardrums, passed the plugs I was smart enough to shove into place at the start of this shitshow, and somehow the muffled sounds were still making my temples pound. The first sign that I was teetering dangerously close to another blackout.

I took a deep breath, held it for two seconds, and released it to try to center myself. While Benny continued flailing on top of his desk, his T-Rex limbs flapping around like a parrot that had its wings clipped a little too short.

Before I knew what I was doing, my hand was reaching into my bra outta muscle memory. My palm tugging my pink Kershaw free and running the clean edge across the fucker's jugular. He made a gurgling noise in the back of his throat, what was left of his neck craning to one side as his head tapped itself out on the veneer surface.

I grabbed a handful of Benny's sweat-slick hair and lifted it up off the desk to look the fucker in the eye. "That's another thing my pops taught me. Don't keep shit nearby that can be used against ya. Especially something as stupid as a fucking letter opener. I mean, really, Benny? Who even uses a letter opener in this day and age? Or were ya just tryin' to look sophisticated?"

I released my grip, allowing his head to hit the desk with another audible thud as I eyed the length of him. The various knickknacks on his office shelves. The brass accents.

"Hate to break it to ya, Uncle Ben, but the whole old-school vibe... it just ain't working for ya."

Then I smeared the blood splatter across my forehead and made a beeline for the door just as the second bomb went off in the distance.

Two down, three to go.

63

The shriek coming down the hall was like nothing I'd ever heard before. But it was the eerie silence that followed it a few minutes later that would really live on in my nightmares. Like a goddamn horror movie come to life. The type of shit that got sexed-up teenagers killed. Got your ass turned into leather masks and your body chopped up into tiny bits.

What could I say? I had an active fucking imagination as a kid. Guess that shit stayed with ya into adulthood too.

I cracked my neck from side to side to alleviate some of the chill traveling up my spine and turned the corner, the floor vibrating beneath my boots as another blast went off somewhere that wasn't here. An explosion that had nothing to do with me this time around. Though I had a pretty good idea as to who *was* behind it.

The same woman who was slipping out of Benny's office with a bloody knife in her hand and a blank expression on her face.

I reached out an arm and tipped up her chin, forcing her

glassy eyes to meet mine. But she wasn't there. "Dani, you okay?"

She narrowed her glare, and whatever she saw staring back at her... it wasn't fucking me. Because she immediately lifted her blade to my throat, pressing it deep enough to draw a line of blood. Then she began walking me down the hall. Towards the chaos. When we shoulda been running from it.

"Dani, it's me. Do ya know who I am?"

"Leo...?" she whispered the name, a name that sure as fuck wasn't mine, and the knife clinked against the floor as baby girl appeared to blink herself outta ona her weird-ass trances. "Connor?"

"Yeah, though I'm not sure how I feel about being option number two," I grunted, grabbing her palm in mine and dragging her back the way we came.

We pushed out the closest fire exit seconds before another bout of explosions sent the building crumbling in on itself. The sounds of sirens were already going off in the not-too-distant distance, but for some fucked-up reason, my feet were glued to the concrete as I eyed what was left of the club I called home for the last few years.

It was an odd feeling. The not knowing what was coming next. What life would be like now that someone didn't own you. Own me. 'Cept they did. Only it was a different someone, in an entirely different way. And that same someone seemed to still be hung up on her ex.

"Come on." I tried to tug Dani towards the side alley. And she dug her boots into the ground, refusing to follow me. "We gotta go, dollface. It won't be a good look if the hats and bats find us standing 'round an active arson site, 'specially when they discover there's a shit-ton of bodies beneath that rubble."

She held up a hand, gesturing for me to wait. To listen. And I clamped my mouth shut in time to hear a familiar rumble come barreling down the street moments before a dark-blue car pulled up in front of us.

64

"Zeke…?"

I watched the way Connor's face contorted with his obvious confusion, his eyebrows knit and his head tipped to one side like a pup trying to learn his first commands. As amusing as it was, we didn't have time to clue pretty boy in to what was turning out to be a perfectly orchestrated plan, if I said so myself. So I quickly shoved him into the back of the Civic and signaled for Zeke to hit the gas.

"What the fuck is going on?" Connor turned his head in my direction as we sped off down the street. Missing the barrage of cop cars and swat vans that surrounded Mollies with seconds to spare.

Zeke's eyes flicked up in the rearview to meet mine before refocusing on the road in front of him, and I clapped a hand down on his shoulder, a silent instruction for him to continue with phase two of our plan.

That's what I liked about the guy. He was the quiet type. Didn't need the words to understand what was expected of him. Unlike some people…

Connor hadn't shut his trap since we started moving, and I didn't have it in me to listen to him right now. So I'd been tuning the fucker out. Trying to piece my mind together. I lost myself back there. I knew it. I could feel it. And I needed to shake the haze from my system before I even considered answering all the questions that were currently being tossed my way.

A few short miles later, we were pulling back up to our hole-in-the-wall motel. The adrenaline draining from my body along with my patience. I jumped out of the car, escorted the boys into our room, and slammed the door behind us. Away from the prying eyes and ears of anyone who'd care enough to listen.

I shoved Connor down on the mattress and waved a hand in his direction. "Go on. Ask away."

"Oh? You need me to repeat myself?" he grunted. "Okay, fine. What the fuck is going on, Dani? And what the fuck is he doing here?" Connor flung an arm out towards Zeke.

"Him?" I hitched a thumb while peering over one shoulder. Then I landed my glare back on the man in front of me. "You mean your best friend?"

"No, I mean the fucker who was too busy suckin' Benny's asshole to trust that I'd always have his fuckin' back." Connor pushed up from the mattress, and I pressed my fingers over the pressure point in his shoulder, watched his arm slump, and slammed him down again.

"Nope. I said you could ask questions but only if you're gonna listen to the answers. If not, you may as well pack your shit and leave." I lifted a challenging brow.

Connor crossed his good arm over his chest while grabbing the limp one to hold it there too. His stubborn-ass way of agreeing while showing me he wasn't happy about it.

"Right, well, if you woulda kept quiet long enough for

me to explain, I woulda mentioned the part about how your *best friend* was only doin' what he was told. For your sake. So you weren't forced to choose sides."

"What the fuck are you talkin' about?"

"I told ya you needed to trust me with this shit. This is the world I grew up in, one I learned to navigate before I learned to walk."

"What the fuck does that even mean, Dani?"

"It means that when it comes to dealin' with sons of bitches like Benny Mulligan, you have to have an ace up your sleeve. You can't play fair. Because he sure as fuck won't." I waved a hand towards Zeke. "Say hello to our ace. Oh, and ya might wanna apologize too."

"I don't understand..." Connor's eyes bounced between me and his friend. Then back again.

"What's there to understand? I did what any good head of the family woulda done in my shoes. Planted a rat, made it look like he was workin' against us. Meanwhile your boy here was a double agent. If that sick Irish fuck was half the man my father was, he woulda seen that shit comin' a mile away. Lucky for us, Benny is—*was*—as dumb as the day is long."

"So...?"

"*So*, kiss and make up. 'Cause Zeke never turned my ass in. I went willingly. Got that girl outta there. And then had 'em plant the real bombs. Yours were decoys."

That had Connor jumping up on his feet and towering over me again. "Decoys? Are you fucking kiddin' me? What the actual fuck, Dani?"

I shrugged a shoulder and folded my arms over my chest, my hip cocked and my glare lethal. "See? And that's exactly why. You're too impulsive, MacCullagh. I needed someone with a clear head. Someone who knew how to listen and wouldn't go in there and accidentally blow us up. More than that, I needed real emotion coming from *you*. That look on your face when you thought the man you considered a brother stabbed you in the fuckin' back. I needed that authenticity to really sell it to Benny. Otherwise it all woulda been for nothin'.'"

I dropped an arm before quickly reaching up and placing my open palm on Connor's cheek.

"You wear your heart on your sleeve, pretty boy. Which, believe it or not, I find admirable. Unfortunately, it also means you can't lie for shit. So we had to do it for ya. Hopin' you'd forgive us later." A small smirk quirked up one side of my lips as I peered up at him through my lashes in that way I knew he liked. "So do ya, MacCullagh? Do ya forgive us?"

"Before I answer that, I got one more question for ya..."

"What's that?"

"No, not you. *Him.*" Connor craned his neck to the side to peer over my shoulder. "If you didn't rat us out, how'd they track us to that creepy-ass motel? We were in the middle of fucking nowhere, no cell service, no nothin'. And the only person I told was *you*."

Zeke's brows knitted together as he leaned back against the wall. "No fuckin' idea, man. I just know it wasn't me."

I trailed a hand along the waistband of Connor's jeans, drawing his attention to me as my fingers dipped into his back pocket. Where I pinched his badge from Mollies between the tips and plucked it free. Then I fisted the white keycard between my palms and snapped the shit in half to reveal the chip-sized tracker that was embedded in the plastic.

"How the fuck did you know that was there?"

I shrugged. "I didn't. Till just now. But figured there was a good chance I was right. Probably had all of ya chipped.

Slimy fucker didn't know what it meant to earn his loyalties. Let alone keep 'em."

Connor shook his head, an amused grin already playing on his lips as he slammed his mouth on mine and forcibly slipped his tongue inside. His free hand landing on my waist and tugging me forward at the same time his cock ground itself against my stomach. Then the little cunt-tease was pulling away again. Much too fucking quickly if ya asked me.

"Okay, pretty little liar, so what now? Where do we go from here?"

"I honestly don't know. New York? Cali?" I shrugged. "Pick a coast and we'll head that way. I just can't be Danica Rossi anymore. Not in this city."

Another slow grin split Connor's lips as he looked down at me with a strange-ass twinkle in his eye. "How about Danica MacCullagh? Ya think ya can stay and be her for a bit? Or, ya know, maybe even forever?"

65

"Hey, Doc, Laney sent me. Said you'd know what that means." I shrugged while grinding the Spearmint against my teeth, the popping sound it created not nearly as soothing as the puff of a cigarette. But shit would do for now. The nicotine was messin' with my sleep and my brain did enough of that on its own.

Which brought me here. To this bullshit building. To see yet another medical professional who I was sure would do nothin' more than talk circles around me like all the rest of 'em.

The old man in question eyed me for a few moments longer than was appropriate, and I could tell the fucker was none too happy about my late-night appearance. Truth was I was none too happy about it either.

And misery loved fucking company.

But Officer Gallagher insisted this was the way shit worked. Show up at this bullshit medical office. Outside the city. And ask for *Doc.* Said I would know him when I saw him. And this crotchety old bastard in a white lab coat screamed quack with a capital K. While the woman coming up his rear was a glorified Nurse Ratched if I ever saw one.

If he thought I was gonna beg him for help, *Doctor Kevorkian* had the wrong fuckin' girl. Wasn't about to let him walk past me either though.

A few more awkward beats and the old man shook his head, a grin softening his features as he directed me to the first door on the left.

My eyes flicked around the room. The all-white walls. The little jars of cotton balls and Q-tips. The too-sterile countertops. And back over to the man perched up on ona those little doctor stools. The bleach smell was fuckin' with my head and eating away at my resolve. I hated hospitals. Hated doctors more. But something had to give before I did.

The old man watched me with an odd expression on his face—one I couldn't quite read—before passing me a shit-ton of papers attached to a plastic clipboard. I glanced down, back up again, then tossed his bullshit forms onto the metal tray table in front of me.

"Yeah, I'm not really the formal type."

"Right, well, I at least need a name for the file," he said in that condescending doctor voice they all seemed to have while peering up at me through his tiny glasses.

"Dani. That should be enough for your *file*," I ground out, my patience as thin as the hair on the old fucker's shiny-ass head, which he nodded once before gesturing for me to continue. "So, Doc, tell me..." I hummed as I sat back with a knee crossed over an ankle. "How familiar are ya with lost time?"

66

FOUR MONTHS LATER

The gray slabs of stone were popping up in the distance like morbid jack-in-the-boxes the closer we got to the towering gates, the white arches of Calvary Cemetery looming overhead and the words "thy will be done" mocking a certain Irish Catholic boy turned heathen. It took everything in my power to stop myself from making the sign of the cross over my chest. Sister Mary's voice taunting me in my head with the familiar disdain that to this day still haunted my nightmares.

"That's not gonna save your soul now, son."

My former grade school teacher was a real ball-buster, her daily scoldings sticking to my brain worse than the gum I liked to press under my desk. Even a decade later.

Dani tugged at my arm, guiding me farther down the walking path while reminding me why we were really here. And that I'd gladly burn in hell for her. I mean, according to good ol' Sister Mary and her trusty ruler, I was headed there anyway.

She came to a stop in front of a row of headstones, each with the same last name scrawled across the front. *Mulligan*. An entire family tree wiped out and lined up along the grass. There was no fanfare, no crowds of mourners, no one throwing themselves on the graves and sobbing into the dirt.

It was a startling realization. That one day we'd all end up here—well, maybe not here. *Here* cost more money than I'd hope to make in a year. But like this. Trapped six feet under in a box, if we could afford it, with nothing to show for ourselves but a few words carved in stone.

I shuddered at the thought, my claustrophobia getting the best of me. *Wonder if my girl would chip in for an open-air casket?* Because I was certain I'd be going first. I had no doubt this woman would be the death of me one way or another.

She glanced up at me with a small smirk playing on her lips as she reached into her pocket and pulled out a folded piece of paper. Setting it on top of the headstone directly in front of us before dropping my hand and walking away.

I watched her go for a few moments. Because the sway of those hips was a sight to behold, even with the grim surroundings. And shifted my cock in my pants. Baby girl was gonna get it when we got home. Though I was pretty sure that was her intention as she glanced back at me from over one shoulder.

My gaze flicked to the yellow legal paper that was one good gust of air away from disappearing before landing on Dani's back again.

"You gonna tell me why we're here?" I called out.

"Nope," she called back without bothering to look at me.

"You know I'm gonna read it, right?"

"Yup."

I watched her take two more steps, then quickly swiped up the note, opened it up, and began skimming the contents.

67

Leo,

It's been a while since I've visited, eh? But what can I say? I've always been good at holding a grudge. And, well, as I'm sure you're aware, I thought your dumb ass shot me.

Found out not all that long ago that I was wrong. I know. Me? Wrong? I'm just as shocked as you are. There's a first time for everything, I guess. So here I am.

It took me a bit to come up with what I wanted to say to you. If I wanted to say anything at all. Since there ain't much of a chance you can hear me. But my new therapist insisted this was more about me than you. No surprise there. 'Cause when isn't it about me? And, yes, you heard me right. I said therapist.

Look at your girl, getting healthy and shit.

According to Doc, it's PTSD and the blackouts are my brain's way of protecting itself when something's especially triggering.

I know. Sounded like a crock of bull to me too. In the beginning. But his voodoo nonsense... it's been working. I've figured out ways to stay in the present. Even got a rubber band around my wrist that I can snap whenever I feel that familiar darkness coming on.

Anyway, what I'm trying to say is... I'm sorry. I'm sorry for being angry for so long. For blaming you and myself for the way things turned out between us. I've been fucked in the head for a while now. And it had nothing to do with the bullet your brother put there and everything to do with me thinking you'd fooled me. Betrayed my ass and broke my heart.

Because you did, Leo. You broke my fucking heart, shattered it to bits without even meaning to. It seems. There've been moments when I wondered what things would have been like for us. But some part of me believes it was always gonna end up this way. With one of us in the ground.

We were young and dumb. And there was just too much bad blood surrounding us. I was never gonna stay, and as much as you liked to argue with me about it, you were never gonna leave. You would have got fed up with me refusing to settle down, and I would have resented you for trying to change me. We would have hated each other. Eventually.

At least that's the conclusion I've come to in my head. Though I admit it's been a lot to process over the last few weeks.

Maybe, as time goes on, I'll think differently on the matter. Who knows what the future will bring? It's not like I ever thought I'd step foot in this cemetery again. Surprise, surprise.

Well, as nice as it's been catching up, I won't be back. And I mean it this time. Ya see, I've met someone and I'm not sure hanging out with my ex (dead or otherwise) is the right thing to do if I want him to stick around.

And I do want him to stick around, Leo. I like this one. Love him, if I'm being honest. But don't you dare tell him that. Gotta keep the guy on his toes or he might just get bored with me.

In summary, I really am sorry. And I really did love you. But I love someone else now.

Yours in memory only,
Dani

68

"Ya hear that, pal?" I folded the note back up into four perfect squares and glanced at the name embedded in the stone. "Sorry to break it to ya, León, but she loves me now. Yeah, I know. I'm a little shocked myself but ya had a good run. And I wish ya the best wherever you are."

I slapped a hand over the top of the slab and watched the sun set in the distance for a few minutes, letting Dani's words sink in. And, if I were being honest, gloating a bit in front of my silent rival. The guy really was taking it like a champ though. No whining or nothin'. A real gentlemanly approach if I said so myself.

"Too bad things didn't end better for ya. From what our girl told me, I think we coulda been friends, shared a beer, watched the game, enjoyed some of my ma's ale pie—*shit's to die for.* Sorry. Couldn't help myself." I grinned and some part of me knew the fucker in the grave was grinning too. "I mean, I would have had to kick your ass eventually. Because there's no universe where that woman wasn't meant to be mine. But I think it woulda been a fair fight.

And in the end, something tells me we woulda shook hands and you woulda asked me to take good care of her. Which is exactly what I plan to do. Take care of her for as long as she'll let me. And long after that too."

I pushed off the cold stone, rubbing my palms together before stepping forward again. There was definitely a fresh chill in the air now that the last rays of sunlight were gone. I glanced over my shoulder one last time, my spine tingling with that feeling of someone watching me.

"You're off the hook, brother. I got her now." I allowed the wind to carry my words off into the early evening sky as I stalked back up the path to my girl and whatever craziness the future would bring us. Together.

EPILOGUE

ONE YEAR AND ELEVEN MONTHS LATER

The tacky substance stuck to my skin like honey, my eyes fixated on the way the translucent film popped when I pinched my fingers together before prying my thumb from my middle digit.

As much as I still loved the feel of it coating my hands, this wasn't blood. No, this was another of my preferred bodily fluids.

The light sheen of precum coated pretty boy's cock as it glistened under the light of our bedside table, the lickable V of his abdominal muscles mine for the taking, and the darkened raised skin a reminder that this man had and would take a knife for me now bouncing with each sharp intake of his breath. I lowered my mouth to the tip, needing a taste of what I did to him, what he could do to me as soon as I let him do it.

Connor groaned, his arms thrashing against the cuffs I'd secured to the metal hooks drilled into the headboard. Sometimes the fucker needed a lesson when it came to remembering who was in control. Though we both knew he liked it *and* the feel of me slowly impaling myself on his cock, my palms flat on his chest and my head thrown back.

I'd loved to tell ya the shit dissipated over time, that the sex got boring and less addictive. It didn't. If anything, a daily dose was hardly enough. For us at least. While the tapping of Mrs. Johnson's broom on the ceiling above us told me it was *more than enough* for the elderly tenant presently living in the second-floor apartment of our small rent-controlled duplex. The crazy old bat was less than pleased with her new neighbors. It was a matter of time before we gave the poor woman a heart attack.

My lips curled at the thought before the ringing of my burner phone had them dropping into a frown just as quickly. I pulled up and off Connor, stomped over to the dresser, and swiped up the device with a frustrated hand. My eyes glued to the man still strapped to our bed with an irritated expression on his face and a heavy set of blue balls between his thighs.

"Who is it?" he mouthed from across the room.

It took some time, but pretty boy finally learned to keep quiet whenever this particular phone started ringing. It was safer for everyone involved. I lifted a finger, gesturing for him to give me a minute, and returned my focus to whomever the fuck was on the other end of my discreet line.

"Danica… it's been too long."

"Just under two years," I replied. The caller didn't have to introduce themselves. I might not have recognized the number but I knew the voice all too well.

"Glad you remembered."

I could hear his grin through the phone, and it sent that familiar chill up my spine. "When and wher—?"

Before I could finish asking the question, the line was cut and a text came through with an address for a location somewhere in downtown Chicago.

I slammed the phone back onto the dresser and glanced up at Connor, as my mouth tipped into what I was hoping at least appeared to be an apologetic smile. "Think your parents would mind us dropping in for a little visit?"

THE END

Interested in finding out more about the Renegades? Those masked psychopaths and their secret bunker?

Keep reading for a sneak peek of *SKIN*!
(Frankie's story and book one in the Renegades Series)

SKIN

BLURB

Obsession was a five-letter word. Ten years in the making. And her name was Emily.

But the real question was who was I?

When my pretty little pet leaned forward, offered me a view of her cleavage, and tried to make a deal, I said why the hell not?

Five days. Thirty minutes. She could ask me anything to her heart's content. Anything but my name. She had to figure that one out on her own.

It should have been easy enough. I was the man she stole from, whose life she ruined, whose future she destroyed.

I was the man she left behind and she was... MINE.

SKIN IS A DARK *RUMPELSTILTSKIN* RETELLING AND BOOK ONE IN <u>THE RENEGADES SERIES</u>. EACH TITLE IS A STANDALONE IN AN INTERCONNECTED WORLD WHILE EACH STORY IS A RETELLING OF A FAIRY TALE, NURSERY RHYME, FABLE, ETC. THE FOCUS IS DARK ROMANCE SO PLEASE HEED THE TRIGGER WARNINGS AT THE BEGIN-NING OF EVERY BOOK.

SKIN
PROLOGUE

HER

It was the feeling of being watched that first had my eyes moving under my lids, my lashes fluttering just enough to be noticeable as I fought to pry them apart. They were heavy, so fucking heavy. Like two bricks were placed on my face to hold me down and there wasn't shit I could do to swat them away. Because my hands... weren't moving either.

I didn't have time to question the gravity of my situation before the damp air was bristling my skin, causing my muscles to spasm involuntarily as the antiseptic smell—a mix of alcohol and too much bleach—burned the insides of my nostrils. Followed by the buzzing of the harsh fluorescent lighting penetrating my eardrums. My temples throbbing in rhythm with my quickening heartbeat. Which was all I could hear now.

The *thump, thump, thumping* against my rib cage.

I was in a hospital. That had to be it. But why? What happened? Was I in some sort of accident?

I couldn't remember anything since the airport. Since grabbing my suitcase from baggage claim and following my boss to her town car. Everything after that felt fuzzy. I didn't know what day it was or where I was supposed to be right now. Or if I even had a job anymore.

And I still couldn't move my arms or legs...

My internal panic was rising to the surface as I tried to take a mental inventory of the rest of my anatomy and quickly realized my fingers and toes were twitching. My breathing slowed along with the pounding in my chest until I heard his voice... the one that accompanied the eyes I could still feel boring past the layers of flesh and bone, severing all nerve connections and rendering me immobile.

I didn't need the drugs I was certain were rushing through my system. Not with the weight of those eyes watching me.

"Welcome back, pet." His tone was low, raspy. Like someone who'd spent far too many hours screaming at the top of their lungs and was now forcing air through a set of damaged vocal cords.

I didn't have much more time to think on it as I felt a pair of heavy palms slam down on each side of my head. My lids flung open, forcing me to stare into two black holes where eyes should be. And weren't. But I could still feel them. Staring at me. Through me.

That's when I realized I wasn't in a hospital. Doctors didn't wear black tactical pants or have knives strapped to their hips. And emergency room walls weren't made of concrete. No, I was below ground. Maybe in some sort of basement?

Before I had a chance to piece it all together, or at least try to, the figure was pushing back from the mattress and positioning himself across the dank room, drawing my attention to what I could only assume was the biggest threat to me getting out of here—wherever here was—*alive.*

Him. The man in the cloth mask. His head tipped to the side as he continued to glare at me through the thin fabric that kept his identity as much a mystery as the rest of him.

SKIN

CHAPTER ONE

HER

"**W**hat do you want?"

"I already told you. And I'm not a fan of repeating myself."

He tossed the small wooden chair across the room, watching it hit the concrete wall and splinter before turning his icy glare on me—I could feel the chill behind his eyes even if I still couldn't see them. Then he stalked forward, pinching my cheeks between his thumb and index finger.

"I want everything you took from me, my pretty little thief." He sank his teeth into my earlobe, piercing flesh through the thin material of his mask. There was an audible pop as he imprinted the likeness of his canines into the malleable cartilage.

I bit into my lip, trying to hold back the tears. I didn't want to give him the satisfaction of seeing me cry. "I've never stolen anything in my life..."

"A thief and a fucking liar, I see... Honestly, I'm disappointed in you, Emily."

I watched him pull away and circle me, his steps measured, precise, nearly soundless until he forced his boots to squeak when he pivoted to look at me again. Sensation was finally returning to my upper limbs, but only enough so that I recognized the weight of the chains currently riveting me in place. There was no point in fighting against them. I knew it wouldn't get me anywhere.

I needed to be smart. Not impulsive, no matter how hard my fight-or-flight instincts were urging me otherwise.

He knew me, my name, but how? Or did he…? Maybe he'd just found my driver's license… Or overheard my name somewhere… Honestly, his knowing who I was did little to tell me who *he* was… and I needed to know that, to also know what he wanted.

"Who are you?" It was the next obvious question, not that I thought it would be that easy.

"I already told you, pet. I'm the man you stole from." I could hear the grin curling his lips. But it wasn't something pleasant. No, it was the sort of grin that preceded a sudden bout of rage. A violent grin.

"How am I supposed to know what I took from you, if I don't even know who you are?" I tried again.

"Not my problem," he hissed in response.

"It is your problem if you want it back…"

Keep him engaged, Em. Interested in continuing to play whatever game this is.

My subconscious urged me to maintain the façade. Be whatever, whoever it was he needed me to be. Part of me knew my inner voice was right, while another part was wondering how long it would take to chew through the meat of my wrist in order to free myself. The same part that realized I would bleed out long before I was able to make it to the door.

He was growing impatient—who was I kidding? The psycho was impatient from the moment I first laid eyes on him, likely long before that too. It was evident in the tense posturing of his shoulders. In the way the biceps of his crossed arms flexed and loosened as though he were moments away from closing the distance between us and landing the full force of his knuckles into my face.

He hated me but why?

There was nothing about his voice that was recognizable, nothing about his build that was the slightest bit familiar. The man was a stranger to me. I was sure of it, as sure as he was that I'd taken something from him...

He pushed off the wall and stalked towards me again. I closed my eyes and held my breath, waiting for the blow that never came. Until I chanced a glance through my lashes and watched as he stomped to the only entry point instead. A metal door. Fireproof, I was certain. And not something I could break down.

"Wait!" I couldn't be left alone in here. Alone with my thoughts and rising panic... I just couldn't... "Let me help you—"

His laughter broke through my plea. The sound was humorless and bitter. "Help me? How the fuck do you expect to help me, pet? Do you even realize how fucked you are right now?" It took seconds for him to appear at my side again, less than that for him to bring us nose to nose.

"That's not what I meant—"

"Then tell me what the fuck you meant, my sweet girl..." His tone was suddenly gentle, like something you'd use to soothe a small child, and I didn't know what to make of all the mood swings.

"If you won't tell me who you are, or what it is you *think* I stole..."

He raised a questioning eyebrow, the tight material of the mask lifting with the movement, but I continued all the same.

"...then at least give me an opportunity to figure it out... please?"

He threw his head back in genuine laughter this time. "*Please?*" He wheezed in a breath, obviously amused. With himself or me? I couldn't tell. "Yes, because proper manners will get you out of this one." He dropped his jaw and glared at me with his neck cocked to one side, as if observing me for a moment. "Go on. What's your proposal? I'm just dying to hear it, pet."

Coming Soon:

SKIN (Frankie's story)
LAMB (The Surgeon's story)
BELLS (Casper's story)

ACKNOWLEDGMENTS

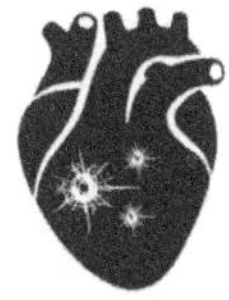

Thanks to everyone who has been a continuous part of this long-ass process. Especially my sounding board, D and Kat. Couldn't do this shit without you bitches!

ALSO BY SYBIL KNIGHT

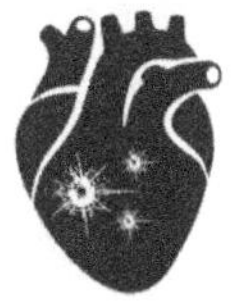

THE HARSHER THE TRUTH

THE SWEETER THE LIES

SINS OF OUR FATHERS

HALF COCKED

SKIN

MORE TITLES TO COME...

ABOUT THE AUTHOR

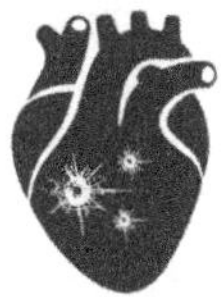

Sybil is a career-driven Philadelphian native. A crime show enthusiast by day, and a BDSM club hopper by night. When she isn't working or writing, she is talking about working or writing. She is a single mom to her beta fish (Fish) and way too many dead houseplants.

Her stories range from gray to black, with darker themes throughout. She prefers heroines with a kick-ass mentality and the heroes who know how to rein them in. The mental and medical aspects of her books are well-researched, though they are given a humanistic approach and diagnoses aren't the focal points. She believes her characters don't need to wear labels in order to get their messages across.

Her books are mostly standalones, though her characters may interact and intersect worlds. Additionally, she works closely with and writes alongside author Dahlia Reign and some characters will appear in cameos in each of their publications.

Sybil welcomes emails from readers if there are concerns or questions regarding any of her publications.

Email: authorsybilknight@gmail.com